DARK ANGELS

Katherine Langrish

DARK ANGELS

HarperCollins *Children's Books*

First published in paperback in Great Britain by
HarperCollins *Children's Books* in 2009
HarperCollins *Children's Books* is a division of HarperCollins*Publishers* Ltd,
77-85 Fulham Palace Road, Hammersmith, London, W6 8JB.

Visit our website at:
www.harpercollins.co.uk

1 3 5 7 9 10 8 6 4 2

Text copyright © Katherine Langrish 2009

ISBN-13 978-0-00-721489-1

Printed and bound in England by Clays Ltd, St Ives plc

FOR DAVID

*

Warm thanks to:
My daughters for reading it and
telling me it was all right really

Sally Martin for insightful and tactful editing
Michele Topham for level-headed calm and Huw Tegid
from Menter Môn for advising on Welsh phrases

The Beginning of the Elves

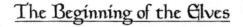ne day, some years after Adam and Eve had been cast out of Paradise, the Lord God came to visit them in the cool of the evening.

By now, Adam and Eve had lots of children, too many to look after properly. Some of them hadn't been washed, and Eve was ashamed of them. "Hide," she told the dirty ones. "You aren't fit to be seen by God. Keep out of His sight."

"Are these all the children you have?" asked God, looking at the scuffling parade of clean children lined up before Him.

"Yes," said Eve.

"Then what you have hidden from Me shall be hidden from everyone," said God.

The dirty children became invisible to human eyes, and from then on they were outcasts, forced to hide in hills, caves and rocks.

This was the beginning of the elves.

CHAPTER 1

The first time the horn sounded on the hill, Wolf mistook it for a sheep bleating or a bird crying, and thought no more of it. He had other things to worry about.

There were no proper paths up here. He hadn't known it would take so long to climb out of the valley. He'd expected to be miles away by now, dropping into the shelter of the woods – not still forcing his way up through waist-high heather towards the long, saw-blade ridge of Devil's Edge. But there were no proper paths up here. Wolf cursed the boggy sheep tracks that never lasted more than a few yards before twisting the wrong way.

He was picking his way across a brook when he heard it: a faint, mournful wailing, more like a stain on the wind than a real sound. He checked mid-stream to listen, teetered on a wobbly stone, whirled his arms, jumped for the next and missed, and landed on his hands and knees in the brawling water.

"Hell's *bones!*"

He waded over slimy pebbles to the bank. By then the sound had faded, and who cared, anyway? *A bird*, he told himself in disgust. *Or an old sheep crying.* He was soaked from the knees down, and his long sleeves flapped like wet washing.

Shivering, wringing the water out of his black robes, he looked back. West, into Wales, the hills were half sponged out by rainclouds. In the valley, the river looped like a scrawl of silver ink. And he could still see the dark lead roof of the Abbey of Christ and Saint Ethelbert at Wenford where, just about now, the monks would be lighting the candles and filing into chapel to sing the evening prayers. Without him.

Good!

But his mind flew back there, swift as a bird.

He heard again the biting drawl of Brother Thomas, master of the boys: "You – Wolfstan. *Take that smile off your face.* I heard you singing in the cloister this morning. Singing like a veritable nightingale! A holy song, no doubt. A psalm, no doubt! Strange that I did not recognise it. What psalm were you singing, Wolfstan?"

Wolf gritted his teeth. It hadn't been a psalm, and the skinny old devil knew it.

"It was a *French song*!" Brother Thomas made the words sound like '*a dead rat*'. "About *love* and *springtime* and *women*!" He'd seized the back of Wolf's neck. "Blasphemous boy!" he hissed. "'*Timor Domini initium sapienti est.*' Do you know what that means, you villain? '*The fear of the Lord is the beginning of wisdom.*' And if you will not learn from fear of the Lord, you will learn from fear of me. Pass me the rod. Strip off your robe."

"I hate you!" Wolf screamed down the hillside.

He snatched up some stones, wincing as his shirt twitched unstuck from his blood-stained back, and hurled one after another down the slope as hard as he could. "I hate you! I'm never coming back!"

He buried his face in his hands. *It's not my fault*!

But it was. He, Wolf, had run away from the household of God. And now he would pay for it by spending the night on the hill, alone and shelterless.

But if he went back…

If he went back, the rest of his life would be bound by the Rule, the endless circle of prayers and duties. *Walk, don't run. Pray, don't talk. Rise when the bell rings. Eat when the bell rings. Sleep when the bell rings.* Till one day he'd be an old man shuffling between refectory and chapel, coughing in the dormitory at night and keeping the boys awake.

Wolf lifted his head. It wasn't dark yet, and when it was he'd find somewhere safe to rest – a dry spot under a gorse bush, or if he was lucky, a shepherd's hut. He turned to go on.

Above him rose Devil's Edge, stark against the sky with its crest of jagged rocks like broken castles – like a ruined city where monsters lived and demons lurked. In a clump of bracken nearby, something uttered a deep wheezing cough, and Wolf leaped like a hare. *But it must be a sheep. Only a sheep.*

He squelched around the edge of a bog. Last year workmen digging peat for winter fuel had discovered a body in one of these bogs. Some unlucky traveller had drowned there – or been murdered and thrown in by robbers – but centuries ago, in the time of the old Romans, maybe. The workmen had carried the body down to the abbey on a hurdle, and Wolf had seen it – creased like old leather, muddy and dripping, stained deep brown from the dark water. Now he wished he hadn't.

He imagined it, or something like it, with glowing eyes and long, thin arms and huge, dark hands, stalking him through the heather. And why not? There were plenty of scary tales about this hill. Stories of blue elf-fires, burning at the mouths of long-abandoned mineshafts and tunnels. Stories of bogeymen and ghosts.

He took another glance at the ridge. Up on the very top, he had heard there was a road. A road leading nowhere, a road no one used. For if anyone was so bold as to walk along it, especially at night, he'd hear the clamour of hounds and the blowing of horns, the cracking of whips and the rumbling of a cart. And out of the dark would burst the Devil's own dog pack, dashing beside a black wagon drawn by goats with fiery eyes, crammed full of screaming souls bound for the pits of Hell.

Wolf crossed himself, shivering. "Blessed Saint Ethelbert, protect me." Then realised that Saint Ethelbert would have no time for a disobedient, sinful boy, and was probably scowling down at him over the battlements of Heaven, hoping the demons and elves that undoubtedly lived on this wild hill would be keeping a special lookout, just for him.

Rain flicked his cheek like a cold finger. The day was ending early. The ridge was still high above him.

So hurry! Get moving, Wolf. Get over the top before nightfall!

He broke into a panicked trot. But it wasn't possible to keep it up for long. Soon he was puffing, clambering, wading through the heather, stumbling again and again into unexpected holes and hidden watercourses.

13

He began to feel almost sure something *was* following him, a little way behind and on the edge of sight, a furtive, scuttling smudge at the corner of his eye. It couldn't be an animal: animals wouldn't act like that. *No good looking round*, he thought unhappily. It would either duck into the heather, or – far worse – stand erect, and stare back at him. And then what?

I won't look, he swore. *I won't look.*

He looked. Not a soul was in sight, not a wayfarer, not a peat-cutter, not a solitary shepherd. The wind gusted up the hill towards him. On it, faint but clear, floated the same lamenting wail he'd heard before.

Something pale scurried over a nearby rock.

He snapped round to look. It whipped out of sight. Naked, whitish, running on all fours. A thin stalk of a neck and a big, round head. It couldn't be human.

A demon!

Wolf bolted up the hillside.

I'm sorry! His prayer was a mental shriek. *Please, please don't let it get me!* He scrambled over a rocky outcrop, floundered into a marshy hollow that sucked at his boots like the slobbering mouth of Hell. Snatching handfuls of tough heather which ripped his palms, he hauled himself out, hearing a distant clamour that swelled on the wind and faded again. The baying of dogs.

Who was out hunting – who was blowing horns on

Devil's Edge? Wolf really, really didn't want to know. He dived into a clump of bracken and curled into a ball, arms wrapped over his head, eyes screwed shut.

The wind hissed and the bracken rattled. Nothing pounced on him. Wolf sat up. He peered this way and that, first fearfully and then with rising hope. Where was the demon? Perhaps he'd lost it.

Two yards away, a grey puffball head with glittering eyes rose over the ferns. Half of the face was white, half dark red.

Wolf bounced to his feet and went tearing up the slope. The skyline was close, so close it looked as though he could leap over it into the sky. With bursting lungs he struggled up one last steep bank and found himself on the top.

So high! So windy! He could see for miles – hills lying in rows like a giant's ploughland. And all along the length of the ridge, linking crag to crag, a broad roadway of pale stones gleamed in the last of the light.

The Devil's Road.

Wolf was frightened to set foot on it, but he didn't dare stop. Any minute now, the Devil would be coming home from his day's work of roaming the world, stalking through the air to set one black, clawed foot on his mountain! Wolf hopped and stumbled across, feeling uniquely visible, like a mouse trying to cross a room where a cat was hiding. The stones poked out of the black turf at all angles, a jumble of unforgiving points and edges that tripped and turned his feet.

The horn sounded again, a flat, sinister wail, followed by the uneven, choppy barking of a large pack of dogs. Wolf reached the far side of the Devil's Road and jumped into the heather. Bleating sheep scattered ahead of him. He ran jolting down the slope, not knowing what else to do. There was nowhere to hide. The ground transmitted an insistent, dull drumming. Hoofbeats.

A cramp tore through Wolf's side. He limped on, throwing agonised glances over his shoulder at the ridge. The gabble of the hounds became louder as they crested the hill. They poured over in a mottled flood, spilling down the slope. Two or three were out in front, running after him with enormous, raking strides. Behind flickered a shape with a blotched, blobby head.

The demon was with them – driving them on! Wolf ran faster. He hit a patch of slippery grass, his feet shot away and he fell, knocking the breath from his lungs.

A band of horsemen rode over the skyline, thin spears pricking the wind. The clamour of the dog pack was close now, savage and eager. Wolf scrambled up, his heart banging in clumsy strokes. *Here they come*! The front-runners were huge. He saw the grinning white teeth in sharp black jaws, the laid-back ears and mad light eyes, the long mud-splattered legs that reached and stretched in fluent bounds…

Wolves! Not dogs at all, but wolves!

He shrieked and brandished his arms. The leading wolf leaped aside in a racing swerve. The other two followed, dashing by at a safe distance. He saw now how tired they were, with glazed eyes and lolling tongues. And with a strange hoarse cry the demon brushed past him, mushroom white except for the red blotch like spilled wine down half its face. Wolf shrank back. It ran stooping, on its hind legs, and was smaller than he'd thought. It had no tail and—

"Hey!" he yelled incredulously, straightening up. "Hey!"

A narrow, bare back and thin buttocks disappeared into the bracken. What he'd thought was a huge head was a tangled mass of greyish-blond hair.

A child? A dirty little child?

No time to think. Horses were coming down the slope at a drumming gallop, and he was in the way – trapped between the wolves and the hunt. The riders had seen him. The horn sounded a bevy of urgent notes, and over the din of the approaching hounds he heard a furious shout:

"*Dex aie! Garson! Gar les chiens!*"

For God's sake, boy, beware of the dogs! Wolf was already running again. Those deep broken barks and yammering yells frightened him to the core. The riders were hollering: "*Sy, sy avaunt!*"

"*Avaunt, ha ha! Sy, dons sy!*"

"*A moy, Bailemonde! A moy, Argos! So howe, so howe!*"

Wolf plunged into the bracken where the child had disappeared. The ferns grew breast high, and dragged at his feet and caught at his voluminous robe. He tore through, hearing close behind the crackle and rustle as the dogs threw themselves after him.

Wolf burst out of the bracken. The ground fell away into a V-shaped dingle, a valley like a deep gutter with a white stream spouting over rocks at the bottom. Trees grew up its slopes. Wolf jumped. For a second he was flying, untouchable. Then his boots sank deep into last year's slimy leaves. He pitched on to hands and knees, got up and ran on. The riders would have to be crazy to gallop down such a bank, but nothing would stop the dogs.

Climb something, you fool – get out of their way! He thrust into the bushes that grew up the sides of the dingle and swung into a holly tree, scrambling as high as he could into its bouncing branches. He hung there, his breath whistling. White sparks danced before his eyes.

The dogs came boiling over the edge of the dingle, leaping down the slope, lean, rough-haired greyhounds and powerful, broad-chested alaunts bred to grip and kill. After them, black against the darkening sky came a rider on a big horse. The horse checked at the drop, half rearing. Then it sprang out. Earth flew from its iron-shod hooves. The rider yelled as they crashed into the bushes, and his long spear ripped through the leaves. A second horseman followed, and a third.

Wolf pressed his face against the damp tree bark and closed his eyes. He whispered a faint prayer. Safe! He was safe! They'd gone past without seeing him.

Further down the dingle, hidden by trees, the baying of the dogs rose to a violent crescendo and the men shouted. They had a wolf at bay. Wolf heard the thud of a spear going home, and a long, sobbing howl, which shot up into a wild shriek and ended in a spine-crawling, choking cough.

The horn sounded for the death – a series of hurrying, victorious toots. From the hillside above came answering whoops and horn calls – then curses and laughter as the rest of the huntsmen reached the top of the steep bank and began cautiously urging their horses down.

Safe in the holly, Wolf clung to the branches and listened to the thump and scuffle of hooves. He peered through the darkly prickled leaves. The men and horses sounded solid enough. He could hear the horses snorting and the riders speaking in French like noblemen. There were no devils trotting by on fiery-eyed goats.

Yet hadn't they been hunting a child – that mysterious child? He shivered, and in his mind's eye the real dogs he'd seen faded and blended into the Devil's black hounds chasing the naked and terrified souls of the damned.

No! He shook his head. The child had been real flesh and blood, the dogs had been ordinary dogs, and as for the riders, devils wouldn't speak French.

Or perhaps they would; he didn't know. But he couldn't stay in this tree all night. He dropped stiffly to the ground. At a safe distance he followed the switching tail of the last horse. Soon he saw a hastily lit fire crackling in a trampled clearing, and the dusk turning blue around it.

The fire glowed on reds and browns: the ruddy coats of the steaming horses, and their red leather harness, cut in scallops; the huntsmen wore red tunics and long leather boots. One stood leaning on his spear. He must be the lord, the master of the hunt. He was watching his men skin the one wolf they'd caught. It lay stretched on the ground near the fire. They had cut off the head and stuck it on a spear, where its white teeth gleamed in a frozen snarl.

Wolf lurked in the undergrowth. Just as he gathered his courage to walk out and be seen, there was a roar of rough laughter at some joke. He lost his nerve. They might help him. Or they might punish him, for getting in the way of the hounds.

Smoke blew towards him, and a smell of churned-up leaves. Triumphant dogs ran about wagging their tails and peeing on the bushes. Their mood had completely changed; they were no longer a danger. One of them dashed up to Wolf and seized his wrist in its mouth, play-chewing with blunt teeth. It was a tall white greyhound, a beautiful, lordly creature wearing a broad collar of gilded leather. Wolf pulled his hand away and drew back, afraid of being noticed.

"No," he whispered. "Off with you. Go on!"

The greyhound took no notice. It swung its thin tail, looking eagerly into his face. *It thinks I'm one of the hunters. It's hoping for scraps.* Wolf backed further into the trees, ducking under the spiky branches of a clump of hawthorns, but the dog followed.

"Go away!" Wolf grasped the thick leather band around its throat and tried to make the dog turn. It resisted, lifting a strong, shaggy foreleg and pawing his knee. Wolf found himself rubbing its neck and scratching its ears. It pushed affectionately against his hand – then stiffened, looking sharply beyond him. Wolf turned, his fingers still hooked through the collar. He couldn't see anything, but the dog apparently could. It set off with a bound.

Wolf followed without even thinking. With the friendly dog at his side he felt safe for the first time in hours. As it dragged him deeper into the wood, a glorious idea dawned on him. If a valuable hound ran off, wouldn't there be a reward for the person who found it? He could wait a while, and then take it back and say he'd found it straying, which was almost true. The lord of the hunt would be a rich knight, a nobleman. Men like that had to act generously.

He could see it all: the grateful knight offering money. *You have brought back my best hunting dog. Take this purse!* Himself bowing low. *It was nothing, my lord. All I want to do is serve you.* The knight exclaiming: *Then you shall join my household. I have need of an honest lad to be my squire…*

He laughed at himself. All the same, it could happen! Then, instead of monkish black, he'd have bright clothes to wear, green and scarlet. He would take care of his master's clothes and weapons. He would learn to ride and hunt and fight.

He hung on to the collar, trying to restrain the big greyhound as it bounded up the steep side of the dingle, under scratching branches, through a patch of tall stinging nettles, and over an ankle-breaking pile of moss-covered stones. Wolf hopped and swore and rubbed his shins. "That's enough!" He tugged the dog to a standstill under a rock face which leaned out overhead. There was a dank, sour smell. A bad feeling hung over the place. "We're not going any further," he said, shivering. "It's time to go back."

The greyhound strained at the collar, growling. A prickle of sweat started under Wolf's armpits. He remembered he was still on the slopes of Devil's Edge. And he was alone, and a long way from the fire.

In the black tangle of thorn trees and brambles at the base of the cliff, a chalky oval gradually formed.

With eyes in it.

A face like a half-moon, white one side and dark the other, floating in a aureole of insubstantial hair like dandelion fluff. It vanished, pulling back into blackness, and Wolf saw that it had been peering from the mouth of a low cave set under an overgrown rocky ledge.

Dry mouthed, Wolf recognised it. The thing he'd mistaken for a demon – the strange child. This was what they had been following. The dog had brought him straight to its lair!

CHAPTER 2

The greyhound threw itself at the spot where the white face had vanished. Wolf jerked it roughly back. "Leave it!" he said in a fierce undertone. "*Leave it!*"

He dragged the dog away over the rockspill and nettles – through thickets of hawthorn and hazel and over piles of rotting leaves. The wood closed behind them and the horror faded. At last Wolf risked a glance over his shoulder and his headlong pace slowed to a shaken walk.

It hasn't followed. We've lost it.

He thanked every saint he could think of for his narrow escape from – well, from what? A demon? He wasn't sure. It didn't look like the ones he'd seen in pictures, the ochre and vermilion demons gleefully gambolling on the Doomsday wall of the abbey church. The strange child-thing wasn't hairy or horned.

But no earthly child would roam the hillside naked in this haunted twilight. No mortal child would take refuge in such a dark and frightening cave.

Then it must be an elf. And that was almost worse. Elves were uncanny, like ghosts. Pale, malicious creatures, which lived in the dark places under hills and mounds, just like that cave, tempting mortals away to waste their lives in false enchantments.

Wolf remembered the creature's fleeting expression as it looked out – narrow-eyed with terror like a hunted fox. Perhaps it hadn't meant him any harm. Perhaps it had only been running from the hounds – caught, like him, between the hunters and their prey. And what if it wasn't an elf? Suppose – just suppose – he had left a frightened child in a cold, dripping cave in the middle of a dark wood?

"Of course it was an elf!" he told himself furiously. He thought of its weird face, its glittering eyes. No need to feel sorry for an elf, no reason to go back.

The distant fire winked behind a black scribble of branches. He had himself to look after. He'd take this valuable hunting dog back to its master, claim his reward and never think about the elf again. He set off through the clutching wood. Twigs tugged his hair, wet grass snaked about his ankles. Cursing, he tore free from another bramble – and blundered nearly into the arms of a giant figure straddling the way.

Wolf recoiled, bursting with terror, and tugged the greyhound in front of him. "Keep off!" he snarled. "Keep right away from me! Or I'll set my dog on you!"

"*Your* dog?" The voice was deep, human and angry. "That's *my* dog, you thief! Take your dirty fingers off his collar! What are you doing with him? Are you the boy who got in my way on the hill?"

"Yes – no!" Wolf's heart was bumping about like a rabbit in a sack. This was the lord of the hunt, the reckless rider who had leaped his horse into the dingle. "Nothing – I wasn't stealing him, sir!"

"Let go of him, I said!" the man roared.

Wolf's fingers slipped from the collar, and the dog leaped happily forwards. "Believe me; I was bringing him back—"

"Yes, after you stole him in the first place. Don't lie to me! D'you think I'm a fool? Who are you? What's your name?"

"Wolf Osmundson." They were talking English. He tried to make himself sound more important – more French. "Wolf fitz Osmund. My father was—"

"Wolf, is it?" The man gave a hard laugh. "Ho!

The second wolf I've caught today." He stabbed a finger into Wolf's chest. "We've already skinned the first. You'll be next. Or perhaps I'll slice your ears off. Who's your master?"

"I'm not a peasant!" Wolf went stiff with scared rage. The man wasn't joking. The laws were savage: a thief could lose a foot, a hand, his eyes. "I'm from St Ethelbert's at Wenford – I'm a clerk, a scholar! My father held a manor. Let's speak French if it's easier for you, lord. Or Latin – I know them both. And I can read and write." Too late, he heard his own voice ringing with insolent defiance. He clenched his teeth. But instead of hitting him the man said merely, "If you can do all that, why are you here?"

Wolf looked away, unable to think of a good lie, sullenly aware that silence would be taken for more insolence. He curled numb toes in his wet boots. His back ached. His face and arms stung with the slashes of countless twigs. Bitterly he remembered his ambition to become a squire. Well, that dream was over.

"You've run away, haven't you?" The man's voice was gentler.

Wolf cleared his throat. "I didn't – I don't want to be a monk."

It sounded weak – feeble.

"I suppose they beat you," said the man with tolerant scorn.

Wolf burned. He remembered the bold and powerful shapes of horse and rider tearing into the trees. How could someone like that ever understand? He burst out, "Maybe they did! But that's not why! I'm not fit for that life. It's like being shut up in a box. A stone box. And outside, everything's going on – without me."

"A stone box!" the man muttered. "Now that I can understand. Where are you running to? Home?"

"I have no home. My father's dead."

There was a moment of silence. They were standing in shadows as black as well water, and Wolf couldn't see the man's face. "Who are you, lord?" he asked, shivering.

"My name is Hugo fitz Warin."

"Lord Hugo?" Wolf stammered slightly. "Hugo of the Red M-mound?"

The man stretched his arms wide. "Hugo of the Red Mound – Hugo of La Motte Rouge – Huw of Domen Goch. See? I too can speak in tongues. Lord of everything that creeps or runs or flies between Crow Moor and Devil's Edge. Anything else you want to know, my young wolf in shepherd's clothing?"

Every single person at the abbey had heard of Hugo fitz Warin, troubadour and knight crusader, as famous for his love songs as for his courage. "Lord Hugo?" Wolf drew a reverent breath. "You took the Cross. You went to the Holy Land with the king and the archbishop. You fought at the siege of Acre!" And that song that had got him into so much trouble with Brother Thomas had been one of Lord Hugo's.

"I did all those things," the man agreed grimly, "and I'm still waiting to hear why you ran off with Argos – my dog."

"Oh!" Wolf came out of a dream of beautiful ladies, battles, broken lances, blood-red pennants and dying Saracens. "That was because of the elf—"

The blow took him by surprise, cracking him across the side of the head. Lord Hugo seemed to grow, like a great bear bristling with black fur. "*Are you making fun of me, boy?*"

"No, sir!" Wolf couldn't understand this sudden fury. He backed, rubbing his stinging ear. "The elf," he gabbled, "the one you were hunting."

"*What* elf?"

"But," Wolf squeaked. He swallowed and began again. "I thought you'd seen it, running down the hill. Didn't you? It was following me. And it got caught up in the hunt, like me, between the dogs and the wolves." The recollection of his awful journey over the mountain overcame him, and he blurted everything out: "I heard the horns blowing, and I thought the Devil was coming, like the stories say. And there was this thing, bobbing about in the heather – I thought it was a demon coming after me because I'd run away from the abbey. And afterwards it must have been creeping around your fire: your dog saw it and went after it – and I went with him."

"You snivelling little clerk," Hugo said after a pause. "Trying to make yourself interesting by telling lies."

"I'm not lying!" Wolf's voice rose again.

"So where is this *elf* now?"

"Back there." Wolf twisted, pointing. "In a cave under the cliff."

"Show me."

"But—"

"I want you to *show me*!"

"All right! I will!" Wolf tried to clap the lid back on his temper. It was madness to shout at this lord, who could have him hanged. He added more moderately, "Do you want to call your men, sir? They could bring torches…"

"So you can claim they scared it away? If anything's there at all? No," said Hugo. A heavy hand landed on Wolf's shoulder, steering him deeper into the thicket. "We'll do this together. And if you've lied to me…" Wolf heard a scrape of metal. His heart started off at a rapid scamper. Hugo had drawn his knife.

It couldn't be far, the cave: but at first he couldn't find it. They stumbled about, linked by Hugo's firm grip on Wolf's shoulder, ducking under the scratching twigs. The sky was a grainy grey above the black branches. There was a patter of rain like aerial feet running over the treetops. *That* could be elves. But it rattled down on them in large, cold drops.

Wolf shook with excitement. He was afraid of failure. Not just because of the knife; what really bothered him was that Hugo would think he had lied. And he hadn't; he'd seen an elf. He forgot his doubts. Lord Hugo wanted an elf, and an elf it must be.

But he was mortally afraid of losing his way – making a fool out of this great lord, this crusader. Hugo had *listened*. He might be hot-tempered, he might lose patience. If he wanted, he could cut Wolf's throat and leave him lying, and no one would ever know. *But he listened. And he's giving me a chance to show I spoke the truth. He's rough, but he's fair. And here's me, Wolf, walking beside Lord Hugo of the Red Mound, looking for an elf.*

It felt like something out of an old song.

They pushed onwards, upwards. The soft ground got steeper, and there was the sour, pungent smell Wolf remembered from before. His heart lifted. Here was the place, the tumbled stones at the bottom of the cliff, and the clump of nettles. He strained his eyes. And there was the cave: a black crack under a shelf of rock.

"Here," he whispered in triumph.

"That? That's one of the old mines." Hugo shook his shoulder. "So where's the elf?"

"I don't know." And he didn't; in dismay he realised that the elf might have come scuttling out by now. "Somewhere inside," he said hopefully.

"Easy to say," Hugo began. But the greyhound, which had followed them back through the wood, let out a strangled whine and dashed past. It disappeared into the dark hole. The glimmer of its white coat went out like a snuffed candle.

"You see?" Wolf pulled free from Hugo's hand. He scrambled over the stones and dropped on all fours, peering under the dripping lip of rock. Just past the entrance the darkness was absolute. From further in, perhaps not far, came a knock, click and rattle of tumbling rocks. And the dog barked, a flat sound like a muffled handclap.

"Splendour of God." Hugo was close behind him. "There's something there after all. Argos!" He leaned over Wolf, calling into the darkness. "Argos!" He whistled, but the dog didn't come. He leaned in further. "Eluned?" he called, and Wolf was startled by the change in him. He sounded eager, desperate, imploring. "Eluned, are you there? Oh, where are you?" He listened with his whole body, as if straining for an answer, but the cave seemed to eat the sound and there wasn't even an echo. He grabbed at Wolf.

"This elf – what was it like? Did it look like a woman?"

Wolf longed to say yes, for plainly this was what Hugo hoped to hear. "No… it looked like a child. But the face –" he shivered "– it's all red down one side, like a dark stain." He checked his memory. "It could be a girl, but only a very young one. A little, naked child."

"An elf-child. A fay." Hugo blew out a long, strained breath. "And you think it's in there still?"

"Yes, sir. And the dog knows."

"That could be anything. A badger."

"I told you, I saw its face." *Its sharp, frightened face.*

It began to rain properly: earnest, steady, soaking rain that would go on all night. Hugo stood, staring at the cave. "Is it possible?" It was a rough whisper, full of doubt and wonder. "That's the gate of Elfland? That *hole*?"

"I'll go in," Wolf said impulsively. Sudden excitement boiled through him. He'd do it. He'd do anything to impress Hugo, prove himself right, show that he wasn't a *snivelling little clerk*. "I'll go in and scare it out. And I'll find your dog. I'll do it now." Now – this very minute, while his blood was up – without thinking twice.

"In the dark?" Hugo's voice rang with disbelief. "You wouldn't dare."

Watch this, Wolf thought. He hitched up his robe and ducked under the rim of the cave.

"Wolf…"

Wolf looked back, expecting a word of encouragement. Hugo was a black shape against the grey. "If you've been lying to me, don't even think about coming back out."

"I've not been lying!" Wolf said fiercely – and hit his head on the roof. "Ouch!" He blundered on. Behind him he could hear Hugo laughing.

The entrance sloped down and was too low to walk upright. It was like going downstairs at night, but stairs made for dwarfs and buried in loose rubble. He was forced to bend in half, bracing his hands against the wall, feeling for each foothold. Soon the roof got lower. He had to crawl.

It was cold and wet – cold as a fresh-dug grave. And dark! Of all the different shades of black in the wood, none had been like this. Soot black – dead black, pressing on his eyes.

The ground levelled. He explored around him with his hands. Mud and gravel and heaps of stones. Shallow puddles. Something curved with sharp edges, like a broken pot. Who had left *that* here? And there was that smell again, that sour, foxy reek. Lord Hugo was right. This dirty hole couldn't lead to Elfland, could it?

It must. It has to, or why would the elf be here? He listened, holding his breath. Nothing but a horrid, dripping silence. But what was that? That pattering, rustling sound?

Out of nowhere, something pushed a wet nose into his face and slipped away again. "Argos?" Wolf called, but the dog was out of reach. He crawled painfully after it, guided by the slip and splash of its paws on the wet floor. The cave went on further than he'd thought, even though the roof was so low.

His breath came quick and raw. What if elves were all around – unseen, but somehow watching him? And what if Lord Hugo got tired of waiting and went away? Or blocked up the entrance to wall him in? He screwed his neck round to look behind him, and could see nothing.

I'm lost!

No. It's all right. Even if I can't see it, the entrance is there, not far away. Lord Hugo won't leave me. And of course he won't shut me in. Not when his dog is here with me.

He rubbed his eyes, and saw floating colours, spectral greens and blues. This must be the beginning of elfish enchantments. Soon, perhaps, a weird light would blossom, and he would see—

What would he see?

Through clacking teeth he began to mutter his prayers. "*Pater noster qui es in caelis…*" He crept, wincing, over sharp rubble. "*…sed libera nos a malo. Amen.*" The familiar prayer made him feel better and safer – it was a lifeline to God. He took a calming breath and began again. "*Pater noster…*" How much further did this cave go? He crawled on over the cold, wet stones. "…*Amen. Pater noster…*"

He broke off. Somewhere just ahead, an animal was growling.

"Argos?"

And then everything happened at once. He bumped into the dog's hindquarters, feeling its long, bony legs and thin tail like a long, wet feather. It snarled in shock and turned on him. Teeth clicked somewhere near his ear. Wolf flung himself aside, shouting, "Argos – it's me!" – and smashed into the wall.

A flash of bright agony tore through his head. The darkness split open like a pea pod. Colours swirled in the gap and settled into a vision of low, green hills on the other side of a rust-red, lazily flowing river.

Wolf stretched out unbelieving fingers.

Elfland! he thought. The rocks had opened, and he was seeing into the kingdom of Elfland! As he stared, it slowly faded into a ghostly image of itself. The red river turned green, the green hills turned red, as if covered with blood. It was a mockery of a landscape, as if the elves were showing him he could trust in nothing. Then, like a dark sphincter closing, it shrank and dwindled. All went black.

Wolf pushed himself up on all fours. Tears of pain and shock ran down his cheeks. All he wanted was to grab Argos and get out.

Or had the dog already scrambled over him? "Argos?" he whispered, waving a groping hand around him. "Argos?" He touched something cold and hairless that shrank and quivered.

The elf! He snatched his hand away. Close to him, cornered! Feverishly he rubbed his fingers. He couldn't bear the thought of touching it again. But he'd boasted that he would bring out the elf, and now he had to. Lord Hugo was waiting. Prodding the darkness, he realised the elf had bunched and burrowed into the scooped-out end of a blind tunnel. Perhaps this was the very doorway to Elfland, but the other elves had closed the rocks, shutting it out. Elves were cruel and heartless, even to each other.

He heard a muffled whimper.

A warm, painful feeling uncurled inside Wolf's chest – pity, mixed with horror. That whimpering sounded exactly like a child. Whatever she was, elf or changeling, he couldn't leave her like this, cowering in a black slot in the ground.

"Don't be frightened," he whispered. "I won't hurt you." The only answer was a scuffling sound as the creature rammed herself more firmly into her hiding place. Wolf hesitated.

"God's blessing on you," he said at last, half-ashamed. He didn't know if it was right to bless an elf.

He reached forward. His fingers skated quickly over a bony back and shoulder, and closed around a thin arm.

Wolf shuffled backwards and yanked her after him. Shuffle, yank. Shuffle, yank. He dragged her through the tunnel. He found himself talking to her in gasps. "I'm sorry. I'm sorry." It was a horrible thing to do. But she couldn't stay here, could she? The pointed stones hurt his knees, and he kept cracking his head on the low roof. The elf-child didn't struggle. She was as light and stiff as a dead bird. Fervently he hoped she hadn't really died – of fright or the damage he was causing by tugging her over the rocks.

The gradient changed, and he grunted and panted till he could turn around. It was much harder going up than it had been coming down. On hands and knees he hauled the elf-child up the shifting slope until soil and clay glued the stones together, the roof rose, and he could see a patch of grey night ahead. *At last!*

"Sir?" he called. "Lord Hugo?"

The entrance blackened and pinched small. Wolf heard grunts and curses. Hugo was crawling into the cave.

"What happened? Were you afraid to come out?" He sounded impatient and suspicious. "There was never any elf, was there?

"Yes there was," Wolf panted. "Help me pull her out."

"Argos came out long ago. *Pull her out*? You mean you've got her?"

"Yes." Triumph vibrated in Wolf's voice.

"Splendour of God," Hugo swore. He squeezed closer, breathing heavily. "Where? Could I get down there? Is it really the way to Elfland?"

He was entirely blocking the passage. All the light vanished. Wolf felt a wave of suffocating panic.

"What did you see?" Hugo whispered harshly.

Wolf suppressed the urge to scream and thrash his way out. "I'll tell you later – later," he gasped. "Help me with her, please!"

"Hand her up then," Hugo commanded.

Lying with his legs deep in the tunnel, Wolf dragged the child past his own body. She had curled into a tight, cold ball and was doing nothing to help herself. He felt her vanish upwards as Hugo pulled her away.

Wolf followed as fast as he could. He scrambled into the fresh, open night. The rain fell on him like a blessing, and Argos pranced to meet him.

Hugo turned, holding the elf-girl in his arms. "Well done! Well done," he said fiercely. Then he threw back his head and yelled, a war cry that sent thrills down Wolf's spine: "Rollo! Geraint! Roger! *A moy, gens de la Motte Rouge*! Men of the Red Mound, to me! Bring torches!"

He strode down through the dark wood, shouting, and his men came crashing through the bushes to meet him, trailing spears and brandishing flaming sticks.

"My lord? Lord Hugo?"

"By the Holy Face, who's with him? And what's that?"

"Wait till you see," Hugo roared. "A better quarry than a wolf, men!" He shouldered his way out into the clearing, and dumped the child on the ground.

The men, eight or nine of them, clustered around swearing incredulously and kicking away inquisitive dogs. Their makeshift torches were already flickering out in the wind, but the light of the sinking fire played over the elf-girl where she crouched at Lord Hugo's feet, smeared with red mud, all sharp spine and bony ribs, her disfigured face hidden against her knees. Her sides heaved and sank, heaved and sank in rapid breaths. The weird puffball of matted hair looked as unreal as when Wolf had first seen her. On her fingers and toes, long brownish nails curled like claws.

"By the bones of Saint Thomas, what is it?"

"It's a kiddie, eh?"

"No kiddie ever looked like that."

"It's an elf!" Hugo flung an arm around Wolf's shoulders. "We were hunting elves as well as wolves, men, though we didn't know it. There's a cave under the cliff back there. One of the old, lost mines. It leads down to Elfland! Argos was lost inside. And this boy went in after him and brought out the elf."

Wolf swayed where he stood. The rain beat into his

face and shoulders. He was deathly cold, but burning pride ran like hot metal through the marrow of his bones at Hugo's praise. Surely – surely now there was a good chance Lord Hugo would make him a squire?

The men growled. "Let it go, lord," said one of them bluntly, to mutters of agreement. "It's not safe to meddle with such things."

"Let it go? Splendour of God, no! Not for any danger. How many men, think you, have chased and caught an elf? Rollo, look after the boy."

"I've got him." A rough hand gripped his arm. "Hey, you – hold up!"

Wolf's tired eyes jerked open. Kneeling beside the fire, some of the men were knotting the elf-girl into a cloak. He heard snatches of low-voiced, horrified conversation.

"Say your prayers, boys – we're bringing it home!"

The man holding Wolf said into his ear, "Oh, you've done it now, young fellow. Do you *know* what you've done?"

"Lord Hugo w-wanted me to find an elf," Wolf mumbled.

The man shook him: "So you look! Next time, you look, but you don't find anything! Got that?"

"Is Hugo mad?" A Welsh voice, hissing with disapproval. "Those old mines, they go right down to Annwn, to Elfland – and deeper for all I know: full of devils and ghosts and *Duw* knows what? This'll bring bad luck: terrible luck. We'll be riding home with the Wild Host on our heels."

"Shut up, Geraint," said the man holding Wolf.

"I'll say what I like!" The Welsh voice again. "And I won't touch a finger to the creature. *Duw*! I'd sooner touch a viper."

There was a pause.

"What'll we do with the clerk, Rollo?"

"Hoist him up behind me," Rollo grunted.

Unfriendly hands boosted Wolf on to the wet hindquarters of a horse. He wrapped his arms around Rollo's thick waist and clung on as they jounced downhill. They scrambled across a ditch and turned south with a ringing clatter of iron horseshoes along a straight, stone road.

Wolf's head kept nodding forwards on to Rollo's shoulder. Then he'd wake with a lurch of panic, and grip Rollo harder to stop himself falling. On they rode through the rain-blurred darkness – men, horses and dogs all hurrying, all eager to get home.

CHAPTER 3

Nest – that was her true name, though she tried to think of herself as Agnes – came out of her freezing bedchamber, clasping a cushion in front of her chest like some kind of round, padded shield. She'd endured the cold as long as she could, just for the luxury of being on her own. She'd sat reading by candlelight until her fingers were numb and shaking, and she was afraid she'd tear the precious pages. Now she stood on the high landing at the top of the stairs, her shivers gradually decreasing in the mild smoky air of the Great Hall, and looked over the rail into the vast, fire-flickering space below.

Rain burst against the shutters. The Hall was warm,

silent and pleasantly gloomy. Soon it would fill up with noisy men and their muddy boots, and the smells of sweat and wet wool and wet dogs. But for now they were all out – except the unlucky few stuck at their posts on the watchtower and the gate. The only two people downstairs were Howell the priest, and her nurse Angharad. It was probably safe to go down…

She leaned further over the rail. Just as she'd thought, Angharad and old Howell were both asleep. Howell's white head nodded forward over his stick, which he clasped between his knees. Angharad was sitting on a stool near the fire. Her sewing had slipped from her lap, and she snored softly.

Nest drummed her fingers on the taut fabric of the cushion. She didn't mind Howell, but Angharad was such a chatterbox. If she woke up, she would want to start gossiping about Godfrey of La Blanche Land. Again. Nothing could stop Angharad once she started. She would go on talking even if Nest refused to answer.

"You're very quiet," she would giggle. "Dreaming of Lord Godfrey? Don't you worry, my *cariad,* it won't be long before he comes and then we'll know all about him. What a handsome little boy he was, the day you were betrothed! You won't remember, you were only little. He had dark hair just like yours – though I prefer a fair-haired man myself, like your noble father. My own second husband was a fair-haired man, God rest him. The first was an old dotard I would never have picked for myself, but of course I had no choice in the matter. Thirteen I was at the time, just the same age as you are now. But it wasn't long before a cold on the chest carried him off, the poor silly fellow. He should have listened to me when I told him to wear his old brown cloak with the double lining. 'You should wrap up,' I said, 'you're not as young as you were. At your time of life it's better to be warm than smart.' But oh no, he knew best, off he went and came back coughing. 'It's your own fault,' I told him, as I sat at his sickbed. 'You have nobody to blame but yourself.' He died, in spite of the fact that I never left his side, and then I was free to marry my Dafydd. Thirteen is young to wed, but I believe in girls marrying young. It keeps them steady. If only you hadn't lost your dear lady mother, and your noble father hadn't taken the Cross and gone off to fight those wicked Saracens –" here she would cross herself "– curse them, then you might have been married already! At least Lord Godfrey's a *young* man. Many a poor lady has to marry a greybeard old enough to be her father. I don't hold with *that*. Winter marrying spring, I call it. January and May should never wed, but with you and Lord Godfrey it will be like May marrying June!"

Nest picked viciously at the cushion, tugging out a loose thread. She didn't feel a bit May-like. If she had to be a month, she thought it would be a very early, chilly March, with frost on the ground and ice on the puddles. But it was no use saying that kind of thing to Angharad, because Angharad never listened. She could go on for hours, wondering aloud whether Godfrey was tall or short, sporting or bookish, plain or handsome – until Nest had to bite the insides of her cheeks and twist her ankles around each other and clench her fingers in her lap to stop herself from flying to pieces.

Down by the fire, Angharad twitched and let out a soft snore. Nest decided to risk it. Plucking up her skirt she tiptoed quickly downstairs. In the pool of light cast by the fire, the rushes covering the floor glowed a bright, summery green. They were clean – swept out and replaced every week – and gave off a faint, fresh scent. Nest dropped her cushion, sat on it, and kicked off her leather shoes. She wrapped her arms around her knees and pushed out stockinged feet to the blaze.

The hearth was octagonal, flat, with a border of old roof tiles sunk edgewise into the earth in a herringbone pattern. The big logs burned on an iron grid, dripping bright flakes on to a dragon-hoard of glowing embers. The heat played on her skin. Her face baked, and the folds of her green woollen dress were soon almost scorching. The last of her shivers died. It was glorious.

In the warm drift of ashes at the edge of the hearth something stirred – something the size of a very big tomcat. It shook off a snowfall of ash, sneezed, and said in a wheezing voice like a leaky bagpipe, "Come down for a bit of a warm, have you, young missis?"

"It's Lady Agnes to you!"

"That's right," the thing went on, ignoring this, "you wiggle them pretty little toes." It stretched a horny hand towards her feet, as if to rub them.

Nest pulled her skirt over her toes. "Oh no, you don't!"

"Ho ho!" It clicked its tongue annoyingly and sniggered. "Standoffish, eh? You'll have to be nicer than that to Lord *Godfrey*, when he comes. What's the matter? I've known you since you was a babby. Don't you like me any more?"

"I don't approve of you," Nest told it crisply.

"What for? Just acos I'm a *bwbach* – a poor old hearth-hob?"

"Not because you're a hob," Nest said. "Because you're so *lazy*. We had a hearth-hob at Our Lady's In-the-Wood, and it was always busy. The nuns used to say they didn't know what they would do without it. It swept and cleaned and polished, and it would leave sweet little bunches of flowers for Mother Aethelflaed to put in front of the shrine of Our Lady, just as if it was a Christian."

The hearth-hob made a rude noise with its lips, but it saw that Nest wasn't listening. Glassy tears swam in her eyes and looked in danger of spilling over. She hugged her knees tight and bent her head.

"I wish I was still there," she said, muffled into her skirt.

"Oh, I dunno," the hob said awkwardly. "Can't have been much fun, stuck in a convent – eh?"

"Oh, it was!" Nest sniffed. "It was so civilised. Every evening we would sit, and Mother Aethelflaed or one of the sisters would read aloud, and then we would converse—"

"What d'you call this?" said the hob. "We'm conversating now, ain't we?"

"Oh, but about *interesting* things," said Nest passionately. "About stars and planets – about saints and miracles – about beasts and birds and far-off lands—"

The hob coughed. "There's a rat's nest in the pantry, I knows that," it offered.

"Don't be stupid!" Nest lifted a wet face and glared at it. "That's exactly what I mean. Nobody here can talk about anything but wolves and dogs and horses."

"Rats ain't exactly—" the hob began, but Nest swept on.

"And there were lots of books there, and music – we would sing together. Play harps. I wanted to do something great, hob."

"Er?"

"I don't know what." Nest stared into the smoky heights above the fire. "Write about a saint's life so that everyone could read it, perhaps. Or become the abbess of a holy house and inspire people and save souls. Or go on a pilgrimage to Rome or Jerusalem."

She dropped her face back on to her knees. "But I've got to get married."

"That'll be all right," the hob encouraged her. "You'll have lots of lovely bouncing babbies, right?" It gave her a sly glance. "I loves babbies. Cunning little things – dribbling and burping and crying…"

Nest shuddered. She screwed her eyes shut. *Sweet blessed Saviour*, she prayed into the folds of her skirt, *I know that I must get married, but let that not be all that ever happens to me. Send me a miracle. Let me have some wonderful work to do for You.*

"Oh well." The hob crooked a hairy elbow to scratch its back. It grunted and strained, trying to reach the bit in the middle, gave up and yawned, showing a lot of blunt yellow teeth. "What's for supper tonight? Roast pork and crackling?"

"It's Friday," said Nest, wiping her eyes.

"Is it?" The hob's face fell. "No meat," it grumbled. "Fasting on a Friday. Who thought that one up? What's the point?"

Nest sat up. "Fasting brings us closer to the angels," she said coldly. "Angels never eat. They spend all their time praising God."

"Only cos they ain't got stummicks," the hob muttered. "Go on, then, what's for supper? Herbert's not the worst cook I've ever known. We won't starve. Fish, I s'pose? A nice bit of carp or trout?"

"At Our Lady's," Nest began, "the hob was perfectly satisfied with a simple bowl of gruel…"

She stopped as the hob sat up. Its hairy ears pricked and swivelled. Nest tilted her head. Beyond the thick walls and shutters, from far over the staked and defended ramparts and the deep ditch, horns were blowing. Then, loud and near, an answering blast from the gatehouse, and the shouts of the porters as they ran to swing back the heavy gate.

"They'm back." The hob gave her a wink. "Don't forget the fish. Not the tail. A nice juicy piece from the middle, with just a spoonful of sauce: Herbert does a good sauce. No need to finnick about with the bones; I eats 'em." With a flurry of ash it burrowed out of sight.

"Greedy thing." Nest clicked her tongue in irritation and stood, dusting ashes from her skirt. The big Hall door creaked open. In ran Walter and Mattie, dark rain-spatters on their clothes. They wrestled the door shut against the night wind, and with a nod and a curtsy to Nest, began setting up the Hall for supper. Scrape! Crash! They dragged the benches out from the walls and lowered the wooden table tops on to the trestles. Old Howell sat up with a start. Flap! The white linen cloth sank billowing on to the High Table. Angharad yawned and groped to straighten her veil and headband. "Dearie me, did I drop off? Is my lord your father back, Nest *cariad*?"

"He's just ridden in." Nest raised her voice. "What's for supper, Mattie?"

"Eels in batter with a sharp sauce, madam. And then a sweet omelette, and apples stewed in wine and honey. S'cuse me, madam, I'm in such a hurry." Mattie scurried to and from the pantry with cups and handfuls of spoons. "Herbert's in one of his moods, what with the hunt coming back so late. And now there's an awful rush on in the kitchen..."

Nest pulled on her shoes. She threw her veil over her hair, went to the door and stuck her head out into the wild night. The wind tore flames from a single torch flaring on a post down near the gatehouse. A bobbing river of excited dogs streamed into the kennels. Men dropped stiffly from their saddles, and the dark shapes of tired horses clopped over the wet cobbles and into the stable.

"Nest! Nest!" Angharad shrilled behind her. "Run and lay out some dry clothes for your father. He'll need to change before supper."

Instead, Nest leaned further into the rain. The last horse to come under the gateway was carrying two riders. It plodded wearily into the torchlight, and the second rider slid clumsily down over the animal's tail. As the horse walked away he staggered and nearly fell.

"They've brought someone home with them!" Nest exclaimed. "A stranger – riding behind Rollo."

"Oh, who can it be?" Angharad hurried across and peered out, breathing hard and squeezing Nest against the doorpost.

The stranger rubbed dirty hands down the front of his ragged dark robe and looked around as though he wasn't sure what to do next. On top of his head, a shaved patch shone pale in the torchlight.

"A tonsure! By Saint Mary, one of the holy brothers!" Angharad's face was alight with curiosity. "Young, too – only a boy. How tired he looks! Wherever has he come from? Not Ystrad Marcella, for sure: they're all white monks there, and that's a black robe he's wearing. Couldn't be Wenford, surely, the other side of the mountain? Or, I wonder now—"

"He can tell us himself in a minute," Nest said. Her voice shook with excitement. A clerk – young, educated! If only he would stay and be someone she could read and write and talk with! She dug an elbow into Angharad's doughy side. "Angharad, let me get past. My father will want me to go out and welcome them all."

In fact Lord Hugo was still in the saddle and hadn't glanced at the open doorway. With one hand he controlled his horse, which turned and trampled, tugging the reins, eager to get to the stable. With the other he was holding some kind of bundle at his saddle bow. "Splendour of God!" he bellowed at his men. "Take it, one of you! I can't sit here all night!"

But the men were slow to obey. It was the young clerk who reached for the bundle – something all swaddled up in a cloak. He took it clumsily, leaning back and averting his face as though he was afraid it would bite.

"Whatever can it be?" Nest muttered.

"Take it inside!" Hugo ordered as he swung down from his horse. Obediently the boy headed for the Hall door. As the light from the doorway reached him, Nest took in every detail. Below the shaven scalp he had a ring of thick, fair hair. His face was fresh, bold and open; but he looked as if he had rolled in mud. Why was he so filthy? *I'll have to send Mattie for gallons of hot water and towels. Supper will have to wait even longer, and oh dear, Herbert will be furious.*

Her eyes widened. There was a patch of sticky blood in the boy's hair and smeared across his cheek. He must have been attacked by robbers. Her father must have rescued him. Poor boy! Her heart swelled in sympathy.

But before she could speak to him, the bundle he was carrying suddenly kicked and squirmed. The boy let go, yelping. He stepped back on the torn hem of his robe, and sat down in the mud.

The bundle humped up like a caterpillar. The corners had been tied in clumsy rabbit-ear knots, with a belt buckled around the middle. Now the knots came apart and a little girl struggled out on to the doorstep, almost at Nest's feet. She was small, pale, surely no more than five years old. Her bony knees were dark with calluses. She had skinny shanks, sharp elbows, claw-like hands and feet and a vast tangle of colourless hair. She looked up. Half her face was dark red, like bread dipped in wine.

For a frozen heartbeat nobody moved.

My miracle, Nest thought with appalled certainty. She had prayed for some good work to do, and God had promptly sent her this. She stretched out a trembling hand. The child spat like an angry cat and shot away.

"Close the gate!" Lord Hugo yelled. But the child wasn't aiming for the gate. She disappeared around the corner of the Great Hall.

Nest didn't pause to think. She snatched up her skirts and raced after. As she turned the corner into the rutted track that ran between the Hall and the cookhouse, rain blew into her face like showers of arrows, and her feet slipped in the mud. Ahead, the dark bulk of the motte with its tall watchtower loomed up into the night.

From their high vantage point on the boardwalk along the ramparts, the guards began yelling, pointing into the yard. "There it goes – past the cookhouse!"

"I see it! Shall I shoot?"

"That's Lady Agnes, you fool – *put that bow down!*"

"It's gone – I've lost it."

"It's doubled back!"

Dogs barked, horses whinnied in terror, men shouted and stamped along the hollow planking. Nest saw the castle as the child must see it – a frightening place of black shadows and glaring flames. The cookhouse door stood open like an entrance into Hell, the fires within colouring the cloud of smoke which rose from the vented roof. Inside, Herbert the cook was bellowing at some underling.

Squelching footsteps sounded behind her. The young clerk came panting up, his bare legs spattered with mud. He called out in rough-sounding English. She didn't understand a word.

"Can't you speak French?"

"You mean you can?" The boy sounded taken aback. "Quick," he added just as roughly, "which way did she go?"

Does he think I'm a servant? Nest opened her mouth to say something sharp. But he could hardly expect to meet Lord Hugo's daughter chasing a beggar child across a muddy yard. And he would be dreadfully embarrassed when he found out. She forgave him…

"WHICH – WAY?" the boy repeated loudly and slowly, as if to an idiot.

"I don't know! When I got round the corner, she'd vanished." Nest clutched her veil as the wind threatened to blow it off her head. "Who is she? And who are you? Where have you come from?"

"Never mind that now." He threw the words over his shoulder, already striding off into the rainy darkness. "What's over here?"

"Only the midden – the dunghill." Affronted, Nest ran after him. "Wait. What's her name? And yours?"

"I'm called Wolf. Don't know about her. Lord Hugo and me – we think she's an elf."

"*Lord Hugo and you*?" Nest caught up. "An elf? What do you mean?"

"You know what an elf is, don't you?" he said impatiently. "A fairy; a fay."

"How dare you speak to me—" Nest forgot what she was saying. A cart stood beside the cookhouse wall. Behind the dark shelter of the wheels, a pale shape lurked. "There! She's there, see? Hiding under the cart!"

The boy seized her arm. "Quick, run and fetch Lord Hugo."

"*You* run and fetch him, you impudent – fellow!"

Nest flashed. She jerked her arm free and stepped towards the cart, lifting her skirt out of the mud in a bunched handful. "God bless you, my poor child," she called in what she hoped was a soothing voice. "Don't be frightened. No one will hurt you." But the child dodged around the wheels and sped away like a fleeing ghost.

"Now see what you've done, you *stupid* girl!" hissed the boy. He shoved past her, bawling at the top of his voice, "She went this way! Come quickly!"

Geraint and Rollo came running, hooting and shouting, waving their arms. From the stables came young Madog, chubby Roger Bach and grizzled Walter with pitchforks and hay rakes. The child jinked and doubled back. She couldn't go around the back of the Hall without passing Nest and the boy. There was only one bolt-hole left to try, and she took it. She shot straight through the open door of the cookhouse. The men piled after her, with Nest and the boy close behind.

The cookhouse erupted in screams, cries and smashing dishes. "Catch her – catch the elf!" roared Rollo. Past his burly back, Nest caught glimpses of the wild child rushing around and around the kitchen like a trapped squirrel – jumping at the walls, clutching at shelves, bringing crocks and pans clattering down – leaping over tables, dodging past the oven.

"Be careful!" Nest screamed. "Mind the fire!" In the

centre of the room, waist-high flames licked the sides of the huge black cooking pot where broth for the garrison was briskly boiling. "Quick, someone – catch her!"

But how could she be caught? No one wanted to touch her. The kitchen cats streaked for the door. Tall, fierce Bronwen the kitchen maid rushed out of the scullery with a pail of water and threw it wildly over everything. Round-faced Gwenny shrieked and shrieked.

"Catch the elf!"

The child leaped at a dresser and tipped over a basketful of eggs. A row of frying pans full of sizzling hot fat capsized into the fire. Furious yellow flames crackled up. Chopping boards, bowls and trays of loaves went flying.

"*By all the devils in Hell!*" Scarlet-faced and terrible, Herbert the cook revolved yelling in the midst of the chaos. He plucked a huge iron ladle from a rack and waved it in the air. "*Get out of my kitchen!*"

The boy pushed past Nest and launched himself at the child, seizing her shoulder. She turned, clawing like a wildcat. Together they crashed to the floor and disappeared under a pile of bodies as Rollo, Bernard and the others hurled themselves on top. "She'll be squashed! Don't hurt her!" Nest screamed, dancing from foot to foot in anguish.

Herbert waded into the scrum, eyes popping with

fury. "*Out, the whole boiling lot of you, before I cut every one of you to collops!*" He whirled the ladle and began indiscriminately whacking exposed heads, arms and elbows. Geraint yelled and staggered away clutching his head. Rollo and Bernard scrambled up, cursing.

Herbert caught the boy by the scruff and the seat, and tossed him aside.

"By Saint Laurence roasting on his griddle! Half a dozen of you, and you can't catch one little brat with less meat on her bones than a picked goose the day after Michaelmas?" He advanced on the child, swinging his ladle. "Don't move, you. Not so much as an eyeball!" She froze, staring at him in terror. Herbert snapped his fingers. He seized a piece of bread and threw it to her. "Here! Sink your little teeth into that and stop wrecking my kitchen."

The child flinched from the missile as if it was a stone, but she watched it fall and darted towards it on all fours. She sniffed it. Finally she grabbed it. With a suspicious glance at the staring crowd, she turned her back, pressed herself close to the wall, and crammed the bread into her mouth with spidery fingers.

"Why, the child's starving!" Bronwen exclaimed.

"That's no child – it's one of the Fair Family!" shouted Geraint.

"That's right! It's an elf! Lord Hugo found it on the hill!"

"*Silence!*" Herbert roared. He scowled around the room, scratching the back of his thick neck, lingering on the spillages, the breakages, the smashed and dripping eggs. The kitchen servants quailed. Even the men-at-arms avoided his eye. "Right!" he bellowed, "I don't care if it's an elf, or a beggar's brat, or an imp out of Hell, I want to know which of you ignorant, flea-bitten fools let it loose in my—" For the first time, he noticed Nest standing in the doorway. Crimson veins popped out on his forehead.

"Madam!" In a gesture of angry duty he snatched off his cook's cap, wiped his glistening face with the back of a hairy wrist, and glared at her. *What are you doing here?* his face plainly said. *How dare you see me lose control of my own kitchen!*

Nest stood flushing, the focus of all eyes. The men pulled off their caps, while Gwenny and Bronwen bobbed curtsies. And the boy, Wolf, gave her an astounded, furious glance – as though she had deliberately made a fool of him. Nest tried to carry it off. She lifted her chin. "W-well done, Herbert."

Three loud handclaps sounded behind her. "Well done, indeed!" Nest spun around and saw her father. He gave her a sharp, hard look, and she began to stammer excuses. But he ignored them and said laughing to Herbert, "If only you had been with me in the Holy Land, Herbert.

You would have been more use to me than a whole troop of knights. Can you salvage our supper?"

Herbert's face darkened to quivering purple as he choked down his temper. At the same time, Nest saw his meaty chest heave with pride at Lord Hugo's praise. In an unnaturally mild, piping voice he said, "Certainly, my lord – if only I can get these *people* out of my *way*." He glowered at the intruding men-at-arms. "But supper may be late."

"No matter," Lord Hugo drawled. "Clear up here, and then we'll eat."

Under Herbert's gimlet eye, the kitchen staff began very obviously to bustle about. Bronwen clapped her hands at Roger and Bernard, Geraint and Rollo, shooing them out of the door. Plump Gwenny found a brush and shovel. She got down on her knees and started sweeping up broken crocks. And over by the wall, the strange child gnawed the remains of her bread. Nest picked up another piece and slipped closer.

Absorbed by her food, the child didn't react until Nest was right beside her. How thin she was! As she wrenched at the bread, her shoulder blades were snap-sharp under the skin. Nest held the bread out. "Hello…"

The child's eyes flashed up. In the light, they shone a beautiful light green, like clear glass. Nest caught her breath. *But she's pretty*! In spite of the dirt, in spite of the dark red birthmark and the matted, tangled hair, this strange child was pretty.

A hand jerked Nest away. She stumbled against her father. He let go, and indignantly she rubbed her arm. "Too close, Agnes," he said, fierce and low. "What are you doing here? You're not to go anywhere near the creature, do you understand? Keep away from her."

"But she's just a child," Nest began.

The child hissed. Her lips drew back over sharp, white teeth. Nest threw the bread, and stepped back.

"An elf-child," corrected her father. "Look at her face. Look at those nails – they're like claws. She came out of the mines on Devil's Edge. The boy here found her."

A little shudder ran down Nest's spine. An elf-girl in their own castle – a fairy child from the underworld come to live at La Motte Rouge! She clenched her fingers in excitement, trying to think what she knew about elves. Some kind of lost spirits, weren't they, midway between Heaven and Hell, doomed to pass away forever at the Day of Judgement? *Maybe this one can be saved. Maybe that's what I've got to do. Tame her and teach her and save her!* She saw the child transformed: clean, clothed and happy. The first step would be to choose her a name. *I'll be her godmother. I'll call her—*

"Elfgift," said the boy, interrupting her thoughts. He cleared his throat and looked at her father. "I thought we could call her Elfgift. It's an English name," he added, colouring. "It means—"

"I know what it means," said Hugo. "Well, why not? It's too late to do anything with her tonight, but tomorrow," he added grimly, "we'll find out whether she can speak and tell us a different name." He raised his voice. "Bronwen, make sure that this *gift of the elves* is washed and clothed, and then lock her up somewhere safe for the night."

Bronwen grimaced. She flung back her head and squared her strong shoulders. "I'll try, lord – if Gwenny can help me. We can shut her up in one of the stables – if my lord really wants to keep her." A question lilted in her voice, but Hugo ignored it.

"I want to help, too," said Nest.

"You will not," said her father.

"Oh, but—" Nest looked into his hard face and cast her eyes down. Arguing would be useless. And Bronwen clapped both hands over a shocked snort. "God's mercy, madam! Not you! That won't be a job fit for Lady Agnes."

Was Bronwen laughing at her? Something inside Nest crinkled up with shame and resentment. Her father was treating her like a child. And Bronwen, Bronwen with her mane of black hair, as strong as a mountain pony, as brown as a berry, clearly thought

Nest too weak and timid to be useful. Bronwen was only a kitchen maid, and it was stupid to care what she thought… but Nest did care. She cared a lot.

And that Wolf boy was grinning.

Him!

She already didn't like him. Now she liked him even less. Anger crackled inside her like a newly lit fire. Why was it funny? Why did being Lady Agnes mean that she was never allowed to do anything? At least, *at least* her father should answer one last question. She would make him. Swinging round, she dipped him a stiff, challenging curtsy, and said very loudly and clearly, "But what do you mean to do with the child, my lord?"

Anger darkened Hugo's face, but he hesitated. For a moment, triumphant, she thought she'd won. He could not refuse to answer her in front of the servants. The kitchen fell quiet. Herbert's small eyes narrowed to the size of currants. Bronwen's eyes widened. Gwenny gaped at Lord Hugo, slack-mouthed and expectant. What did Lord Hugo want the elf-girl *for*?

"Lady Agnes! Madam! Oh, my *Lady Agnes*!" Angharad scuttled into the kitchen like a plump, flustered hen. "You naughty, naughty girl!" she scolded Nest, and turned to Lord Hugo. "Don't think I haven't taught her better than this, my lord, because I have. Running off into the night and romping in the kitchen?

My goodness. Now you come back with me this minute and behave like a lady."

Nest gulped down a great lump of anger and pride. Silently she curtsied again to her father. *I won't make a scene. I won't make a fuss!*

The moment was over. Herbert turned to shout at a couple of dogs that had sneaked in to lick up the smashed eggs. And the boy, Wolf, caught her eye for a fleeting second and looked quickly away. His mouth twitched – as if he was trying not to laugh. Nest hated him. She held her head high and let her gaze sweep coldly past.

Then Angharad gripped her by the arm like a prisoner and towed her away.

CHAPTER 4

Wolf woke from a dream of riding in a wild cavalcade that went sweeping through dark skies over the reeling countryside, while he looked down in terror on hills which lay huddled together like hogs in a pen.

He opened his eyes, not in relief, but with a feeling of guilt and restlessness.

He was lying on a pallet not far from the fire. The floor was warm from the glow of the heaped embers. There was a smell of soft smoke and green rushes. Somewhere nearby, a mouse squeaked as a cat pounced on it. Around him, Lord Hugo's household lay snoring, coddled in cloaks on their straw mattresses.

Wolf's back was sore. He rolled on to his side. It must

be about the second hour after midnight, he thought. At the abbey right now, shivering boys were dragging each other out of bed, splashing icy water on their hands and faces, and stumbling down draughty stone steps to the chancel for the fourteen psalms and lengthy readings of the Night Office.

He drew his knees up and snuggled the blanket to his chin, trying to enjoy the warmth. He wasn't at the abbey any more. He could sleep as long as he liked and not get up till morning… But sleep would not return. He itched, twitched, tossed, scratched and at last sat up, pushing the blanket aside.

The Hall was a vast shell of space enclosing warm air and shadows. He tipped back his head and stared up at the vaulting rafters, and the dim paintings on the plaster walls: bands of chequers and rosettes, and between each shuttered window a great fierce animal: a leopard, a griffon, or a lion. The High Table at the end of the room was a dark cave under its silken canopy. Behind it the stairs climbed to the solar – the private chamber of Lord Hugo and his heiress, the Lady Agnes.

Wolf sat mulling gloomily over the past hours.

Supper had been an ordeal. He'd washed off the worst of the mud in a tub of tepid water. Hugo had promised him new clothes to wear; but so far nobody had brought them. In his tattered robe, he felt like a shabby black crow amidst the peacock colours of Hugo and his men.

He'd not known where to sit, so at first it was a relief to be shown to one of the lower tables, amongst the men-at-arms. At the abbey, food was served and eaten in strict silence. But here, once Hugo's chaplain – a white-haired old man whose voice was hardly audible – had pronounced the blessing, everyone crossed themselves and burst into noisy conversation. Wolf sat dumb and miserable while the talk raged over him. It wasn't just that they ignored him; they talked such a muddle of French, Welsh and English that he only picked up about one word in three. He shared a platter with a bald, cheery faced man called Roger Bach, whose single remark to Wolf as he sat down was, "Pass the salt," and who spent most of the meal shouting incomprehensible jests to a tall, skinny fellow called Stephen le Beau on the other side of the board – and then roaring with laughter at his own jokes.

Then – far worse than being ignored – there had been a sudden hush. Wolf had looked up to see the girl, Lady Agnes, standing at his elbow. Covered in confusion he'd scrambled to his feet, but she'd bowed slightly and said in a voice colder than icicles, "Lord Hugo sends you this dish from his own table and begs that you will enjoy it with him." With that, she'd shoved a plate of some kind of special food into his hands and retreated without another word.

Roger Bach nudged him in the ribs. "*You're* in favour," he'd said disapprovingly. "What's she given you?"

Flushed to the ears, Wolf investigated. It turned out to be chunks of fresh, white eel meat in a crisp batter, with a wine sauce, both sharp and sweet. It tasted delicious, but under the envious noses of his table companions (who were eating a perfectly good but ordinary broth), Wolf could hardly choke it down.

"Funny old life," Roger sniffed. "Some of us serve Lord Hugo for years and years, and never get to share a dish from his table. Then some *other* people turn up out of the blue and get made a big fuss of for digging out a scrawny little elf-girl.

"But we're only *soldiers*," he'd added nastily.

He doesn't like me, Wolf thought now. *I don't think any of them like me – except Lord Hugo. And Argos! Certainly not Lady Agnes.* With a hot prickle of discomfort he thought how he'd ordered her about, and called her a stupid girl.

Anyone would have made the same mistake, he decided indignantly. She ought to have behaved properly, instead of running around the yard like a servant. She obviously had no sense of humour – he'd tried to catch her eye and smile when her interfering nurse dragged her out: and she'd looked straight through him.

So what? He shrugged. He wouldn't have much to do with her. And perhaps the men would change their minds about him, once he was out of these monkish clothes.

He hugged his knees. Coloured clothes tomorrow! He'd worn shapeless black robes for years. And with rising excitement he thought there was a really good chance now that Lord Hugo would make him a squire. He'd done far more for Lord Hugo than finding his dog. It was Lord Hugo who mattered.

He thought about Hugo, who had sat at the supper table with his long legs stretched out in soft leather boots stamped with little gold rosettes, a mantle of chequered black and green flung over his broad shoulders. Tall, strong and blue-eyed, his fair hair cut short, his handsome face clean shaven, Hugo looked the mirror of knightly splendour. But his expression was hot and impatient, flashing easily between laughter and anger. He might be a hard lord to please.

Wolf realised he'd succeeded almost by accident. If he hadn't made friends with Hugo's hound – if the hound hadn't followed the elf-girl – if his own impulsive pride hadn't driven him to enter the cave and fetch her out – would he be sitting here now? Or would Hugo have left him wandering on the mountain?

He crushed the thought. *Lord Hugo's a crusader, a hero. Of course he wouldn't have left me!* And yet a serpent voice whispered, *It isn't me Hugo's interested in. It's the elf-girl.*

Why *had* Hugo carried Elfgift home, against the wishes of all his men? Wolf was sure it had something to do with that other mystery. Eluned. Hugo had trembled as he leaned into the cave and called the name. It was a woman's name; but whose? There didn't seem to be a wife in the castle; Lady Agnes' mother must be dead. Perhaps Eluned was some girl Hugo loved. But why would any girl go wandering about on Devil's Edge, or hiding in a cave? It made no sense.

The wind shook the walls. Wolf shivered. He thought of the elf-child, shut up in the stables. Was she wakeful too, and listening to the wind? Had he done the right thing, taking her away? If he'd left her in the cave, what would have happened? Would the gates of Elfland have opened to let her in?

"At least she's warm and dry," he said to himself. "And safe from the wolves. I'm glad I did it. I'm glad I brought her out."

From the bright margins of the fire came a soft and evil chuckle: "*Ho ho ho…!*"

Wolf's head snapped round. For a moment, he could have sworn someone with hot, glowing eyes sat cross-legged in the ashes, grinning at him. But there was nothing there. Only an unburned, crooked log and a heap of crumbling ash.

As for the strange chuckling sound, one of the snoring sleepers must have muttered something. Unless… Wolf threw an uneasy glance around the great, shadowy Hall. Back at the abbey, the prayers of the Night Office would continue until dawn. Often he'd heard the Devil whispering in his ear, "*Go back to sleep… it's cold in the chapel but it's warm in bed… lovely and warm…*" It was the duty of the brothers to roust each other out. Now here he was, miles away. A deserter, a traitor to Christ. No wonder if fiends were keeping an eye on him…

Suddenly Wolf knew he'd never get back to sleep unless he got up, found Lord Hugo's chapel, and said his prayers. He wrapped the blanket around him like a cloak and threaded his way between the mattresses to the door. It stirred in the wind, clicking against the latch as though someone outside were testing its strength. Wolf put his shoulder against it and opened it a crack. He slid outside and eased it silently shut.

The wind was cold, but at least it had stopped raining. The high castle ramparts closed off the view everywhere but upwards: when he tipped back his head he saw a half circle of sky interrupted by rooftops and streaked with a few windswept stars. An owl whooped overhead, and something howled on the hillside. Maybe one of the wolves he'd seen. "You can't get me," he jeered softly. "I'm safe." The huge wooden gates were firmly shut, and the torch by the gateway had burned out. Even the guards were probably asleep. He was free to roam where he liked within the circuit of the walls.

To the right lay the cookhouse, the stables and the dunghill. The chapel must lie in the other direction. Trailing a hand along the plastered wall, he walked the length of the Great Hall. Unlit buildings ahead looked like a granary and a small house, but there was a gap between them and the end of the Hall. He slipped through and found himself in a little yard. To his left reared the massive slope of the mound.

Across the yard was the chapel, overshadowed by trees. He could distinguish the dark curve of an arched doorway, and a faint light glimmered from a tiny window set deep in the wall. Of course! There would be a lamp burning all night in front of the altar. Wolf strode confidently forward – and stumbled over a firm, fleshy hummock that heaved to its feet with a devilish shriek and leaped away, screaming.

A pig!

Wolf nearly screamed, too. He clapped a hand to his heart to stop it jumping out of his side, and waited for the watchmen to shout. But perhaps they were used to the alarms of pigs. No one called out. In a few moments the pig's squeals died to angry grunts as it trotted off through the mud, hunting for a new place to sleep. Shaking with painful giggles, Wolf splashed across the yard to the shelter of the chapel doorway, where he recovered his nerves and twisted the ring handle of the heavy wooden door.

Inside, the cold holy air smelled of stone and candle smoke, and the rich scent of incense. Wolf's eyes opened wide. Every wall was covered with paintings, whose colours glowed in the light of two candles standing on tall prickets against the south wall. A row of saints gazed down at him with calm, stern faces: Saint Agnes with her lamb, Saint Catherine with her wheel, Saint Winifred holding her decapitated head under her arm, Saint Margaret leading a chained dragon. On the opposite wall Saint Martin cut his cloak in two to give half to a grateful and adoring beggar. In the sanctuary a tiny, bright flame peeked through a pierced silver lamp holder and flung ornate shadows over the chancel walls. Wolf fell to his knees. He thanked God for bringing him safely over the mountain and out of the cave.

Then his tongue stuck. He wanted to be forgiven for running away. But he didn't feel sorry at all, and if he said he was, the sin of lying would be added to his account. And sinners went to Hell.

This was tricky.

"Holy Saint Agnes, Saint Winifred, Saint Martin, help me," he said carefully. "Please ask Saint Ethelred not to be too angry with me for running away from the abbey. And, holy Saint Martin, please let Lord Hugo reward me by making me his squire…"

His mouth curved in a dreamy smile. He imagined himself on a tall white horse, riding behind Hugo's black charger – a lance clasped under his arm, the scarlet and gold skirts of his long surcoat fluttering in the wind. Hugo turned, gave him a fierce grin. "Come on, Wolf – together now, charge! For God and King Richard!" The horses thundered into a gallop…

Wolf heaved a deep sigh. Then, in a voice that sounded thin and solitary compared with the richness of sixty men and boys chanting in unison at the abbey, he repeated the third psalm and the ninety-fourth, which were always sung at the Night Office.

He rose and dusted off his knees. He'd done his best. The chapel was full of silence. Accepting or rejecting him? He didn't know.

He turned to go. He had knelt for a long time. The candles on the south wall were guttering low. Between them was an alcove he hadn't noticed before. In the darkness of the alcove – Wolf drew a cold breath of quivering shock – a woman lay motionless on a low bed.

It wasn't a bed, he realised after the first stab of horror. It was a tomb. And the woman – he crept closer – wasn't real. She was a stone statue, an effigy; so cleverly painted that she looked almost alive. She lay staring upwards, her head propped on a small stone pillow. Her dark hair was covered with a white veil, her hands were crossed on her breast, and her toes poked stiffly from the folds of her rust red dress.

Wolf let go his breath with a sigh. The saints on the walls leaned over him, the air over the candle flames seemed to dance with invisible angels, and their heat struck him under the eyes. Around the base of the tomb, words had been painted. He bent to spell them out.

HOC+SEPVLCRVM+HUGO+WARINI+FILIVS+ VXORI+ELVNEDI+FACIENDVM+CURAVIT

Hugo son of Warin had this tomb raised for Eluned his wife.

Wolf was very still. Everything he thought he had worked out about Hugo fell down like a child's tower of wooden bricks, and lay scattered. '*Eluned his wife!*'

So, when Hugo had called so desperately into the darkness of the cave for a woman named Eluned, he had been calling the name of someone he knew to be dead.

One of the guttering candles went out, leaving all

the shadows twice as dark. The flame on the other flared and then shrank to a wobbling blue blob. Wolf felt the hairs rise on the back of his neck. He bowed to the altar and scuttled for the door, half expecting the stone woman to sit up and beckon him.

He blundered night-blind into the yard.

The moon was up behind the clouds, lighting them to watery vagueness. The wind blew farmyard smells. After the strangeness of the chapel, it was a perfectly ordinary night. Wolf leaned his cheek against the cold, iron studs in the thick door, his teeth chattering. Nothing had happened! There was nothing to fear – but, even if the men sleeping in the Hall weren't exactly friendly, he wanted to be back in the middle of them, in the safety of the walls and the glow of the fire.

In the faint moonlight he could see the yard – an expanse of greyish mud. He hurried across, and was about to slip around the corner of the Hall, where the huddled buildings made a darkness as intense as ink – when instinct made him pause, and a woman stepped around the corner from the opposite direction. She saw him and held up a warning finger. At the same time, part of the blackness at his feet stirred and grunted. An ear flapped – a trotter twitched. Wolf had been saved from falling over the pig for the second time that night.

"Thanks!" he gasped. His rescuer was wrapped in

flimsy clothing for this time of night: fluttering white garments with a light veil pulled across her face. She must be a lady of the household, one of Lady Agnes' women, though he hadn't noticed anyone like her at supper. Mist blew around her as she swayed towards him and murmured in a melancholy, musical voice: "*Dwi methu mynd i mewn.*"

"I'm sorry, I don't speak Welsh…"

Plainly disapproving of his ignorance, the lady shook her head sadly. After a moment she tried again, in the same mournful voice, but this time in Latin. Her accent was strange, but Wolf understood her. "I can't get in," she said softly, clasping her hands.

"You can't get in? You mean, into the chapel?"

"I can't get in."

"But it's not locked. Look, it's easy." Wolf retraced his steps across the yard and the lady followed. It was certainly getting colder; damper too: the mist was rising all around them like pale breath. He twisted the handle, pushed the heavy door ajar and stepped back politely for her to enter.

She peered in, twisting her hands together, but drew back and turned entreatingly towards him.

"I can't get in."

"But of course you—"

Wolf paused. Perhaps she was mad… Through the

transparent veil he glimpsed a sweet, wild face. "What's your name, lady?" he asked gently. But the question appeared to distress her. "I can't remember," she moaned, swaying in a sort of absent-minded dance. "*Gwae fi*! I can't remember!"

Wolf stared at her feet. She had crossed that dirty yard right behind him. His own shoes were clotted with mud. Yet there wasn't a single stain on her little white slippers.

He looked up. She was gazing at him through the veil with owl-black eyes. Surely eyes shouldn't be so round and so big – like dark coins? He began to back away.

"I can't get in!" she wailed.

"Sorry – sorry," Wolf gabbled. "I don't know what to…" It wasn't just the lady's fluttering clothes that were almost transparent. He could see the dark stones of the arched chapel doorway curving right through her body.

"Help!" Wolf shouted, stumbling away. "Help!"

From the other side of the bailey, a guard dog barked, deep and echoing. Someone shouted from the ramparts, "Shut up! Stop that racket! *How-ell-ll*!" And a nearby door creaked open, disclosing a glimmer of firelight. A white-haired old man limped out into the yard. The priest who had said the blessing at supper!

Wolf rushed at him. "Help me!" He clung to the old man's arm. "A ghost! She spoke to me! She wants to get into the chapel!"

The old man nodded as though he expected this. "No, no, that's no ghost, that's just our little *ladi wen,* our White Lady. No, she can't get in, the poor child. Don't worry, I'll soon deal with it."

He stepped forward so briskly that Wolf felt compelled to follow. Billows of mist floated across the yard, and the pale lady was still moaning and wringing her hands at the chapel door. "Hush now, hush!" the old man called in a soothing voice. The lady turned to him like a frightened child.

"I can't remember my name…"

"Dear, dear." The old man put on a pretence of surprise; Wolf got the impression he had done this many times before. "But that's all right, because, you see, we have a name for you. Dame Blanche; our White Lady. Our sweet Ladi Wen." He dropped into musical Welsh, and the lady listened very attentively. When he finished, she bowed her head in sorrowful consent, and walked smoothly away. The mist followed her. Her feet moved a fraction above the ground, and she drifted at a slight angle to the way she was facing, as though the wind had caught her – and when she reached the dark corner where the pig lay, Wolf wasn't sure if she went around it, or just vanished.

"There's better, now," said the old man cheerfully. "I suggested she takes a bath, see? She loves to have a splash in the cistern, and it's still an hour or two from daybreak."

Wolf wetted his lips. "But – but—"

The old man patted him. "Come in and see if my Hunith can make us both a nice hot drink."

Wolf followed him into a small, homely room containing a bed, a hearth, a few pots and pans hanging on the walls, and a tiny little woman. She was as wrinkled as a walnut, and gave him a toothless smile of pure delight as she drew him warmly to the fireside, patting and stroking his hand and murmuring some Welsh greeting.

"This is my Hunith," said the old man, "she cannot speak a word of French or English, but she wants me to tell you how happy she is, see? – to welcome you to our house."

Hunith was still holding his hand. Wolf managed to pull it gently away just before she kissed his fingers.

"And I am Howell," added the old man, beaming. He had a snub nose, a wide mouth, a bald forehead, and a fringe of hair as white as thistle-floss circling the back of his head. "And you are Wolf, and you have come all the way over *Brig y Diafol*, I hear – over Devil's Edge – from the great Abbey of Christ and St Ethelbert at Wenford?"

"Yes, sir—"

"I would like to hear more about that," said Howell wistfully. "It is my dream one day to visit that great abbey where the bones of Saint Ethelred rest."

Wolf interrupted. "Sir, please! What *was* that thing outside? I could see right through her. I—" He stopped. In a dry whisper he added, "In the chapel – there's a tomb. With a woman lying on it. Lord Hugo's wife. Eluned."

Old Howell's eyebrows shot up, and his forehead wrinkled. With his halo of downy white hair and his rosy apple of a face, he couldn't look really stern, but he did his best. "The Lady Eluned died almost seven years ago in the faith of Our Lord and is assuredly now in Paradise with holy Saint Catherine and blessed Saint Margaret. Do you really suppose she would leave the bliss of Heaven to wander about our yard?" His tone was severe.

"No sir. I suppose not." Grimly, Wolf wondered what Howell would say if he knew that Lord Hugo had been calling his wife's name into a black cave on Devil's Edge.

"No, indeed!" The old man's face relaxed. "But our little White Lady," he said almost tenderly. "Everyone knows her. Nobody minds her. She does no harm at all."

"But what is she? Why does she want to get into the chapel?"

"Ah, she often flits about the chapel. She can't get in, and that makes her curious, you see. As for her nature, I don't know for sure, but –" Howell rubbed his nose thoughtfully "– do you know the history of this island of Britain?"

"No." Wolf blinked at the sudden change of subject.

"Then it will be my pleasure to instruct you!" Howell lifted a gnarled finger. "The first settlers came here not long after the city of Troy burned to the ground, fully one thousand years before the birth of Our Lord! And what did those first men find? Giants (which they killed), and spirits such as pans, fauns and naiads, which our Lord God set from the beginning of the world to dwell in every element, some in air, some in fire, and some in water. If you stay here you'll notice our White Lady loves the cistern. There's a spring bubbles up in the corner, and often a bit of a mist floating over it, and the water is the sweetest you'll ever taste. And it's my belief she's nothing other than an elemental spirit, placed there long ago as the keeper of the spring by the will of the Creator, blessed be He."

"Oh?" Wolf hesitated. He knew what Brother Thomas would have called such creatures. Demons, without a shadow of a doubt. But poor, mournful Ladi Wen didn't seem very demonic.

"Shouldn't you sprinkle her with holy water?" he mumbled. "Wouldn't that get rid of her?"

"Why should I want to get rid of her?" Howell asked. "What harm does the poor creature do? They even say that if she ever leaves, the luck of the place will go with her. She belongs here, and always has.

Doubtless, she has no soul, and perhaps she and all her kind will pass away forever at the dreadful Day of Judgement, but let us leave that to the mercy of God."

Wolf felt rather ashamed. "She did save me from falling over the pig," he admitted. Old Howell's face creased into a million merry wrinkles.

"My Morwenna! I heard her squealing. So it was you who disturbed her, was it? A wonderful pig she is. And clever, my goodness!" He turned and spoke to Hunith, who clapped her hands in delight. Her face shone.

They were a lovely old couple, Wolf decided. Of course, priests weren't supposed to get married, but a lot of the Welsh clergy did. Brother Thomas used to sneer at them. *A priest's woman is not a wife,* he'd say, *but a concubine*! Wolf almost laughed. He'd imagined a concubine as some impossibly gorgeous girl – not ancient little Hunith with her sweet, toothless smile.

"Hunith says, no sense in falling over Morwenna again!" Howell patted Wolf on the shoulder. "Stay with us now, until morning."

"I'd like that," said Wolf with gratitude. For the first time since arriving at La Motte Rouge, he felt welcome, befriended and comfortable. Hunith pressed a mug of hot milk into his hand, sweetened with honey and flavoured with nutmeg. He took a long, satisfying swig, and wiped his mouth.

Tomorrow, he decided, *when Lord Hugo gives me my new clothes, I'm going to ask straight out if I can be his squire.* Tomorrow would be the beginning of his new life.

CHAPTER 5

Wolf stepped out of Howell's house into a windy, damp morning. Yellow leaves fluttered from the tall elm trees that shaded the chapel. Just to the left of Howell's door, an enormous pig lay snoring in the shelter of the wall. Her bulging, hairy sides were a mottled purply black. She opened a pink eye fringed with pale lashes and looked at him slyly.

"Hey, Morwenna. You *are* a beautiful pig, aren't you? This is for you!" Wolf threw her a crust from the loaf Hunith had given him. Morwenna twisted her thick neck without getting up and caught the crust in one snapping gulp. Wolf laughed.

In daylight, La Motte Rouge looked smaller than

Wolf had expected. It was an old-fashioned stronghold, built mainly of wood. The Great Hall had been plastered, and the plaster had been painted in red and white checks, but the paint had faded, and in some places the plaster was falling off. The tall watchtower on the mound was painted red too. Wolf looked up, shading his eyes. It seemed to move against the clouds like a warning finger. But he thought it would be fun to climb to the top and see for miles. Down here in the yard was a bit like standing at the bottom of a well, and the only thing he could see beyond the walls was the brown backbone of Devil's Edge, just showing above the ramparts like a lurking lion.

It felt strange, having nothing to do. He stood watching the rooks circling from their untidy nests in the elms, but kept one eye on the door of the chapel. Lord Hugo and his household were inside hearing Mass, and Wolf was missing it. Rolled up in a rug at Hunith's fireside, he'd slept late for the first time in his life. *Anyway,* he told himself, *I'm not at the abbey. Who's going to care or even notice whether I'm there or not?*

Presently he heard a hearty "Amen", and the chapel door swung open. Out came Lord Hugo, with Argos loping at his heels. Behind him came his daughter. Wolf picked out faces. That plump elderly woman bustling along beside Lady Agnes was her nurse, Dame Angharad.

The stocky man at Lord Hugo's shoulder was Rollo. Wolf winced. By daylight he saw Rollo had a deep, hairless dent on one side of his head. It looked like an old sword cut.

"Wolf!" Hugo snapped his fingers and Wolf ran eagerly to greet him.

"Good day to you, lord!"

"God be good to you." Hugo looked him up and down. "So you found your way to the chapel last night! More of a monk than you thought, eh?" He laughed as Wolf looked confused. "Go with my daughter; she has new clothes for you. Then come and find me in the stables. I'm going to see the elf."

New clothes! Wolf felt his face split into a smile. He looked around eagerly for Lady Agnes. She frowned at him and jerked her head. "This way."

Stiff necked, she walked ahead of him into the Hall, which seemed bigger and gloomier than the night before, though slats of cold daylight gleamed through the shutters. Wolf followed the girl to the foot of the stairs, where she paused and turned. "Wait here. I'll send Angharad down with your clothes."

Wolf waited. He thought about clothes coloured like jewels, red, blue, green. There would be a tunic, for sure. A new shirt to wear under it. Tight-fitting hose for his legs; boots; a surcoat or a cloak. Perhaps even a sword or a dagger? He bit his lip to prevent himself grinning from sheer pleasure. At last Angharad came waddling down again with an armful of drab drapery.

"Here you are, Master Clerk," she puffed, holding out a set of blackish brown robes almost identical to the ragged clothes he was wearing. Wolf stepped back in dismay.

"What's the matter?" Angharad demanded. "Take them!"

"But I thought – I hoped—" His voice dried.

"They're clean and new: what more do you want?" Angharad flapped them angrily. "My lady and I sit up half the night sewing, and that's the thanks we get? You may be a clerk, Master Wolfstan, but you're only a boy, and you'll feel the weight of my hand if you don't mend your manners this instant!"

"I'm sorry." Wolf gulped. "I do thank you. But there's been a mistake. I don't want to dress like that any more."

Angharad pointed to his head. "You came from the abbey, didn't you?"

"Yes, but—"

"And that's a tonsure, isn't it? So you're a monk!"

"I'm growing it out!" Wolf shouted. "I ran away! I'm not a monk! I never wanted to be one!"

Angharad's eyes glittered, and her cheeks bunched as tight and hard as two pincushions. "Don't you shout at me like that! Go and complain to Lady Agnes, if you dare! New clothes, that's all Lord Hugo said – and that's what you've been given!"

Wolf grabbed the robes, flung them over his arm, and ran up the staircase two at a time. He knocked. After a moment, Lady Agnes put her head out. Tresses of dark hair tumbled loose about her face and she held a comb in her hand.

"What do you want? Was it you doing all that yelling?"

Wolf thrust the robes at her. "Lord Hugo didn't mean me to have clothes like these!"

She lifted an eyebrow. "What sort of clothes did you think you were going to get?"

Wolf glared at her. He saw a thin-faced, black-haired girl with a pale skin and big, bold, brilliant eyes. Her front teeth stuck out slightly. He thought she was very ugly.

"I've left the abbey," he said curtly. "I'm not a monk. I never took vows. Lord Hugo w-wants me to have ordinary clothes."

"Really?" Lady Agnes jeered. "I suppose they threw you out. I suppose you were stupid. I suppose you couldn't do your lessons and got beaten."

"Suppose what you like," said Wolf through gritted teeth.

"You should call me 'madam'. Or 'my lady'!"

"Then *suppose what you like, my lady*!" Wolf made an exaggerated bow.

"You stupid, ignorant boy!" Her face was pinched with envy: Wolf took it for spite. "You lived in St Ethelbert's Abbey, full of wise, holy men, and you could have stayed there your whole life and gone on learning more and more. And you chose to run away!"

"They weren't all wise and holy," Wolf muttered.

"Lucky for you my father took pity on you, or you'd be a beggar by now."

"He did not *take pity on me*! We met in the woods up on the mountain. And it was me that got him the elf-girl. I went right into one of the caves up there on Devil's Edge and pulled her out," Wolf bragged.

"Yes!" Lady Agnes flashed. "And now he wants you to look after her, and *I'm* forbidden to go anywhere near her. Even though I begged and prayed, and it's my last chance to do something really important!"

"Me? What are you talking about?" said Wolf, appalled.

"Didn't you know? Isn't that what you were after?" Lady Agnes' eyes narrowed. "Wait – you weren't hoping to be my father's squire?" Wolf felt his face grow hot. She laughed. "You were! Oh, that's rich! That's funny!"

"Why?" Wolf growled.

"For one thing, my father already has a squire. Rollo!" She caught his expression. "Yes! Squires don't all have to be young and handsome, you know! He's old and ugly, and he has a big dent in his head, but he's served my father for years and years. And how could *you* be a squire? Can you even ride a horse? Have you ever held a sword?"

Wolf spun on his heel. He had to clutch the rail to save himself from falling downstairs. He didn't look back – she was bound to laugh at him. Instead he heard something very much like a sob, and the door to the solar slammed heavily shut.

Stuffing the horrible robe under his arm, he ran through the Hall, catching curious and disapproving stares from a middle-aged man and woman putting up trestle tables ready for the noon meal. They must have heard everything. He hurried outside to find Lord Hugo.

A cock yelled from the dunghill. Over the gatehouse a long, red banner rattled and snapped in the wind. The head of the wolf that had been killed last night grinned on a stake near the open gate. Beneath it, a bored guard leaned on his spear and scratched his armpit. Wolf recognised the round, chubby face of Roger Bach. On seeing Wolf, he hitched up a shoulder and spat.

Wolf headed for the stables, his temper cooling. He had few friends here. Shouting at Lady Agnes hadn't been clever. He passed the kennels. The hounds were out in the yard, thronging around a thin, dark-haired kennel boy who was feeding them a mixture of broken bread and scraps. Wolf saw Argos' white tail waving.

Between the kennels and the stables was a deep pond – or rather a cistern, rimmed with a low stone wall. A restless dimpling showed where a spring bubbled up at one end. Halfway along, an overflow gurgled into a stone trough where horses could drink and people could fill buckets. Wolf leaned over, thinking of the White Lady. It looked as if you could jump right through the bottom and fall out into another sky. A face was down there, glimmering up at him, and he wasn't sure it was his.

Wolf scooped up a shallow handful and drank. It was cold and clean. He listened to the noises of the morning: rooks calling; the kennel boy whistling; the voices of guards gossiping up on the gatehouse; the rising note of an argument in the cookhouse, ending on a slap and a cry. Everyone had a job to do – except him.

With a sigh he stripped off the torn robe with its muddy hem, and ducked swiftly into the new one. It dropped around him in warm folds of crisp, new wool. Things could be worse. *If Lord Hugo really wants me to look after the elf-girl,* he thought gloomily, *then I suppose I will.* There was no alternative – except returning to the abbey in disgrace.

"There you are!" Bronwen came briskly across the yard, carrying a baby astride her hip. "Lord Hugo wants you right away! Sooner, if possible!"

With her free arm she gave Wolf a push. "Sharpish now, come along." She hustled him into the dark stables. Tethered horses laid their ears back and twisted their heads to look at Wolf as he made his way down the long line of stalls.

At the far end, where the light from the doorway was dimmest, Lord Hugo was leaning on a long, slender pole. As Wolf got nearer, he saw it was a hunting spear with a gleaming iron point and a crosspiece. "I've been waiting."

"Your pardon, lord." Wolf bent one knee in a hasty bow.

"Very well. Come and look at the elf."

Wolf peered over a barrier of hurdles and fence posts into the dim pen where the elf-girl was being kept. He couldn't see her. Then he realised she had dragged up the straw to half bury herself. A bowl of water and a shallow pan of scraps, looking suspiciously like dog food, stood in one corner.

Without speaking, Hugo reversed the spear and prodded the straw with the blunt end. He did it twice, and suddenly Elfgift scuttled out of the straw and into the opposite corner, turning her blotched face to the wall. Bronwen clutched her baby, and Hugo plucked his spear back, as if he'd teased out a spider.

"Her hair's gone!" Wolf exclaimed, shocked. Elfgift's huge puff of wild hair had been cut off. Her cropped head looked defenceless and small.

"We had to cut it, lord," Bronwen said hoarsely, turning to Hugo. "It was all matted, and jumping with fleas, and we broke the comb. We had our hands full with her, I can tell you. It took Gwenny and me and Mattie too to hold her down while we bathed her. It's a good thing my Lady Nest didn't try to help," she added. "Soaked, we were! And then we had to hold her down again for Madog to clip her nails."

Wolf felt sorry for Elfgift, who had curled up with her back to the world like a wounded animal. "She must have thought you were murdering her."

Bronwen laughed crossly. "We were the ones that got hurt. Look where she bit me! As for clothes – well!" She pointed to a torn rag in the straw. "We tried to put a smock on her, but she ripped and fought till she clawed it off again. You might as well try dressing a cat."

Hugo looked at the dim, crouching figure of Elfgift. "Can she understand you? Has she spoken? Said anything at all?"

"Not a word, no more than my little *dwt* here." Bronwen kissed her baby on the head. "Nothing but spitting and hissing. And did you really see her running across the hills with a wolf on each side of her?"

"It wasn't quite like that," Wolf began, but Hugo cut across him. "Bronwen, the old mines under Devil's Edge – do you know any tales about them?"

"Oh, plenty! But nothing good, nothing good at all."
Bronwen shuddered, hitching the baby up. "They used
to find silver and lead up there, but that was ages back."

"I've heard they were dug by the Romans," Wolf put
in, eager to help.

Bronwen's dark eyebrows lifted. "And when was that,
those old Romans?"

"About the time of the birth of Our Lord," Wolf
said. "Nearly twelve hundred years ago. Howell would
know," he added.

"So long a time?" Bronwen shook her head in
wonder. "*Duw*, it can't be long till Judgement Day!" She
crossed herself. "Well, no one goes in them now. Some
of them have names. *Ogof yr Esgyrn*, that's one: 'the cave
of the bones'. A shepherd went in years back looking for
a lamb, and never came out again. Left his bones there,
scattered on the floor. They say that if you knock on the
walls, something knocks back. They say –" her voice fell
even lower "– that if you listen, you can hear a sort of
mumbling, as if people are talking together just out of
sight, but you can never quite hear what they say."

A soft shudder ran down Wolf's back.

"And what happens if you go further in?" Hugo asked.

Bronwen hunched her shoulders. "No one would do that,
lord. Not for gold or silver. You'd get lost. And down there's
where *they* live." She pointed at Elfgift. "Ones like her."

"Fays? Elves?"

Bronwen hugged her baby, pressing it hard against her. "Hush, lord! If they can hear you, they'll be angry. They like to be called the *Tylwyth Têg*, the Fair Family."

"And they live down there – is that what people say?"

Bronwen nodded. Her eyes were bright with speechless anxiety. "In the underworld. In Annwn, lord."

"All right, Bronwen," said Hugo slowly. "Thank you. Off you go."

But Bronwen lingered. She rubbed her nose and coughed. "Who's going to look after her, lord?" she asked. "Herbert's already mad at me for taking time out of the kitchen."

"Wolf will do it," said Hugo.

Wolf was glad he had been half prepared for this. Bronwen's face cleared. "Right! And him being a holy clerk, she won't be able to do *him* any harm! I'll get back to Herbert, then. Thank you, lord!"

She backed out, leaving Wolf and Hugo alone.

"Me?" Wolf said.

"You! Yes! You found her, you tame her. Do you think you can?"

"I don't know." Wolf looked at Elfgift, cowering in the straw. *She's better off here than she was on the hill – isn't she?*

"What do you want me to do?" he asked warily.

"First tell me exactly what you saw and heard when you went into the cave last night."

"No knocking or voices." Wolf shivered. "The tunnel goes down, quite steeply at first, then it levels out into a wide space, but the roof is very low. I had to crawl. And the floor is all covered with sharp stones."

"Could I get down there? The entrance was narrow."

"I don't know, sir." He remembered the awful feeling of being stuck with Hugo blocking the way. "Not easily. It's very tight."

"Unless the elves crawl, there must be other ways," said Hugo. "Go on."

"I was following Argos, and he snapped at me and I hit my head." Just remembering it made Wolf's heart thump faster. "And I saw…"

"What?"

Wolf shut his eyes, trying to see inside his head. Colours came floating back. *Green and red, and a river like a twisting red rope.* "The walls opened. And I saw green hills on the other side of a red river." Describing it made him less sure of what he'd seen. It was like trying to shut a sunbeam in a box. The image escaped. But he was certain *something* had happened.

Hugo emptied his lungs in a short, satisfied breath. "Then it's true. The mines lead down to Elfland."

"But it vanished, and I was in the dark again," Wolf said,

alarmed by Hugo's certainty. "Perhaps I was mistaken."

"No, Wolf, no." Hugo smacked a fist into his palm. "There's the elf-girl herself. Besides, there's more. You know the story of the hill?"

"The Devil rides over it with his Wild Host, hunting souls to Hell?"

"Some say the Devil." Hugo's eyes glittered in the dimness of the stable. "Some say the King of Elfland. The lord of the underworld."

Two stalls down, a horse shifted, scraping an iron shoe across the cobbles. The straw rustled in the elf-girl's pen. Was she moving? Or was it just a rat?

What was all this about?

"Who's Eluned?" Wolf burst out.

He hadn't known he was going to say it. The words flew from his lips and couldn't be recalled. He knew who she was, of course. But what would Hugo say? In cold suspense he waited to see.

Hugo leaned stiff-armed on his spear. He bent his head and said with formal simplicity, "Eluned ferch Owain was my wife, and the loveliest, the merriest, the most noble lady I have ever known. I delighted in her company so much that I made songs for her sake that were sung across Christendom. But envious Death took her away from me, and left me in such sorrow that for seven years I have had no heart to sing."

Wolf didn't breathe.

Hugo looked sideways at him. "You've seen her tomb in the chapel, haven't you? I had that made. Then, it was the year Baldwin the Archbishop came into the Marches preaching the Crusade, I took the Cross. I thought I would ride to the Holy Land and leave my sorrow behind. But sorrow has quick ears, Wolf. She sleeps lightly. However quietly you steal away from her, she wakes and follows. Or so I found."

He was silent for a moment. Then, light and delicate, he sang,

> "*My lady, bright of face, without match,*
>   *without peer*
> *The whole world over.*
> *Though I died and went to Paradise,*
> *I would come back*
> *To be your lover.*

"Do you know it? That's one of mine. In the heat and the stink and the flies of our camp outside Acre, sometimes I'd hear the men singing it. 'Though I died and went to Paradise, I would come back'. And in dreams she does come back to me; my lady comes."

He lifted his head, frowning through the stable wall. "In dream after dream she *torments* me. I'm hunting up on the hill, and she comes past in the company of others I can't see – only I hear the footfall of horses, and the jingle of harness, and feel the press of them riding by. I call her name, and spur after, and she turns – I see her pale face looking back, and she's swept away faster than I can follow.

"Or I see her by moonlight, dancing in the hazel woods with a ring of maidens, and when I try to grasp her hand, she slips away as clouds slide over the moon, and leaves me in darkness.

"Or I'm following one of the wild streams that run off the moor. She's standing on the other bank, reaching out, but when I try to cross, the water rises in a white torrent and parts us."

He looked at Wolf, his eyes black and dilated. "Why does she haunt me so? Because she wants me to find her!"

Wolf felt the blood creep under his skin. He said with dry lips, "But, my lord. She's dead. *You buried her.*"

And a movement caught his attention. Beyond Hugo's shoulder, further down the line of stalls, he saw the slender figure of Lady Agnes poised with one hand on a post. Her face was pale and horrified. She met Wolf's eyes, made a half-gesture of appeal, and stepped silently into the nearest stall, sinking out of sight.

"We buried something. But what?"

Wolf wrenched his eyes back to Hugo.

"Don't you see?" Hugo's fingers whitened on his

spear. "They're cunning, the elves. Have you never heard how they can enchant something – a bit of wood, a fence post – so that it could deceive anyone, so that it would look like a woman?"

"No, I mean, yes!" Wolf was distracted by the thought of Hugo's daughter listening – of knowing she was there, when Hugo didn't.

"Maybe that was all we buried. A piece of wood – a mockery, an illusion!" Hugo was full of passionate energy. "*What if my lady is not dead*?"

There was a short, terrible silence, which Wolf felt compelled to break. "Well, lord –" he began wretchedly, guessing the answer "– in that case – where is she?"

"Under the hill!" Hugo set the spear against the wall, took a pace away, then turned back. "Consider, in all those dreams – even while I was at sea and in the Holy Land – in all those dreams it was here I saw her, always here, among these hills and woods. And the night she died – it was New Year's Eve, and the candles burned so low and blue, and we heard over and over again the sound of thunder. That was the *Mesnie Furieuse* – the Wild Host – riding over the valleys. Between the old year and the new, between life and death – don't you think, when the spirit is loosening from the body, the elves can seize it?"

"Maybe…" Wolf heard a faint, agonised gasp and a

rustle of straw. His neck was stiff with not looking in the direction Lady Agnes was hiding.

"Perhaps they took her, perhaps she's not dead." Hugo ground the heels of his hands into his eyes. "Perhaps all this long time she's been hidden in the deep caves, in Elfland."

"B-but why?" Wolf stammered. "What would they want with her?"

Hugo flashed an almost fearful look at the dim huddle of Elfgift hiding in the straw. He dragged Wolf towards him and spoke low, his breath hot. "I've heard that once every seven years, Elfland pays a fee to Hell. They must draw lots for one of themselves to go there – down to the everlasting fires – unless—" He stopped suddenly, shutting his teeth.

"Unless what?" Wolf whispered.

"Unless they can steal a mortal to pay the price instead. Do you understand me?" He shook Wolf's arm. "It will be seven years at this year's end, seven years since I lost my lady. The time is short. On New Year 's Eve the fee to Hell will be due. *Now* do you see why I need the elf-girl?" He sounded frantic. "I must find my wife. For her precious soul's sake, I must bring her home. The elf-girl can tell me what they have done with her – lead me into Elfland, guide me through the tunnels—"

"But Elfgift can't talk," Wolf said, stupidly.

Hugo threw up his arms. "Teach her! You're a scholar, you told me! Teach her, and I'll give you – what do you want? Money? A position?"

"To – to be your squire, lord." Wolf got it out at last in a frantic mutter. His heart beat hard.

"You shall be," Hugo swore, "if you teach the elf-girl to talk."

"But I don't know how!" Wolf cried. "How am I to do it?"

"*Any way you like!*" Hugo snatched up the spear. For a moment Wolf thought he would hurl it the length of the stables, to the extreme danger of anyone who might be coming in. Instead, he struck downwards as hard as he could. The point sparked. The flagstone cracked. The shaft splintered. The nearest horses flung up their heads and kicked.

Hugo flung down the shattered shaft and opened his hand, breathing deeply. There was a deep red mark across his palm. He looked at Wolf.

"Teach her to talk, or get back to your abbey," he said in a low voice – and strode out.

CHAPTER 6

"Oh, dear God."

It was a tiny whisper from the stall where Lady Agnes was hiding. Wolf squeezed past the shifting barrel-belly of a shaggy grey pony and found her crouching underneath its nose. It snorted nervously as Wolf held out a hand and pulled the girl to her feet. She picked straw from her dress with trembling fingers.

"Did you hear what he said?" Wolf asked. She didn't answer.

"Did you *hear* what he *said*?" Wolf's voice rose, and the pony yanked at the halter rope.

"Of course I heard. I'm not deaf." Lady Agnes bit off the last word and buried her white face in the pony's mane. Wolf realised she was shivering from head to foot. "Steady," she whispered, more to herself than to the pony. "Steady, oh, steady."

Wolf looked at her. She was a girl, and the abbey had taught him nothing about girls. Also, she was a high born lady. He had thought of her as almost a different species. Now, for the first time, he realised she was simply a person his own age – a person who had just heard something terrible about her dead mother. He had no idea what to say to her. "You're not supposed to be here," he mumbled. "Someone'll come in and find you."

"I can visit the stables if I want," she said, through chattering teeth. "Anyway, this is my p-pony."

Wolf was sure that if Lady Agnes wanted her pony, it was the job of some stable lad or groom to fetch it out for her, but he didn't say so. "It's a nice pony."

"She's a mare. She's c-called Douce Amie." Lady Agnes took a deep breath and looked him in the eye. "I should like to go, now. Th-thank you for—" She turned away as if staying with him any longer was unbearable. But this time Wolf didn't mistake her cold courtesy for pride. Her face was raw with shock.

"Wait!" he said impulsively. "Shouldn't we talk?"

"What is there to talk about?"

"Everything – what you just heard—"

"I wasn't supposed to hear it." Lady Agnes sounded

bleak. "It was *you* he was talking to. I disobeyed him.
I w-wanted to see the elf-girl. Serves me right."

"But what about your mother? What if the elves—"

"*I don't believe it!*"

"Your father does."

"Because of dreams!" She clutched her head as if it
ached. "Not all dreams are true."

"But some are." Wolf pressed the point. "What if he's
right? What if your mother's still alive – and in terrible
danger? Don't you want to find out? Didn't he tell you
any of that before?"

"I hardly know my father!" The words stung like a
whip. "My mother and he were these famous lovers; he
made all those songs for her; then *she* died and *he* went
off to the Holy Land and left me with the nuns. He
wishes I'd been a boy! He never talks to me; he's never
even told me what he did on the Crusade. And then
you come along – and you're a boy – and he tells you
everything, even his dreams! Why should I talk to you?
I don't want to have anything at all to do with you. Do
you understand?"

She tried to push past him. Wolf thrust out his arm
to bar the way.

"I've got two brothers," he said hotly. "My father
held a poor manor from Lord William de Braose. He
didn't need three sons. I was the youngest, so he gave

107

me to the abbey. He told me we were going to leave an offering. He gave me money to hold for the abbot. I thought the money was the offering; I was proud to be trusted with it. But he meant me. I was about six years old. I haven't seen any of my family since. I can remember how the edges of the coins dug into my palm. But I can't remember my father's face."

Lady Agnes shot him a stricken glance.

"He's dead now, anyway," Wolf stormed on, "and my brothers have the manor. They don't want me back. Nobody wants me. Nobody ever asked me if I wanted to be a monk. And I'm not going to be one any more. So don't tell me I'm better off than you, Lady Agnes of La Motte Rouge. You belong here. I'm a runaway clerk, and your father will throw me out unless I can be useful."

He stopped, his heart galloping.

Lady Agnes lifted her chin and looked away. Her lips pressed together. Silent tears fled down her face.

Wolf saw, and cursed himself. She was upset already, and he'd made it worse. Now she would hate him more than ever. *Why can't I keep my temper? Why can't I keep my big mouth shut?*

"Please help me!" he blurted in desperation.

"What?" croaked Lady Agnes.

"Please," Wolf begged, "help me with Elfgift. You heard what Lord Hugo said. I've got to teach her to talk. And I don't know how. You came here because you wanted to see her. Can't we look after her together?"

"How can I," said Lady Agnes bitterly, "when my father has forbidden it?" She drew her veil forward to shield her face, and heaved a shuddering sigh. "I wish I could go back to Our Lady's In-the-Wood."

"The convent? Why can't you?"

"Because I'm going to be married. On Saint Stephen's day. The day after Christmas."

She spoke in such a flat voice, Wolf wasn't sure what to think. She seemed very young. But noblewomen often married young, and one thing he did know about girls was that they all wanted to get married. He pulled his mouth down. "I see."

"It will be all right. Only—" Her fingers twisted and jerked at a golden strand of straw. "Only I so wanted to do something first."

"*Do* something?" Wolf was totally out of his depth.

"I was sure the elf-girl was sent here. As an answer to my prayers. Mother Aethelflaed at the convent says women can be just as brave and holy as men. I prayed so hard to have some good work to do, something worthwhile."

"But you can," said Wolf. "I don't know how to even begin teaching Elfgift to talk. At the abbey, if you don't learn your lessons, they beat you."

"You wouldn't beat Elfgift?" Lady Agnes exclaimed.

"No, I wouldn't. It does no good. But what shall I do instead? Can't we talk about it? If you have any ideas, I can try them out."

"It would be you doing it, not me. Father won't let me help."

"Yes, well…" If Hugo believed he had lost his wife to the elves, Wolf could see why he would want to keep his daughter safe. "I suppose he thinks Elfgift's dangerous. But you would be helping, all the same."

She said suspiciously, "You don't care about Elfgift. You just want my father to make you a squire."

Wolf was stung. "I do care! Of course I want to be a squire. But I'll help Elfgift too, if I can. It was me that got her out of the mines. It was horrible down there," he added. "No one should have to live in a place like that."

Lady Agnes swallowed. "I'm sorry. I was being unfair. And I didn't know. About your father, I mean, giving you away."

Wolf scratched his neck, flushing. "S' all right. I don't usually talk about it."

"I don't either. I – I've never talked like that to anyone before." She added, "Though I don't blame *my* father. Going on the Crusade was much more important than staying with me. I do know that."

She held out a stiff hand: he knew now it wasn't pride but shyness. "I'll help if I can, Wolf."

"Thank you! My lady," he added politely, catching her eye. After a moment, a ghost of a smile danced between them.

"All right." Lady Agnes gathered up her skirts. "Let's take a look at Elfgift."

"I must be quick. I told Angharad I was going to the chapel." Lady Agnes leaned over the hurdles. "Elfgift!" she called. "Oh, the poor little thing!" She turned a flushed, indignant face to Wolf. "How could anyone think she's dangerous? Look at her, cowering in the straw like a prisoner! She's terrified. We can't keep her in here."

"We can't let her run away," Wolf pointed out.

"Perhaps some kind of harness…" She bit her thumb reflectively. "At the convent, some of the nuns had little dogs. They taught them tricks by rewarding them with bits of bread dipped in milk, or little pieces of meat. We could try that."

"What – teach her tricks?"

"It's not so different! She's got to trust us."

They stared at the huddled shape in the straw. A hen that had been pecking up grain in the mangers suddenly appeared on the partition between the stalls. It poised there, lifting its yellow feet and turning its head this way and that, before tipping itself clumsily into Elfgift's stall with a whirr of wings.

The straw exploded. Bright-eyed and wild, Elfgift threw herself on top of the hen. There was a deafening squawk and a fountain of feathers. With a shout, Wolf vaulted into the stall to prise the hen from Elfgift's clawing fingers. He wrenched it free, and it flapped hysterically over the barrier and ran drunkenly away, cackling in terror.

"*Poor little thing*?" Wolf asked, breathless. Downy feathers were still rocking through the air.

Lady Agnes began to laugh. "She's like a tiger!"

"Like a hunter," said Wolf. Elfgift sat panting lightly, watching the falling feathers with sharp eyes. She snatched one out of the air, licked it up with a quick dab of her tongue, and spat it out again.

"Elfgift?" Wolf stretched out his hand. Elfgift growled.

"Try her with food from the pan," said Lady Agnes, watching fascinated.

Wolf picked up the pan of broken bread and scraps. Screwing up his nose, he stirred his fingers around in it. "What a mess. Sopping wet bread and porridge. Here's a piece of meat. *Elfgift*…" He drew out the name slowly. "Look – meat. Lovely meat." He waved the gristly morsel between his fingers.

Elfgift watched him. She didn't come closer, but she didn't try to hide.

"She needs better food than this," said Wolf, turning in disgust. "*Ouch!*" He leaped like a frightened hare. As soon as his attention had wandered, Elfgift had clawed the scrap out of his hand with one swipe. She bolted into a corner and ate it.

"That's it, then!" Lady Agnes was laughing again. "We can tame her with food."

"Tame her, maybe." Wolf felt despond settle into his heart. "But how can we get her to talk?"

"We'll do it," said Lady Agnes gallantly. "One thing at a time. Listen, I must go before someone sees me and tells my father. Wolf – come to me in the solar after the noon meal. We can talk there."

With a lively backward glance she whisked out. Wolf watched her go, and shook his head in wonder. She was so different from what he'd thought.

"And so are you," he told Elfgift, turning to look at her where she crouched, her long fingers splayed out in the straw. She drew back her lips, showing her small, sharp teeth. But Wolf thought she wasn't as scared as the night before. To seem less of a threat, he sat down in the straw with his back against the barrier. "Can you talk?" he asked, only half joking. "It would save so much trouble, if you can."

What language did the elves speak? Bronwen and the kitchen servants must have tried Welsh already. He remembered the White Lady last night. Latin?

"*Veni nunc, Elfgift, ad me,*" he tried. "Come to me now, Elfgift." She cocked her head a little: obviously she could hear. No understanding showed in her face. But he didn't think she was stupid.

He sat still, hoping she would begin to get used to him. It was peaceful at first, listening to the horses munching their hay and swishing their tails. Then his legs began to cramp. Sharp bits of straw pricked through his woollen robes. He shifted position, conscious of Elfgift watching him with the alert, terrible patience of a cat. The livid red side of her face was turned to him; the whites of her eyes had a wet, opal gleam to them, and the dark pupils were fixed on him. As he moved, she flinched; and the sharp, jerky movement made him jump in turn. "It's all right," he said uneasily, to himself as much as to her. What *was* she exactly? Elf, or changeling child? Child or elf? He wasn't afraid – at least, not afraid she would attack him. It was just that she was so strange.

He began talking quietly. "I'm Wolf. You mustn't be scared of me. And your name's Elfgift. What do you think of that, Elfgift? Is it a good name? Do you like it?"

Elfgift cocked her head. He thought he heard a faint growl.

"I'm Wolf; that's me." He spoke in a steady, soothing monotone. "You've got to be good, Elfgift. You've got to learn to…" Suddenly exhausted, he found himself yawning, "…talk…"

He tipped his head back against the barrier and closed his eyes, humming softly. It was easier than talking. One half-remembered tune meandered into another. After a while, a lullaby floated out of his memory.

> "*Lullay, my little young child,*
> *Sleep and do not cry:*
> *Your mother and your father*
> *Watch at your cradle side.*
> *And there they will abide.*
>
> "*Lullay, my little young child*
> *Sleep, and do not fear:*
> *You are your father's pride.*
> *You are your mother's dear.*
> *And both of them are near…*"

Wolf sat with lowered head, motionless. Where had that come from? He hadn't heard it in years, hadn't even known he remembered it – but the song came with a memory of warmth and enfolding love. For a moment he felt bitterly lonely. He opened his eyes – and Elfgift sprang backwards with a sharp rustle of straw. Wolf yelped. She had crept to within a couple of feet of him.

"Elfgift…!" He knelt, stretching out his hand. But he'd thoroughly startled her, and she wouldn't approach. "Don't be frightened. You like music? I'll sing it again." Self-consciously he settled back against the barrier and half hummed, half sang the tune over. He didn't look at her directly, but kept an eye on her. She didn't venture closer, however. "*You are your father's pride, you are your mother's dear,*" sang Wolf – and someone came into the stables.

He shut up at once.

Whoever it was didn't stop at any of the stalls but came walking with a quiet, purposeful tread right along the row to the end. Hot with embarrassment, Wolf kept his head low, hoping he hadn't been overheard.

A shadow fell over them both. Wolf heard slow breathing. The person, whoever it was, was standing by the barrier, looking over the top of Wolf without seeing him.

Elfgift shrank into the straw. Wolf didn't move. It was too late to stand up; and perhaps in a moment or too the man – he was certain it was a man – would go away.

Slow moments passed. The man standing above him gave a sharp sigh. Goosebumps rushed across Wolf's skin. Then the makeshift barrier of hurdles and fence posts creaked. The stall darkened even further. *He's climbing in!* Wolf scrambled up.

"*God's bones!*" The man yelled as if a ghost had risen from the straw. He clapped a hand to his barrel of a chest, gasping.

"Rollo!" Wolf recognised the dreadfully scarred forehead.

"God's bones! It's the clerk." Rollo's shock turned to rage. "What are you doing lurking there, you scarecrow?"

"Looking after Elfgift, like Lord Hugo told me. What are *you* doing?" Wolf's voice rose. He pointed. "What's *that*?"

Rollo glanced down at the long, business-like knife in his right hand. He stuck it into the sheath on his belt. "Nothing!"

"You were going to kill her!"

"I wasn't," Rollo shouted.

Wolf stumbled further into the stall, out of arm's reach. "What else were you doing, creeping in here with a knife in your hand? I'll tell Lord Hugo!"

"Calm down! I wasn't going to hurt her! I wanted to touch her with the blade, that's all, because—"

"Because what?"

"Because it's cold iron." Rollo glowered at Wolf. "Cold iron! The fairies can't stand the touch of cold iron, right? Everyone knows that."

"You wanted to test her?" Wolf said slowly. "Find out if she's really an elf?"

"I thought she might fly away through the roof," Rollo said. He craned his neck to see into the back of the stall.

"There she is, brrr, the uncanny thing. Come on, boy. It's your fault she's here. I never heard any good come of keeping a changeling. And it's put maggots into Lord Hugo's head I thought he'd forgotten about. Let's try it."

"Maggots?" said Wolf blankly.

"Notions – fancies!" said Rollo impatiently. "Get out of my way."

"No!" Wolf stood his ground. He didn't think touching Elfgift with iron would make her fly through the roof, but he would get into trouble if she did. And what if it was a trick – what if Rollo just wanted to get close enough to stab her?

Rollo grimaced with frustration, rubbing his thick hands over his face. "See here. Lord Hugo's helped you, right? Brought you home off the moor, taken you in?"

Wolf nodded warily.

"Well, if you want to help him, you'll get rid of the elf-girl. As soon as possible!"

"Why?" Wolf demanded.

Rollo hesitated. "Lord Hugo— look, it's none of your business, but when his wife died, seven years ago, he was half crazy with grief. Then he took the Cross, and that seemed a good idea at the time. Nothing like keeping busy, is there? So off we went to the Holy Land."

"You went too? What was it like?" Wolf couldn't

help asking. He imagined proud walls, and long banners streaming on the bright wind.

Rollo eyed him. "What was it like? Four years of bad food, filthy water, rats and disease. I lost six teeth. And it didn't do Lord Hugo any good, either. He started having dreams − nightmares, really − that'd wake him up in a cold sweat."

"He told *you* about his dreams?"

"Why not? What's strange about that? A man can't keep many secrets in a tent, or on shipboard. 'Rollo,' he said to me once, 'it's my Lady Eluned who comes walking into my sleep. And sometimes,' he says, 'it's as if she's alive, dancing on the moors or in the woods. And sometimes I see her in a great hall, surrounded by people. And I wake,' he says, 'and I know she's dead.'

"Well, that was bad enough. We set off home. Then one day on the road, I think it was somewhere between Poitiers and Tours, we fell in with a whey-faced, gangling strip of a fellow riding on a mule. I forget his name, Breton or Flemish, something outlandish I could never get the hang of, but he was a *jongleur* − wandering from place to place, singing and juggling, and telling tales. He kept up with us for a few days. He made my lord laugh, and we all thought that had to be a good thing. But if I'd known what he was going to do, I'd have stuffed that *jongleur* head-first down a well and drowned him!"

"Why, what did he do?"

"Only told Hugo some story about a dead woman coming back," Rollo growled. "God knows why he picked that one, out of all the tales he knew. He told it well. Too well. Well enough to give you the shivers. Next morning he was off, mule and all. *I'll see you again one day,* he said, but we never did see him again. After that, my lord was very quiet. *Very* quiet. You could see him thinking about the tale he'd heard. More than thinking. *Brooding* on it, know what I mean? And now you come along with your elf. I reckon I know what Hugo thinks. He thinks his dreams are telling him his lady isn't dead after all. He thinks the fairies have got her. He thinks he could go down into the mines and look for her." Rollo jabbed a finger at Wolf. "Am I right?"

Wolf nodded, subdued. "But, Rollo. Dreams like that have to mean something. Maybe it's all true."

Rollo gave him a hard stare. "Maybe. His lady was a strange one anyway, to my way of thinking. Always up in her chamber, reading out of thick books. I've never been up there myself, but the maids tell me she painted magical signs on the walls. She was a foreigner, too – a Welsh princess from Powys with a white face and black eyebrows and long, black hair. I like blonde girls, myself. But she cast a spell over Hugo, all right.

"But, if Hugo goes down into Elfland, what's the

odds he'll ever come out? He's the best master I've ever served. So what if his wife died? Other wives die, and their husbands get over it. There's no shortage of women, and *I* never met one it was worth risking your immortal soul for, which is what Hugo will do if he meddles with elves. You seem to be a sensible lad, even if you are a clerk. So off you go for a walk now, and I'll do what I came to do, and if the elf's not here when you come back, well, she'll have flown away home, and everyone'll be much happier. Right?"

Wolf bit his lip. Rollo made it sound like straight-forward common sense. And he could use a friend in the garrison. *All I have to do is walk away. He's not going to hurt her. Only touch her with iron…*

And you believe that, do you? added a more cynical voice in his mind.

Elfgift was burrowing in the straw at his back. He turned, and she looked up at him, pin-points of light glinting in her eyes. It was true that there was something eerie about her. But she'd trusted him. She'd crept up close while he was singing. And she was managing to keep him between her and Rollo – as though she sensed danger, as though he was her shield.

Wasn't that enough?

"Well?" said Rollo. "You don't want to spend your time nannying a thing like that, do you? Off with you."

"No!" said Wolf recklessly. And as soon as the word was out, his spirits soared. Like an eagle casting itself into the air he flung himself into his element. Freedom – seizing life by the scruff and shaking it – no more dithering about, wondering what to do—

"No!" Almost joyfully he looked Rollo in the eye. "Lord Hugo told me to look after her. I'm not going for any walks. Get out! And if you come back – if anything happens to Elfgift, or if she's hurt, or disappears – I'll tell Lord Hugo everything you said!"

He braced himself. If he'd spoken like that to Brother Thomas, he'd have got a blast of cold rage followed by a thrashing. Rollo breathed hard and his fists knotted, but he controlled himself. Contemptuously he said, "A boy's threat. Do you think I give a damn if Hugo's angry, so long as he's safe? All right, have it your way – for now. But you'd better look after that elf well, Master Clerk. Elves are no better than demons. And if any harm comes to Lord Hugo through her, I'll hold you responsible. I'll see you both hanging from the same tree!"

CHAPTER 7

"Good for you!" said Lady Agnes fiercely. Her pale face flushed. "As for Rollo – shame on him! You should tell my father."

"I can't do that!" Wolf exclaimed. "He meant well."

They were alone together in the solar. A book lay open on a stand in front of them. If anyone came in, Lady Agnes and Wolfstan the Clerk were studying *Lives of the Saints* – though neither of them had turned a single page.

Wolf thought the solar was the grandest room he had ever been in. It was lofty and cold, open to the rafters. A great curtained bed stood in the centre of the floor. A small door led through into Lord Hugo's private chamber.

The plaster walls had been whitewashed and then

123

painted – but not with magical signs, as Rollo had thought. On the south wall was a picture of the universe, with Christ in Glory presiding over it, one hand lifted in blessing. On the north wall, someone had painted a map of the world, the green lands rimmed with a great blue circle of ocean. Afternoon sunlight ruled a stripe up the map, gleaming on the gilded names of Britain at the bottom, Jerusalem at the centre, and the Earthly Paradise at the top.

"Meant well?" Lady Agnes exploded. "He was going to murder her!"

"I know," said Wolf, "but he was doing it for Hugo. He thinks Elfgift – well, he thinks she's a danger to your father. And I suppose he could be right."

The girl sprang to her feet. "Very well! Perhaps he is right. Perhaps they're all right! My father's dreams are true. My mother didn't really die. She was carried away by the elves or the Fair Family or whatever you want to call them…" She broke off. "I don't believe it! This was where it happened. This room, that bed. I was only six; they'd promised me a baby brother or sister. I wasn't allowed in. So I sat on the stairs for hours, till Angharad came out and cuddled me up – she was crying. She said, 'Nest, my poor *cariad*, your Mam's gone away to Heaven and you'll never see her again.' Just like that! And you know what I did? I hit her! I hit her with my fists and I screamed, 'It's not true!'"

She crossed the room with quick strides. "But it was true. They made me believe it. My mother was dead." She lifted her face and glared at him. "*And now they're changing their minds?*"

Wolf looked down at the book in front of him, searching for something to say. From its bold, black script, little tendrils and dragons escaped up the margins. He muttered, "I don't know what to think."

"I'll tell you. Come here. Come!" Imperiously she waved him over to the painting on the south wall. "See this picture, how beautiful it is? A map of the whole of Creation! Mam painted it herself. I used to sit on a stool eating nuts and watching her."

She pointed. "Look, here's the Earth in the middle, like a little ball. All around it is the air. Above that, the Moon." She traced a line up the wall. "Next, Mercury and Venus." Her finger landed on a fiery little sun with a human face, crackling with life. "Here's the Sun. Then Mars, Jupiter, Saturn, spinning around and around the Earth, all of them set in crystal spheres, each one bigger than the last! Then, this dark blue circle with the stars painted in it – that's the Fixed Stars, all turning around together. And then the sphere that makes them all move, and beyond that—" Her finger burst through the last ring, like a chicken pecking through an eggshell. "Heaven."

She drew a deep breath. "*That's* where my Mam is!

Outside the universe. Safe in Heaven. Safe with God!"

Wolf believed her. She sounded so sure.

"You know what Mam used to tell me?" Nest went on. "'Compared to Heaven, Nest, the whole world is no bigger than a nutshell.' And it's hollow. Deep in the centre of the Earth is the underworld. The pit of Hell, crowded with devils." She clenched her fists and her eyes flashed. "How can my *own father* believe Mam might be in Hell?"

Wolf thought of Hugo breaking his spear on the flagstones. "He's afraid for her. He's had all those dreams, remember? He thinks she's in Elfland. But Elfland isn't Hell. Not if it's the cave where Elfgift was. I was there. And it was just wet and dark and stony. There weren't any fires or demons."

"Maybe the fires and the demons are further down."

Wolf couldn't deny it. There was a moment's grim silence. Nest added more calmly, "Then it's not true, what the servants are saying – that you found a cavern glowing with light, filled with green hills and castles and rivers?"

"It was completely dark down there," said Wolf. "I did see something. I hit my head, and it's true for a moment I thought the walls opened, and I saw –" he screwed his eyes shut, trying to remember "– *maybe* I saw hills and a river. But I couldn't swear to it. And the next minute it was gone, and I was back in the dark."

Nest nodded. "Because the elves can make things look any way they like. By fairy glamour, magic illusions." She sat down, leaned her elbows on the bookstand, and stared at him. "I've been reading. This book says the elves are nearly as bad as demons. Is Elfgift really an elf, Wolf?"

"She's not a demon," said Wolf at once.

"You're sure?"

"At the abbey they warned us about demons and devils till we were frightened of our own shadows. So I thought she was a demon the first time I saw her, but I was wrong. Elfgift couldn't harm anyone," said Wolf hotly. "Only someone like Brother Thomas would think that."

"Who's he?"

"My old master at the abbey." Wolf's face darkened. "All the boys hated him. I don't think even the abbot liked him. I've decided, anything Brother Thomas told me, I'm going to believe the opposite. Don't worry about it, Nest. Elfgift's not dangerous."

"You're right," Nest decided. She blew a breath of relief and looked at him, half-smiling. "When did you start calling me *Nest*?"

Wolf was startled. "Did I? Is that what your mother called you? I'm sorry. I must have picked it up without thinking."

"It's only the Welsh for 'Agnes'."

"I like it. It suits you better than 'Agnes'."

She was silent. He added, "I won't do it again. My lady."

"Oh, don't," she burst out. "I'd far rather be Nest. I hate being Agnes. You can call me Nest – at least until I get married…"

Wolf flushed, and bowed. There was a moment when neither of them knew quite what to say. Then they both spoke at once.

"But what about—"

"But Elfgift—"

It was a relief to laugh. Wolf said, "Yes, Elfgift?"

"We'll tame her with kindness," Nest said. "That's what Mother Aethelflaed would do. The first thing is to teach her to know her own name. Try calling her, and give her a titbit if she comes. If we keep talking to her, she'll learn by listening."

It didn't sound like much of a plan, but Wolf couldn't think of anything better. He remembered how Lord Hugo had said the elves paid their fee to Hell at New Year; it was only the beginning of October now. "We've got three months," he said optimistically. "Surely that's long enough?"

The door latch clicked. Angharad came in, pushing aside the embroidered woollen curtain that kept out the draughts. Breathless from the stairs, she puffed, "Long enough for what?"

"Teaching Elfgift to talk," said Nest. "My father has asked Wolf to do it."

Angharad shook her head. "It can talk if it wants to; it's pretending, isn't it? It's a goblin; a *crimbil*! I know how to set about it. Though your father ought to get rid of it, that's my opinion. I nearly dropped dead of fright when I saw it on the doorstep last night. Elves bring disease."

"Oh, Angharad…"

"They do! There's the elf-hiccup, and elf-stroke, and water-elf disease – my own mother's sister suffered dreadfully from the water-elf disease. She couldn't stop sneezing. Besides, what if the elf-lord comes looking for it? None of us will be safe in our beds. I hardly slept last night. I was woken by something screaming just outside the window, screaming like a lost soul!"

"Only the wind," said Nest.

But Wolf said awkwardly, "I think it might have been Howell's pig. You know the one – Morwenna? I tripped over her last night on my way to the chapel, and she squealed awfully."

Angharad bridled, flushing. "It wasn't the wind, my lady. And it was not a pig, either, Master Clerk. *Like a lost soul*, I said, and *like a lost soul* is what I meant. It was the Wild Host of Annwn, whirling round and about the castle, shrieking!"

Wolf caught Nest's eye. "*Still the pig*," he mouthed.

She bit her lip on a smile. Angharad's eyes darted suspiciously between their faces.

"Angharad, *cariad*, what's your advice?" Nest soothed. "You said you know a way to make the elf-girl talk?"

Angharad sank on to the edge of the bed, easing the weight from her feet. "You have to catch it off guard. What you do is this: you get hold of some porridge and an empty eggshell. And then, with the elf in the room, you do something completely strange. You boil up the porridge in the eggshell, and the elf is so astonished, it gives itself away by crying out, '*I have lived for a thousand years, but I never saw anyone cooking porridge in an eggshell before!*' What's the matter?"

Nest doubled over, covering her face.

"What's wrong?" Angharad threw up her hands.

Nest emerged, wet-cheeked and choking with laughter. "I was imagining Wolf – pouring porridge into an eggshell. It would c-collapse and go all over his f-fingers…"

Wolf walked swiftly to the window and stared out, fighting down giggles. A chilly draught blew in, and the sky was full of bright, cold clouds. He could see across the yard to the gate where the guards stood with their crossbows, watching the cart-track that led out across Lord Hugo's fields.

A group of horsemen with hounds at their heels came trotting past the kennels. Hugo led the way on his black horse, white Argos frisking at his side. Rollo rode just behind on a thick-legged bay. The guards straightened, presenting their crossbows and crying, "Lord Hugo goes hunting!" A horn brayed, harsh and valiant. Wolf felt a stab of longing. He'd give anything to be going with them.

One day I will. When I'm a squire. When Elfgift can talk…

"What do you think, Wolf?" said Nest from behind him. Her voice brimmed with laughter. "The eggshell idea. Shall we give it a try?"

"He isn't listening," Angharad said crossly.

It was true. Wolf crammed himself into the window, forcing half his body through the narrow aperture, craning his neck to follow a fleeting movement below.

He pulled back in, bumping his head on the frame. The room looked dark after the brightness outdoors.

"Quick! Elfgift's got out!"

CHAPTER 8

"Wolf – wait for me!"

"Nest! Madam! Oh my lady, *come back here*!"

Wolf bounded down the stairs, aware of Nest darting after him and Angharad wailing in the background. He raced across the Hall, wrenched the heavy door open, and thudded into Walter who was coming in at that moment with an armful of firewood.

"Oy!" Walter yelled. Sticks cascaded to the floor.

"Sorry!" Wolf dodged outside and looked both ways. No sign of Elfgift. But he knew he'd seen her.

Through the half-open door he could hear Nest apologising breathlessly. "Yes, I know, Walter. Wolf was in a hurry – he was doing something for me. Yes – yes, it *was* clumsy. He's sorry!"

She stepped outside, caught Wolf's arm, and said – in what he was beginning to recognise as her 'Lady Agnes' voice – "Wolf, stop rushing about!"

"We've got to find her," he groaned.

"I know. *Listen* to me! If everyone starts chasing Elfgift again, she'll be terrified, like last night. Go up on to the ramparts. You can walk all the way round the castle and see everything from up there. And I'll get something tasty from the kitchen, something to lure her with."

"What if she ran through the gate?" Wolf broke out in a cold sweat at the thought. How stupid to think Elfgift would just sit quietly in her stall. She must have climbed over the barrier, and then sneaked out when they opened the stable door for the horses. He imagined her already halfway up Devil's Edge. "We'll never get her back. Your father will throw me out…"

Nest was still very much Lady Agnes of La Motte Rouge. "If she'd gone through the gate, the guards would have stopped her. That's what they're paid to do!"

"Right." Wolf glanced up at the boardwalk, the narrow platform that ran right around the ramparts behind the stockade. "How do I get up?"

Nest pointed to a ladder of split logs beside the gatehouse, and Wolf scrambled up the splintered and muddy rungs. He set off around the boardwalk, walking not running, for the wet planks were slimy and there was no inner guardrail. Anxiously he scanned the castle yard. Elfgift could have run behind any of the buildings. He hurried past the roof of Howell's house, a new perspective unfolding at every stride. Just before he reached the chapel, the whole structure developed a tremor that vibrated up through the soles of his feet. He knelt, clutching the edge, and looked over. Ten feet below him, Morwenna the pig was scratching herself against one of the supporting posts, scrubbing her sides and grunting happily.

Wolf was tempted to spit on her back. But that was the sort of thing only little boys did. Still kneeling, he looked towards the mound. A few rooks strutted about on the slopes. Near the top, the steep slope was bare earth and grass, but a dense tangle of bramble bushes had grown up around the ditch at its base.

Elfgift scampered out from behind the chapel and disappeared into the brambles like a rabbit.

Swearing, Wolf swung himself down the nearest ladder. He ran across the yard and peered between the arching loops of the briars. There she was, crouching in the ditch, stuffing her mouth with blackberries.

"Elfgift," Wolf called. "It's me, your friend, Wolf." She flashed him a disobedient glance – almost smug, as if she knew she couldn't be reached – and ate another berry, sucking each fingertip with loud smacking sounds like kisses. Exasperated, Wolf tried to get closer. Hooked thorns tore his hand and clung to his woollen sleeve.

"*Elfgift!*" he snapped. She ignored him. Better not call too loud. He looked up. Overhead the tower swung, dark against the clouds. Two-thirds of the way up, a roofed fighting platform ran round all four sides. A helmeted guard looked down at him, leaning over the balustrade. Wolf turned casually away.

"Have you found her?" Nest came running across the chapel yard, holding a small bundle wrapped in a white napkin. To Wolf's dismay, Angharad waddled in her wake, complaining.

"I don't know what's got into you, Nest. It's not at all suitable, dashing about like this. What will your father say? He'll be as mad as a lion if he finds out. You're not supposed to go anywhere near the elf. And you're not to run about the castle by yourself!"

"Angharad, *please* don't fuss," said Nest. "Where is she, Wolf?"

"Under the bushes, eating blackberries. She won't come out."

"Try her with this!" Nest unfolded the napkin and handed him a small pie, heavy with meat, warm from the oven, glazed with shiny trickles of brown gravy. It smelled unbelievably delicious.

"Wasting good Christian pies on a nasty heathen elf!" Angharad muttered. Her face was hot and red. She shot Wolf a look of indignant dislike, and folded her arms.

"Oh, Elfgift," Wolf cooed. "Food! Lovely food!" He stooped to waft the smells into the hollow under the brambles – and straightened sharply. "She's gone!"

"There she is!" Nest pointed. Elfgift had crawled right through the brambles and was scrambling upwards to where a couple of glossy black rooks were walking about the steep slope looking for worms. When she was almost upon them, the rooks hopped lazily into the air, leaving her staring after them like a hopeful kitten. She sneezed, rubbed her nose, and scampered on.

"After her, Wolf – quickly!"

The way up to the tower was by a bridge over the ditch, then a flight of uneven steps cut into the slope. Wolf took the first few at a run. By halfway he had slowed to a plod. Six steps further and he halted, wheezing. His lungs burned. His knees shook. And he'd completely lost sight of Elfgift.

He looked back. The slope dropped away at a frightening angle. Angharad looked like two currant buns stuck together; and a doll-sized Nest waved wildly and pointed.

Through slitted eyes, he glanced up. The tower hung over him, a dizzying sight. The door at the bottom was half open. He was just in time to see a small, bare figure vanish into the dark interior.

Wolf looked up even higher. The guard on the outwork at the top of the tower had missed Elfgift. He was staring at Wolf and Nest and Angharad as if trying to work out what they were all doing. Wolf gestured. "Look out!" he hailed breathlessly. "The elf-girl – catch her – she's in the tower…"

The guard mimed incomprehension, cupping a hand behind his ear.

"All right, never mind," Wolf muttered. He forced his legs to carry him on up the steps. Just as he was about to step under the overhang of the fighting platform, he heard a shout.

"Oy! You below!"

"Yes?" Wolf tipped his face up.

Just in time he jumped aside. A white fleck came flying down. The guard had spat at him, and was now roaring with laughter.

So much for only small boys finding such tricks amusing. But Elfgift was inside the tower. Wolf marched in and firmly latched the door behind him.

He was in a square room, much higher than it was wide. It was cold and smelled of damp. The only light came from two narrow windows high in the left- and right-hand walls, and from an open trapdoor in the high boarded ceiling, which was the floor of the room above. A tall ladder slanted through it.

As his eyes adjusted, Wolf saw that he was in the armoury. Piles of shields were stacked against the walls. Bundles of spears leaned in the corners, and crates of crossbows and arrows crowded much of the floor.

He searched about swiftly, looking behind the crates. "Elfgift? I've got food for you. Smell it? Mutton pie… lovely mutton pie…"

No answer. He looked at the ladder. Had she gone up there?

Grimly he tucked the pie into the breast of his robe and began to climb. A few rungs up, and he could see she was nowhere in the lower room. He kept going. Now he was level with the little slit windows, and a cold draught funnelled through. Higher – higher – and he was through the trapdoor. He clambered out on to the upper level.

This was the top of the tower. There were small windows in three walls and a door in the fourth, leading out on to the fighting platform. The wind rushed in through the windows and out through the open door. There was still no sign of Elfgift.

The planks shook and the doorway darkened. The

guard looked in, ferocious in iron helmet and mail-shirt, brandishing a heavy, loaded crossbow.

"What do you want?" he asked belligerently, and Wolf's heart sank as he recognised stocky Roger Bach – again.

"The elf-girl got out," he said. "She's up here somewhere."

"Up here?" Roger scoffed. "She's not up here. I've been keeping watch."

Wolf pointed silently. Elfgift was peering in through the left-hand window. Her blotched face was streaked with blackberry juice. When she saw them she rolled her eyes weirdly and dropped out of sight.

Roger's ruddy skin drained of colour. "She can fly?"

"She climbed up the ladder. Didn't you notice?" Wolf jeered. "No, of course not, you were too busy spitting. *Excuse* me!"

He pushed past Roger, out on to the fighting platform.

The world burst open around him.

Wolf gasped and gripped the doorway. Balanced in the air, the tower rocked to the gusts of swirling wind. Rooks sailed past in easy curves, like skaters. Below him, the roofs and trees of La Motte Rouge crowded together into a little circle like a child's wooden castle.

To the east the valley tumbled away in farmlands and meadows to the road, and the willow-choked line of

139

the river. Beyond that, the smoke-blue rim of Crow Moor rose into the sky.

To the west, almost close enough to touch, the hunched shoulder of Devil's Edge rose high and threatening, patched with bracken the colour of dry blood. Bright clouds peeped over the edge, puffing their cheeks.

Wolf recovered. "You go that way," he said to Roger. "I'll go this. We'll catch her between us."

Running a hand along the smooth rail, he hurried to the first corner. No Elfgift. Only two sides of the tower left, and nowhere for her to go – unless she *could* fly. He darted round the next corner – and there she was, trotting along ahead of him. Then the bulky figure of Roger stepped out in front of her. "*Gotcha!*" he shouted.

Elfgift recoiled. She looked round, saw Wolf, dodged this way and that – and scrambled up on to the balustrade.

"No!" Wolf's heart almost stopped. Elfgift crouched on the rail, her fingers and toes gripping the edges. She peered over at the long drop.

"She's going to jump!"

"She's going to fly!"

Wolf and Roger spoke at once, equal horror in their voices. Then Wolf remembered the pie.

"Elfgift," he called in a trembling voice. "Elfgift, I've

got something nice for you. Come and get it…" As he fumbled inside his robe for the rather squashed mutton pie, Roger took a pace forward, crossbow levelled.

"Stay where you are," Wolf shouted. "Unless you want to end up explaining to Lord Hugo how she fell?"

"I don't take orders from you," Roger growled. "I'll do what I like, you jumped-up monkey!" An icy gust hit the tower. Elfgift swayed, and Wolf saw her muscles tighten and bunch. She lifted her chin, staring outwards and upwards at Devil's Edge and those dazzling, ominous clouds puffing up over the ridge. Wolf had the awful feeling that maybe she thought she could jump across from the tower to the hillside. It looked so close from up here. But that was an illusion.

"Elfgift, get down or you'll fall!" He knew she couldn't understand a word. He felt helpless – useless. Hailstones began to rattle out of the sky.

"Looks like she can't fly after all," Roger chuckled, taking another step. He must look like a monster to Elfgift – a metal monster in his gleaming chain mail. She turned to face him, wobbling on her narrow perch.

"Roger, you're scaring her," said Wolf urgently. "Back off, or she'll jump!"

"No she won't. I'm going to be the one who catches

her this time. *I'm* going to get the reward." Roger waved his crossbow in a threatening arc. "Come on, you elf. Give yourself up, or I'll shoot!"

"She doesn't know what a crossbow is, you idiot!" Wolf howled. He turned and sped away around the tower. The hail came on harder, freezing and stinging. He whirled around the last corner. Elfgift was still there, poised above the drop. Half blinded by hailstones, Wolf hurled himself at Roger's back.

"Get off!" Roger roared. He jerked the stock of the crossbow so that it struck Wolf in the chest. Wolf sank gasping to his knees. The crossbow triggered. With a loud click, the deadly bolt sped past Elfgift's ear. She let go of the rail, rose to her feet, and screamed; a cry that scraped cold fingernails all the way down Wolf's spine.

As if answering her call, all the rooks of La Motte Rouge burst out of the treetops. They rose screeching about the tower, hurtling and criss-crossing over the fighting platform, tearing the air with their cries. They swerved in over the rail at frightening speed, black missiles with beaks like spear points, claws like hooks. Wolf wrapped his arms over his head. He heard Roger shouting in terror, "Stop it! Stop it! Make it stop!"

"Elfgift!" Wolf screamed. Where was she? In this storm of birds and hailstones, surely she must have fallen? He crawled along the platform to the spot where he had last seen her.

Wings beat the air, slapped and buffeted his ears. Something cold and claw-like touched his cheek. He squinted and saw a skinny foot waving in his face. He grabbed it, and jerked hard. Elfgift tumbled off the rail on top of him.

He clutched her tightly, hauling her in. The rooks were as thick in the air as shaken pepper, bewildering the eye. "Elfgift, it's all right!" Her bony little body was tense with fright. He'd dropped the pie, and had nothing to give her. "Elfgift, hush. Don't be afraid. Hush. Poor little Elfgift, it's all right."

He rocked her, hardly knowing what he was doing. "Hush, Elfgift.

> *"Lullay, my little young child,*
> *Sleep and do not cry:*
> *Your mother and your father*
> *Watch at your cradle side…"*

Squalling and quarrelling, the whirlwind of rooks thinned and sank and blew away. A burst of hailstones rattled against the sides of the tower and bounced along the wooden platform.

> *"And there they will abide…"*

The rooks settled back into the treetops fifty feet

143

below, with a rattle and rustle of wings and a discontented chattering. The last of the hailstones rolled over the edge of the platform and dropped into the void. A banner of intense blue sky unfurled between the storm clouds.

"It was her!" Roger crawled towards them on his hands and knees. He had dropped his crossbow. His helmet was crooked and his eyes glared. He lifted a trembling, accusatory finger. "She did it! As God's my witness! Called up a flock of demons in the shape of crows…"

"They were rooks."

"Rooks – crows – who cares!" Roger's teeth were chattering. "Evil spirits, that's what they were. Birds don't behave that way!"

"Rooks do." Wolf got to his feet: awkwardly, because Elfgift was clinging to his clothes. He lifted her, holding her against his chest. She felt clammy, like a frog. He stared at Roger over the top of her head. "You know they do. Rooks often act that way, when they're alarmed or protecting their young…"

"Yes, protecting *her* – that devil's brat. You know she did it! You heard her, screeching and waving her arms and calling to them. How else do you explain it?"

"She didn't call them!" Wolf insisted, though part of him thought Roger might be right. He felt a pounding headache coming on. "She screamed because you frightened her. But even if she did call them, you know what? I don't care.

You want to bully her and wave your crossbow at her? Then you deserve what you get. Leave her alone, Roger."

Roger leaned on the rail, breathing hard. "I'm telling everyone about this."

Fine! Then I'll tell everyone too! I'll tell them how you fell over and dropped your bow and how your eyes nearly popped out of your head with fright…

Wolf didn't quite say it, but perhaps Roger read his face, for he shook his head. "And you call yourself a clerk," he said with lame dignity. "Encouraging Lord Hugo to keep an uncanny thing like that as if it was a – a pet, or something. You ought to know better."

"Oh, go and milk ducks!"

It was a schoolyard taunt, silly, but satisfying. Wolf stamped away, feeling better. At the top of the ladder he tried to make Elfgift climb down by herself, but she clung to his neck and nearly toppled him headfirst through the trapdoor. He couldn't make her understand about riding on his back, so he had to make a hair-raising descent into the shadowed depths of the armoury, holding her with one arm and grabbing one-handed at each rung in a series of perilous jerks. As he reached solid ground he leaned against the ladder and closed his eyes in a prayer of heartfelt thanks.

"You got her! Oh, well done, Wolf! What happened?"

Wolf nearly jumped out of his skin. Elfgift squeaked

and butted her head into his shoulder.

"Nest! I thought you were down below."

"I ran up here to shelter. That sky – and the hail – and the rooks! The way they went whirling around and around, cawing and screeching!"

"Roger Bach thinks they were evil spirits," said Wolf.

Nest paled. "Oh, but they weren't. Were they?"

"How should I know?" Wolf was still shaken. "They came when Elfgift screamed, that's all. As if they wanted to help her."

"Then they couldn't be evil!" Nest said.

"If Roger starts spreading rumours…"

"If he does, we'll say Elfgift was rescued by the birds of Heaven. Rooks are God's birds, like any others. In the Bible—"

"All right, never mind that for now," said Wolf quickly. "Here she is, safe and sound. Let's get her back to the stables before your father comes home."

"And she's tamer already." Nest brushed Elfgift's stained cheek with the back of her hand. "Look, she trusts us! How did you do it, Wolf? Was it the pie?"

"Must have been," Wolf grunted. The pie had been trodden into paste at the top of the tower, but he wasn't going to admit to singing lullabies.

Nest made for the door, throwing a curious glance around the dark, narrow space. "I haven't been up here for years. When I was little I climbed to the top once, to see the angels dancing in the sun on Easter morning."

Wolf's eyes opened wide. "You saw angels?"

Nest laughed and sighed. "It was the year after Mam died. I remembered her telling me that on Easter morning the angels dance for joy because Christ is risen. So I got out of bed while everyone was still asleep and climbed up the ladder. I was very small. And I did think I saw angels. Like flakes of fire swooping against the sun. But mostly I remember being too frightened to climb back down the ladder. Rollo had to carry me down, and Angharad smacked me and put me to bed."

"Angels!" Wolf was fired with wonder. "I'd like to see that!"

"She told me they dance on Christmas morning too." Nest looked at him. "Shall we find out?"

"What – come here at sunrise on Christmas day?"

"Exactly!" Her eyes sparkled. "There won't even be a guard. Not at Christmas. We'd have it all to ourselves. I could wake up early and slip downstairs. What do you think?"

"Let's do it!" said Wolf promptly.

"It's a promise then. Wolf, I'm glad you came." She put out her hand, and Wolf spared a hand from Elfgift to clasp it briefly. Struck by a sudden thought he looked around. "What happened to Angharad?"

Nest's face lit to a wicked smile. "Didn't you hear me say I *ran* up here when the hail started? But *poor* Angharad is too fat to manage the slope. So she had to go back to the Hall."

They made their way out of the tower together, laughing.

CHAPTER 9

"Hasn't she spoken yet?" Hugo demanded.

"No sir, not yet."

Elfgift crouched by the water trough, dropping pebbles in, apparently fascinated by the plop and splash. Her hair was growing back. A light floss of pale curls danced on her head. And she was wearing a grubby linen smock that came to her knees. Regular food was giving her a better colour. She looked healthier, and – viewed from the right side – disturbingly normal. Argos trotted over to her with a waving tail and stuck his nose in her ear. Elfgift threw an arm over his neck and hugged him. Then she pushed him away and dropped in another pebble.

"She's dressed, I see," said Hugo, snapping his fingers to bring Argos back.

Wolf nodded. "We— she let me do that a few days ago." He didn't tell Hugo that Nest had made the smock, stealing half an hour from sewing clothes for her marriage. "And once we— once I got her arms through the armholes, she seemed to love it. She keeps stroking the skirt and holding it out. It's muddy already, of course. And it's not very warm. But she doesn't seem to feel the cold…"

Hugo interrupted. "Do you know what day it is today?"

Wolf looked at his toes. "Saint Ursula's, sir…"

"Well past the middle of October. And the elf *still* doesn't speak?"

"She knows her name," Wolf said hurriedly. "Elfgift!" Elfgift's head snapped round on its thin little neck, and the dark side of her face became visible.

"Her name!" Hugo laughed shortly. "What good is that? Will she come to you?"

Wolf crossed his fingers. *Don't let me down…* "Elfgift, come here!"

Slowly and deliberately, Elfgift dropped in another pebble. Plunk!

"Wonderful obedience," said Hugo drily. "So. How much does she understand?"

A lot. She understands if I'm angry or happy or sad... But he knew Hugo didn't mean that. "A few more words. *Food*, that's a good one. And *dirty*! And *no*!" It didn't sound much, now he had to say it aloud.

Hugo snapped a pair of gloves back and forth across his palm, and Wolf searched for something extra to tell him. "Music. She likes to be sung to. And sometimes—"

"*Music*?" Hugo's eyebrows drew together. "What sort of music?"

Wolf was getting rattled. "Just any songs..." *The lullaby,* was what he meant; and he'd been going to say that Elfgift sometimes hummed the tune back to him in a gruff little growling voice that raised the hairs on the back of his neck. But now he held his tongue. Hugo might want a demonstration, and that would be awful.

Hugo bit his nails and gazed at Elfgift playing around the trough. "Bring her to me," he said after a moment, and pulled his gloves on.

Wolf crossed the yard, praying that Elfgift wouldn't choose this moment to start on one of her hide-and-seek chases around the castle. She saw him coming and got ready to run. "No!" Wolf pleaded. Something in his voice or face did the trick. She came to him quite sweetly, and with a sigh of relief he led her back.

Confronted with Elfgift, Hugo seemed suddenly uncertain. He hesitated, flashed a glance at Wolf and said to her, "Speak, elf – if you can. Teach me about Elfland. Do you understand me? Nod if you understand."

Elfgift wouldn't look at him. Wolf knelt and grabbed her arms. "Elfgift, listen to Lord Hugo. Please talk to him." Over his shoulder he said urgently, "Sir, I really don't think she can."

Hugo pushed him aside. He took Elfgift's face between his hands, forcing her to look at him. "Have you seen a lady there? A mortal woman? Answer me!"

Elfgift pulled away. Mewing and spitting she raked at Hugo's gloved hands.

Wolf forgot himself. "Let her go!" But Hugo's grip tightened, squashing her cheeks. Elfgift's eyes rolled up, showing the whites. Her tongue came out. "You're throttling her!" Wolf shouted. Up in the trees the rooks chattered and stirred. In the kennels the dogs began to bark.

Elfgift went limp. She hung from Hugo's hands. He let go, and she sprawled to the ground. Wolf leaped to help her.

"Splendour of God, Wolf!" Hugo swore. "Do you never think before you speak? No wonder the monks beat you."

"Frightening her won't help," Wolf said fiercely.

Hugo seemed to hold his breath. Then he said, level and hard, "Do you want to be a squire? Very well. For the moment I'll take your *advice*. There is still time. But remember the seven years are nearly up. I cannot wait forever. Teach her to speak by Christmas, or I'll find other ways. I swear, by all God's angels and saints, your elf-girl will lead me under Devil's Edge. *Do you understand me*?" He strode away. The disturbed rooks circled back to their nests.

Elfgift picked herself up. She looked sideways at Wolf and caught her lower lip between her teeth in a naughty, almost sly smile, as if inviting him to enjoy Hugo's failure. *We got rid of him*, she seemed to say. *Good*! She skipped back to the water trough.

Wolf passed his hands over his face and groaned. Why had he been given this impossible task? Sometimes he almost wished he'd never left the abbey. At least there he'd been anonymous, one black robe among many. Here he was conspicuous, singled out as the elf-girl's keeper.

"*Hi, Nursie! How's the baby, Nursie*?" Roger Bach bellowed at him from the gatehouse. Wolf set his teeth. There was nothing he could do about it. The men all teased him, and it wasn't friendly teasing. They even played tricks on him in the Hall at night. He'd wake with a gasp of fright to find his blankets tugged off, or cold water dripping in his ear. He wasn't sure who was doing it. If he sat up and looked around, everyone lay still, apparently asleep.

"*Has the baby had her pap?*" Roger yelled. His chubby face convulsed with laughter.

Wolf coaxed Elfgift back to the stables and went up to the solar in a gloomy mood to tell Nest what Hugo had said. He put Roger out of his mind. But it turned out that Nest had overheard the incident. As soon as Wolf knocked, she pulled him into the room, boiling with indignation.

"Does he often jeer at you like that? Does he? Oh, I'm sorry, Wolf!"

"I don't care," he said with forced cheerfulness. "He thinks it's funny, that's all."

"How dare he? Do they all pick on you? Is it because of Elfgift?"

Wolf shrugged. "Some of them. Mostly they ignore me. Roger's the worst, because of what happened on the tower."

"I am so sorry," Nest repeated. Frustrated tears stood in her eyes. "If only I could do something…"

"It's all right," said Wolf, impatient but touched. "You can't make people like me. Not even Lord Hugo could do that."

"Mother Aethelflaed could. She rules that whole convent by herself, and everyone does just what she says."

"Oh well, women. Men are different," said Wolf.

Nest's eyes flashed. "I'd like to see the man who could

stand up to Mother Aethelflaed! I wish I was like her."

Wolf imagined some ancient, fierce crone in a wimple, with watery eyes and a bristly upper lip. He almost laughed, till he saw Nest's anguished, unhappy face.

"You'll be married soon," he said, to comfort her. "Then you'll be in charge of your own house. You'll be a grown-up lady, and Angharad won't be able to tell you what to do."

"Yes," said Nest in such a low voice that a shadow fell across Wolf's cheerful assumption that, because she was a girl, she was longing to be married.

He said, "You do want to get married, don't you?"

"Of course." Nest didn't meet his eyes and Wolf wasn't reassured.

"This husband they've got for you – Lord Godfrey – do you like him?"

"I don't know." She was turning crimson.

"You don't know! Haven't you met him?"

"Of course! Just – not for a little while, that's all. Leave me alone, Wolf!"

"How long?" Wolf persisted.

"About eight years ago, when we were betrothed!" Nest snapped. "Happy now? It was before my mother died."

Wolf couldn't believe his ears. "Eight years? How old were you – five? How old is he?"

"Eighteen. He must have been ten at the time.

All I can remember is that he took my doll and flung it in a puddle. Angharad says he was a handsome little boy. It's been arranged for years, Wolf. I'm my father's heir. I've got to marry. I don't really mind. I just – just wish I knew—"

"What he's like now?"

She nodded.

Wolf said bitterly, "Your parents arranged your marriage when you were five years old, and mine packed me off to the abbey when I was six."

Nest looked stubborn. She braced her thin shoulders, as if lifting up some heavy load. "*Honour thy father and thy mother,*" she said quietly. "We owe a duty to our parents. That's one of the Ten Commandments, Wolf. You can't alter it."

They sat together in silence. Wolf rubbed his face and yawned. When he did it again, Nest shot a glance at him. "Are you tired?"

He managed to stifle the third yawn. "I didn't sleep well."

"Why not? Weren't you warm enough? Or is something wrong?"

He was ashamed to tell Nest about the practical jokes. "I'm fine. Don't worry about it."

"But what is it?"

"It's nothing. Really."

"*Tell* me!" It was Lady Agnes speaking, with sharp

command. Wolf gave in. "Someone plays tricks on me at night. That's all."

"Who?"

"I don't know. I keep waking up in the night with the blankets pulled off. Or they splash water on me, or pinch me…"

Nest went very still.

"It might be Roger, I suppose. Once when I woke up I felt someone bending over me. I could see his eyes, gleaming…" He couldn't say it, but *glowing* would have been a better word; it had been like a nightmare. "I couldn't move. I just lay there forever, wondering what would happen. In the end he laughed, a sort of low chuckle, *ho ho ho*! Like that. And then he vanished."

"You should have told me this *days* ago!" Nest cried.

Wolf flung her a startled glance. "It's no good. You can't do anything about it. I've just got to pretend I don't care."

"That's where you're wrong." Her eyes glittered. "This is something I *can* fix! You come with me!"

She caught his hand and dragged him to the door. Wolf resisted. "Stop it, Nest! It will make things worse if I get them into trouble."

"Oh, no it won't. I know who's been playing tricks on you. Come on!" She was halfway down the stairs. As always, the Hall was dim and hazy with fire smoke, pungent with the smell of the rushes and green herbs trodden into the floor. Angharad sat by the fire warming her toes and gossiping with Mattie. They looked extremely comfortable.

Nest bit off a fierce exclamation. "Always there, always keeping an eye on me!" she muttered. "Anything I ever want to do, I have to ask or coax or make excuses. Well, it won't come out with them sitting there. I'll have to get rid of them. Wait here!"

Utterly bewildered, Wolf lingered at the bottom of the stairs. Nest crossed the Hall to sit with Angharad.

"Brrrr!" She wrapped her arms over her chest, shivering dramatically. Angharad took the bait at once.

"Are you chilly, *cariad*? Don't go catching cold. You don't want to be coughing and sneezing when Lord Godfrey comes!" She elbowed Mattie, who tittered. "You ought to be wearing your warm green mantle. I know just where it is; I put it there myself: it's in the second oak chest in the solar, well sprinkled with lavender and wormwood against the fleas. Mattie will fetch it, won't you, Mattie?"

Mattie rose. Nest leaned her head against Angharad and coughed. "I'm not cold at all," she croaked. "I'm hot. I'd rather have a drink."

"Mercy! Has she got a fever?" Angharad felt Nest's brow. "Off to the kitchen, Mattie, and beg Herbert for a cup of hot wine for Lady Agnes. Ask him to sweeten it with honey and thyme – or maybe cloves would be better. Wait, I'll come too. You sit here, Nest, close by the fire where it's warm. And say your prayers: the *Paternoster* and the *Benedicite*: that often helps. Is your throat sore? Are you hungry? Would you like a morsel to eat? A junket? A soft-boiled egg?"

"Just the drink," said Nest faintly. She watched, pale as a lily but sharp-eyed, while the two women bustled out. Then she jumped to her feet, balling her fists, and spoke with fury directly to the hearth.

"Come out of there *immediately*!"

"What are you doing?" demanded Wolf. "Who are you talking to?"

"The *bwbach*. Our hearth-hob! Oh, I'm so sorry, Wolf, that it's behaved like this." She stamped her foot. "Come out! There was one at Our Lady's In-the-Wood, but it would never have *dreamed* of teasing a guest." She addressed the fireplace again. "You ought to be *ashamed* of yourself!"

Wolf stared breathlessly at the hearth. The pale smoke curled up. He listened, but all he could hear was the whining hiss of sap bubbling out of a green log, and the mumbling voice of the fire.

"I know you can hear me." Nest spoke coldly. "Wolf is my friend. Don't you dare play any more tricks on him!

I believe Herbert's cooking roasted capons today, stuffed with rosemary and breadcrumbs." She paused. "Smoked venison sausages with onions and mustard. Apple pastries with almonds and whipped cream! But you're not having any. Until you apologise, you'll eat gruel."

A sudden disturbance in the ash made Wolf jump, but still nothing spoke.

Nest turned to Wolf. "It isn't really wicked," she whispered. "It's been here forever. I used to talk to it a lot when I was little. We leave food out for it every night; it's an awful glutton. And it does like to play tricks on people, especially strangers..."

"Does it live in the flames?" Wolf whispered nervously. If so, he was sure it must be a sort of fiend.

"No, no, it lives under the hearth," said Nest. "There's a hole. A hollow space right under the floor. I saw it one summer when the fire went out. Howell says, hundreds of years ago there was another house here, and our Hall is built on the foundations. Oh, come *out!*" she flung at the hearth, stamping her foot. "Angharad will be back soon. And I'll have to drink some awful concoction to please her. And it's *all your fault.* Come out and apologise!"

The hob wouldn't come out. But, around midnight that night, Wolf opened his eyes. Nothing had pinched him, or dribbled water on to his face. He'd just woken, all by himself. He lay for a while, peeping through half-closed lids and listening to the household snoring. Some whispered, some snorted, some rasped like a saw cutting through a log.

Besides the snoring, the night life of the Hall went about the floor on its private affairs. A mouse ran past a foot from his nose. A hen that had got shut indoors stalked past on yellow feet, pecking up insects. House crickets chirped to and fro across the hearth, persistent, maddening, and shrill.

There was also an odd crackling sound and a smell he couldn't quite identify, like chicken, but fishier. He pushed himself up on one arm. Dark against the glow of the fire, a hunched, squat shape sat with its back to him. The firelight shone reddish through a shock of tufted hair. Knobbly elbows stuck out. Without turning round, it said in a sour, grumpy voice, "Wakened up, have you? T'weren't my doing this time, so don't you go a-blaming me. I reckon you'm used to rousting out o' bed in the middle of the night."

The hairs on Wolf's neck prickled. "I thought it was one of the men waking me up. Or a devil."

"I an't no devil."

"What are you then?"

"Folks find me as they takes me," the hob said

enigmatically, twisting round. Its eyes were dark slits with little glowing cores. In one skinny hand it held a long, wooden skewer with something stuck on the end that looked alarmingly like a miniature human with tiny splayed-out arms and legs. Wolf shrank. "What's that?"

"Toasted frog. Fancy some?" It waved the skewer under his nose.

"No! No, thanks." The fishy chickeny smell wasn't too bad, but the sight of the blackened little morsel made his throat close up.

"No, you wouldn't, would you?" the hob grumbled. "You'm full of roasted chicken, and sausages, and pies."

"Well…" Wolf began. The hob interrupted.

"You think I care? *I* dun't care. I can find me own fare. I can fend for meself. I've et frogs afore. Though they're better with a touch of butter and garlic," it admitted.

"It's not my fault. What did you want to go scaring me for?"

The hob sniggered. "Scared you, did I? T'were only fun! An't you got no sense of yumour? Look at you! All dressed up like a monk, and that bald spot on yer 'ead—"

"It's growing back!" Wolf snarled, passing a hand over his head where his thick fair hair was reasserting itself. The hob ignored this.

"*Course* I played tricks on you. You'd ha' played tricks on yourself, if you could ha' seen yourself." It pulled a leg off the frog and sucked the meat. "'Sides," it mumbled, spitting out bones, "that's my nature." It looked up and fixed him with a sharp, sudden glance. "The young missus, now. Tarrible harsh, she was – stopping my rations an' all. But I don't reckon to get niffy with her, cos she'm even harsher on herself."

"On herself?"

"Right!" The hob nodded. "*She* dun't want to get married, pore young thing."

"I don't think she'd mind so much if she knew more about Lord Godfrey."

"Who are *you* telling?" the hob demanded. "Tarrified o' getting married, she is. Tarrified. But she'll do it. She reckons it her duty. That's *her* nature." It finished the frog and tossed bones and skewer into the fire. "Not bad," it licked its lips, "but I'd ruther not miss another dinner. You tell the young missus we've had a nice gossip, and all's settled. I shan't worrit you no more."

"But she said you had to apologise, and you haven't actually said sorry," Wolf pointed out.

The hob turned right round and stared at him silently. The little sparks in its eyes grew red and hot, till Wolf's hair seemed to rise and creep about his head.

"I'll do better'n that," said the hob at last with restrained menace. "I'll give you a piece of advice. I can see you're a bold young feller. Quick as an arrer! Sharp as a razor! That can get you into trouble that can. You watch that tongue o' your'n dun't *cut your own throat!*"

"Sorry." How had the hob managed to get him apologising to it?

"All right." The hob was stern. "Off to sleep with you now, if you like."

Obediently, Wolf lay down. Then he struggled up again. "Wait! I need to ask you something."

"Woss that, then?"

"You're an elf, aren't you?"

The hob almost choked. "*Me*? I'm a hob!"

"It's the same thing, isn't it? A fairy, then, or a fay. What's the difference?"

"*What's the diff*—?" The hob's hair stood straight up like a dog's hackles. "Me? Catch me moping about in drippy old caves, pretendin' they're palaces! All of it make-believe, like kiddies playing at banquets with a cup o' cold water and a handful o' leaves. You know why the elves learned all that magic? Acos they had to! I've allus lived in housen, I have, and et cooked food every day, regular and decent!" Its eyes glowed like indignant lamps.

"All right! Calm down," said Wolf. "What do you mean, *they had to*? What are the elves, if you're not one?"

"Bunch o' beggars," said the hob sourly. "The elves, they dun't belong nowhere. They an't got nowhere to go, so they lurks about in woods or creeps into holes in the ground. Hiding places for lost things. Some of em claims to be the dark angels what was cast out o' Heaven. So they says: but they'd say anything. They'd claim they was the Princes of Persia if they thought they'd be believed. And some of em's just the children of Eve that she disowned. Anyone that loses himself can end up with the elves, I reckon."

"So they're harmless?"

"Harmless? *Harmless*?" The hob nearly choked again.

"If it's all make-believe?" Wolf said lamely.

"Dun't you know belief is the most powerful thing there is? Hundreds o' years o' make-belief can make most things, I reckon. You keep clear of em, young master. Meddle with the elves and they'll draw you down deeper than you'll want to go. They say the back door of Elfland leads straight down to Hell, and the rivers run with human blood. They'm a raggle-taggle crew."

Human blood? Wolf shuddered. "I only asked because I thought you could tell me about Elfgift. You've seen her?"

"Oh, her?" The hob's hair smoothed back down. "Oh, she'm an elf all right." It spoke with sad anger, as though the words meant "she's crippled".

"Really?" Wolf felt his stomach sink. Which was odd:

this was good news, wasn't it? He ought to be glad to hear Elfgift was really an elf. If she wasn't; if she couldn't help Lord Hugo to find his lost Eluned, how would he ever become a squire?

"With a face like hers? Oh, aye," said the hob bleakly. "She was cast out long ago, that Elfgift o' your'n. Far, far too late to do anything about that."

CHAPTER 10

It was the last day of October, and evening was closing over the castle in a muffle of misty rain. Tonight the Devil would rampage over the hills, probably in the shape of an enormous black sow with no tail. Ghosts would come squeaking out of their graves, lost spirits would wander abroad and sit, plaintively weeping, on every stile.

As Wolf returned from shutting Elfgift safely into the stables for the night, he saw the pulsing glow of a bonfire beyond the open gates, and heard distant sounds of merriment. The All Hallows' fire had been lit, and would burn till dawn to keep elves and sprites and ghosts at bay. Of course, it was also a good excuse for a party.

Wolf had never been to an All Hallows' fire. He raced into the Hall to tell Nest. It was very quiet. On one side of the fire Hugo and Geraint sat with a chessboard between them, heads bent over the bone pieces. Old Howell watched the moves with benign interest. Argos lay flat on his side at Hugo's feet, soaking up warmth from the fire. On the other side of the hearth Angharad and Nest and Mattie sat sewing. As he came in, Wolf saw Nest wearily stab her needle into the fabric that overspread her lap – expensive blue wool. She saw him and brightened. "Wolf! Come and talk to me."

"They've lit the All Hallows' bonfire!" Wolf blurted. "I can see it from the gate!"

Hugo and Geraint looked up. But Angharad got in before anyone else could speak. "My lady's got no interest in that," she said sharply.

Wolf was disconcerted. "H-hasn't she?" he stammered. "I thought she might like to see it."

"No indeed, and my lord will tell you the very same thing!" That put paid to any hope that Hugo might override Angharad's strictures. "A gently born girl of her age wouldn't dream of going to a thing like that, to rub shoulders with kitchen boys and peasants. You wouldn't, would you, my *cariad*?"

Nest pinched her lips together and looked at the floor. "You go if you want, Wolf," she said in a low voice. "I'm not allowed."

Wolf stood on one leg, torn. She glanced up. "Go on! You can't help with the sewing, can you?"

"All right…" He backed out, feeling mean for abandoning her, and angry with Angharad. Why couldn't Nest go and have fun at the bonfire like anyone else? Those *kitchen boys and peasants* were her own servants, who would die rather than let anything happen to a hair on her head.

"Going to the bonfire?" The gate guard was Roger Bach's crony, Stephen le Beau. Tall and skinny, he leaned on his spear in the drizzle like a scarecrow version of Lord Hugo, his lank fair hair dripping in points under his helmet.

"Mind the Black Sow doesn't get you," he said. It was half joke, half threat.

"Thanks," said Wolf. He peered out and almost changed his mind about going. Maybe Angharad had a point after all. The bonfire was further away than he'd thought, and there was a lot of dark, muddy lane to walk down alone.

Stephen threw up his hand so suddenly he made Wolf start. "What's that?"

It was a prolonged bubbling sound from the direction of the cistern, as if the spring had suddenly boiled up with great force. A glimmering white thing rose from the water. It might be a white swan, splashing its wings, but Wolf knew it wasn't. A cloud of dispersing moisture blew across the yard as a cold presence drifted past, weeping softly.

"The White Lady!" Stephen clutched his spear. "She'll be prowling all around the castle tonight."

"But she's harmless," said Wolf. "Isn't she? Howell said so."

"Howell would," said Stephen, "but it's the way she comes up behind you…" He crooked his fingers and raised them over his head. "*Whoo-hoo-hoo…*"

"Stop it!" Wolf stepped defiantly out on to the wooden bridge over the moat.

Stephen waited till he was halfway across. "*Whoo-hoo-hoo!*" he moaned again, and cackled. "Saw you jump!"

Wolf disdained to look around. But Stephen's words had done their work. The glow of the bonfire ahead made the lane seem blacker than ever. He walked quickly downhill, stumbling over the stones and potholes. *I'm not afraid of the White Lady*, he told himself. But what if she was silently gliding after him right now?

He threw a glance over his shoulder. And to his horror there *was* something, drifting through a nebulous swirl of mist between him and the gateway. And it looked just like the blurred figure of a veiled woman. For an awful second Wolf wasn't sure. Was it a wreath of mist? No, there really was a cloaked figure coming after him!

He swung to face it. It was that, or run down the uneven lane not knowing how close it was behind him. Prickles raced down his spine. *The White Lady's harmless. Howell says she's harmless!*

The eerie figure drew closer, its face hidden. Wolf's mouth was dry. He raised his hands to ward her off. "Who's there?" he quavered.

"Ouch!" said the shape, tripping. "I can't see a thing. Is that you, Wolf?"

"Nest!"

"Hush! Don't yell out my name like that!" She grabbed his arm, looking back. "I want to see the bonfire!"

"How did you get away?" Wolf asked weakly.

"I was furious with Angharad," said Nest. "So I told her I was going by myself to pray in the chapel. It wasn't a lie. I meant it. But then in the yard I saw the White Lady wandering ahead of me, and I didn't want to meet her, she's so mournful and clingy—" To Wolf's surprise she giggled. "So I was coming back to the Hall, and there was Stephen le Beau on the gate, looking scared – and I just wrapped my veil over my face and walked straight past him, wailing and wringing my hands."

Wolf gazed at her in delighted awe. "What did he do?"

"He yelped like a puppy and scuttled into the gatehouse without giving me a second glance." Nest's voice trembled with laughter. She tugged his arm.

"Hurry! I don't want to waste a minute."

The bonfire was a long bowshot from the castle, in the corner of a field between the lane and the old stone road. At last they were close enough to see the dark shapes of men dragging branches towards it, and to hear the lively murmur of voices. There were more people clustered around the fire than lived in La Motte Rouge: the villagers who worked on the estate were all gathering. Someone beat on a little drum, while others clapped out a rhythm. Somebody else was dancing a jig.

"Oh, this looks fun!" said Nest. In astonishment she added, "And that's Rollo!" She was right. Rollo was dancing with head thrown back, arms raised, the firelight glistening on his face and the shadowed slash of his deep scar.

"*Birandón, birandón, birandéra!*" he shouted, stamping his heavy boots into the mud. *Pat-a-pat, pat-a-pat, pat-a-pat-pat*, went the drum.

"*Oh, off we went to the fighting*," Rollo sang in a tuneless roar.

"*Yes, off we went to the fighting,*
So off we went to the Ho-oly La-a-and –
Birandón, birandón, tra la la!

"*But all the time we were thinking*

We'd rather be home again drinking,
So back we came from the Ho-oly La-a-and —
Birandón, birandón, tra la la!"

There was a burst of laughter and cheers. Rollo dragged a hand across his sweating forehead and bowed, grinning. Someone thrust a flask at him. "Here y'are, crusader! Drink up!" He took a good swig.

Wolf saw that Nest might not be very welcome here. This was a rough, informal gathering, where people could behave as they liked, without worrying about their social superiors. He couldn't imagine Rollo singing like that if he knew that Lady Agnes was listening.

Maybe Nest had the same thought. She was rearranging her veil to shadow her entire face. They stood on the edge of the crowd, watching, not quite belonging. Most of the garrison seemed to be there, and Wolf spotted Bronwen and Gwenny.

"*Birandón, birandón, birandéra,*" roared Rollo, preparing for another verse.

Just then Roger Bach looked over his shoulder and saw Wolf. He gave a whoop.

"If it isn't the nursemaid! Pipe down, Rollo, here's Wolfie-boy to tuck us all up and send us to lullaby land!"

Wolf felt the blood stinging his face. "Let's go," he said quietly to Nest.

"Wait!" Roger shouted. Against his instincts, Wolf looked back. Roger spun a small coin from one broad thumb nail. "Sing us a psalm, and I'll give you a groat!"

Wolf's eyes narrowed in anger. But before he could think of a reply, Rollo called out, "Is that the value you put on a psalm, Roger? Leave the lad alone. You ought to know better'n to make fun of holy things on All Hallows' Eve."

Roger scowled. But he'd gone too far for the villagers, who murmured sympathetically and opened to let Wolf in. Nest was still hovering in the background, a cloaked, anonymous figure. Wolf flung an agonised glance over his shoulder as Rollo yelled, "Bronwen my lovely, get young Wolf a drink!"

"Bronwen!" Wolf whispered as she handed it to him. "Over there, behind me. That's Lady Agnes. Look after her!"

Bronwen goggled – but only for a moment. She nodded emphatically and strode past, her dark hair tossing. From the corner of his eye, he saw Nest begin to back away, but Bronwen said something and drew her towards the fire. Next time Wolf looked, Nest was standing with Gwenny and Bronwen surrounded by a ring of village women. Deeply grateful to Bronwen, Wolf clutched his earthenware cup of mulled ale and stared about him. The fine, cool rain prickled his cheeks but was almost as soon dried by the heat of the fire.

Rollo stood beside him, snapping his fingers to the pat-a-pat-pat of the drum. "Don't heed Roger," he said in a low voice. "There's no real harm in him. He and I go way back. Have you seen this dent in my head?"

"Er—" It was the first thing anyone would notice about Rollo. "Did a Saracen do it?" He'd been dying to ask.

Rollo laughed. "Nah, a skinny little bare-legged Welshman! Nearly finished me off for good. Would have, too; but Roger got him in the ribs before he could give me another chop. He's not a bad lad, Roger. By the way, I've been thinking."

"Yes?" said Wolf cautiously.

Rollo scratched an ear. "Maybe I was a bit hasty, the day you gave me such a start in the stables. Not many lads would have stood up to me like you did. I'm not saying I was wrong, mind you. I don't hold with elves."

His voice was loud. A few yards away, Wolf saw Nest listening.

"What do you think?" Rollo demanded. "You've had enough time to make your mind up. Is she really an elf? Or just a kiddie who can't talk?"

Wolf squirmed, thinking of the hob. *She'm an elf, all right.* He cleared his throat. "Um…"

But Rollo was rather drunk and didn't wait for him to finish. "You know what? You know what you ought to do? You know how to find out?"

"No…"

"You go to the kitchen," Rollo waved a finger, "and you get an *eggshell*…"

Nest ducked her head into her hands with a snort of laughter. Rollo looked round in surprise, but Wolf said hurriedly, "Yes?"

Rollo turned back. "You fill it with porridge."

Wolf glued his eyes to Rollo's face in an expression of strained interest. "Go on."

"And you stir it up in front of the elf –" Rollo demonstrated holding up an imaginary eggshell and stirring with mincing fingers. "And the elf's so surprised to see anyone *cooking* in an *eggshell*…"

Wolf drew a deep, careful breath. Nest was wiping her cheeks.

"Rollo," he said.

"Hmm?"

"Tell me about the Crusade."

The joviality died out of Rollo. "The Crusade? What bit d'you want to know about?"

"The siege of Acre," Wolf suggested eagerly. He looked to see if Nest was still listening, but she had her head close to Bronwen's and they were laughing. Maybe she was passing on the eggshell joke.

"Nothing to tell," Rollo mumbled. "The Saracens opened the gates and came out to surrender: two and a half thousand of 'em, maybe closer to four thousand with the women and children. Two bitter, bloody years they'd held out, and they came out in good order and gave themselves up."

"But that happened at the very end. What about the actual fighting?"

"The fighting?" Rollo said with a short laugh. "It was a siege, my lad. In sieges, you sit around outside the walls waiting to see who starves first, them or us. It was nearly us. Men died like flies. Even the archbishop died. Finally the king turned up and offered incentives. Anyone who pulled a stone out of the walls got two gold bezants! Later it went up to four. *That* got people moving. Say what you like, those walls came down for money, not for God."

Wolf felt cheated. He'd wanted tales of gallantry and chivalry. "But there must have been *some* fighting," he persisted.

"You want blood?" Rollo twisted round suddenly. "I'll give you blood. Ask me what we did to the prisoners. Go on, ask!"

"Well – what?" Wolf asked apprehensively.

"We butchered them. Every single one of 'em, men, women and children. The king ordered it and we did it. Me, and Lord Hugo, and all the rest of us Christian knights and squires and men-at-arms."

Wolf felt sick. Rollo wiped a hand across his mouth and added, "Killing in battle's one thing. Slaughtering prisoners – it can't be right, now, can it? In your heart of hearts, you know it's wrong. It would be a relief if someone said so. But no. The churchmen and the bishops and the clerks – *people like you* – all say, 'Oh, they were Saracens. It was right to kill them. God approves!'."

He glared at Wolf. "Funny thing, that! Seems to *me* I might have done something bad. Seems to *me* God might not want people climbing up to Heaven on a pile of corpses. But there's the pope and the bishops and Holy Church all a-patting me on the back. What if they're wrong? What if I'm going to Hell instead? Wha's – I mean, what's a man to think?"

Wolf didn't care what Rollo thought. "It's a lie! Lord Hugo didn't kill them – did he? Not *Lord Hugo*!"

Rollo's big face screwed up. "Ah! Sorry. Sorry, Wolf. S'the drink – the drink talking. I forgot you're just a boy. You still need heroes." He rocked back on his heels and stared up into the drizzle. "I need *more* drink. This weather is not good for my bones." He stamped away.

"Wolf!" Nest bobbed up at his elbow, her face alight. She was wearing a different veil, much thicker and coarser. "Bronwen and I have swapped. She's got my veil and I've got hers. Do you know, I always thought Bronwen didn't like me, but she does! This is such fun. I'm so glad I came."

Wolf focused on her slowly. Nest touched his arm. "Did you hear me? Are you all right?" Her eyes widened. "You're not *drunk*, are you?"

Wolf collected his wits. "No, but I think Rollo is." Rollo had begun dancing again and was bawling:

> "*And then I got back to discover*
> *My wife had run off with a lover.*
> *And so my cup runneth o-o-verr –*
> *Birandón, birandón, tra la la!*"

"...*tra la la!*" There was a curious echo from down the lane – higher and clearer than Rollo's voice. Rollo froze in mid-caper. "What the *devil's* that?"

Nest and Wolf turned. For a moment Wolf could have sworn he saw another blaze glittering through the crannies of the hedge, throwing a strong moving shadow ahead of it through the mist and the swirls of bitter smoke. A shadow half man, half beast. Other people saw it too. There were gasps and screams.

Out of the dark and drizzle, a long, swinging head emerged, huge ears twitching. Hooves clattered and squelched. "A mule!" someone yelled. Sitting sideways on its back was a man with horns.

More screams! Some of the boys were running, and hurling stones. Wolf too was groping for a stone. Then he realised the man didn't have horns. He had ears, as huge and pointed as his mule's. And he was flinging gilded balls into the air: they whirled and dropped into his hands and rose again.

In a high, strong voice he sang out some catchy nonsense that trilled off the tongue.

"Fol de rol, tra la la, saladarado,
Nazaza, mirontaine, birondandón!"

A stone struck the mule on the shoulder. It grunted and shied. But the man riding didn't miss a catch or falter in his song. As another stone whizzed past he caught it and threw it into the air to dance up and down with the golden balls.

"Falada, fol de rol, trillivilleros.
Tra la la, nazaza, miramontaine!"

By now everyone was dropping the stones they'd picked up, and Bronwen clouted the ear of the boy who'd thrown the last one.

"It's a juggler!"

"A *jongleur*!"

They began to applaud. Neatly, the *jongleur* let the balls spin down into his hand. He tossed the stone high, high into the air, jumped off the mule and bowed low. The stone was coming down now, hurtling to strike him.

"Look out!" shouted Wolf.

"Look out, look out!"

The *jongleur* straightened up and stuck out his hand. The stone smacked into his palm. He brought it round it front of him, raised it to his mouth and bit. Again everyone gasped, sure his teeth would shatter. "All I ask is bread, my masters, so don't give me stones!" the *jongleur* called in French. And he looked at Wolf, winked broadly, and tossed it straight at him.

Wolf caught it. And it wasn't a stone at all; it was a bitten bread roll. He laughed in admiration, sure he'd seen a simple conjuring trick, and looked round for Nest to show her. She nodded quickly. But most of the peasants were open-mouthed.

"You!" It was Rollo. He blundered forwards clumsily. Wolf saw his face and was chilled. Rollo looked as if he had seen a ghost. "Wha's your name?"

The *jongleur* turned lightly towards him. He was a tall, thin youthful-looking fellow with a pale, freckled face and a hint of frizzy hair escaping from under a close fitting cloth hood with cloth donkey-ears. "Halewyn." The twist of his wide mouth spelled amusement.

"I've seen you before," said Rollo. "Haven't I?"

"Surely," said the *jongleur* after a moment, "if you be one of Lord Hugo's men? Then we met two years ago, on the road—"

Between Poitiers and Tours. It came back to Wolf then, Rollo's words in the stable, a few weeks back. *A whey-faced, gangling strip of a fellow riding on a mule,* Rollo had said, *and he told my lord a story about a dead woman coming back.*

"Where have you come from?" Rollo asked roughly.

"I sprang out of the ground!" The *jongleur* flipped himself backwards. He stood on his hands, brandished his feet under Rollo's nose, and righted himself again. The crowd laughed and clapped, but the *jongleur* inspected his hands and sadly shook his head. "Muddy, alas. I should have thought before I acted. But that's me all over. Just an impulsive boy."

Rollo's face darkened. But the *jongleur* rolled a comically expressive eye, as if to say, "Who *is* this rude fellow?" and stepped past, dismissing him. "Hey, Brother," he said to Wolf, but loud enough for everyone to hear. "I've travelled a long way tonight. Will you take me up to the castle and find me a bite to eat? I can tell a sad tale and a merry one, sing a song and fling a somersault. As for your lord, he knows me. He's seen me before."

With all eyes on him, Wolf dared not look at Nest. He hesitated. But, whatever Rollo thought, he liked the look of Halewyn. It was good to hear a pleasant voice, good to be asked for assistance. "Of course I will. Come with me."

CHAPTER 11

Halewyn walked beside Wolf, leading the mule. Its plate-sized feet chopped and splashed through the mud. From the corner of his eye Wolf was aware of Nest, walking with Bronwen a few paces to the rear. Before they were halfway up the lane, the rain came on harder, and many of the folks from La Motte Rouge caught them up in a rush for the gates. Bronwen and Nest were swept up in the crowd. Hand in hand they ran past Wolf and Halewyn and disappeared together up the lane.

"Look out, Gwenny – the Black Sow's after ye!" bellowed Roger Bach, lunging at Gwenny and tickling her. The girl screamed, between laughter and terror. She tore herself away and dashed after Bronwen. The mule laid back its ears and kicked.

"Softly, Beelzebub. Softly, my friend." Halewyn stroked the mule's damp nose.

"You call your mule *Beelzebub*?" Wolf was glad of the distraction.

"Why not?" said Halewyn blithely. "It's a very good name for a mule. He's a stubborn, disobedient old thing, aren't you, Beelzebub?"

Wolf bit his lip on a shocked smile. He looked sideways at Halewyn. To ride so far on All Hallows' Eve! To name his mule after the Devil! He must be afraid of nothing.

They came to the gate. Stephen le Beau stepped forward sharply, barring the way with his spear. "Who goes there?"

"It's all right, Stephen! This is Halewyn. Don't you remember him? He's a *jongleur*, he's met Lord Hugo, in France I think it was…"

Rollo came past them then, and Wolf saw him give Halewyn a grim, unsmiling glance. But Stephen's face was already splitting into a welcoming grin. "You! *Course* I remember you. You told us that story about the priest and the fleas. Never laughed so hard in me life!" He clapped Halewyn on the back, and chuckled as Halewyn pretended to stagger under the blow. "I'm on guard tonight. You'll stay for a while, won't you? I don't want to miss the fun."

"Till Christmas, if I'm welcome," Halewyn promised.

"Take your mule to the stables." Stephen raised his voice. "Is that everyone?" he shouted to the last-comers. "Everyone in? Lend me a hand, Walter, let's get the gates shut."

They ran the heavy gates shut and slid the huge bar across. Stephen patted it.

To Wolf's surprise he took a deep breath and rattled off some ragged rhyme:

> "*Heaven defend us all this night*
> *From ghosts and every wicked sprite.*
> *Open Heaven gates and shut Hell gates*
> *And keep us safe and sound. Amen.*"

"Amen!" chorused Walter.

"That wasn't a proper prayer!" Wolf exclaimed as he and Halewyn walked away with the mule.

Halewyn looked at him queerly and laughed, showing the pointed tips of long dog-teeth. "It wasn't, was it? But it was very quaint, and it makes them feel safer, so where's the harm? Is this the stable? All barred and bolted, I see. Excellent practice. There's no use barring the stable door after the horse has gone, is there?" He watched while Wolf undid the bolts. "This isn't your job, surely, Brother – what's your name?"

"Wolf," Wolf grunted, heaving the door open.

"Brother Wolf?" Halewyn sounded delighted.

"Just Wolf. And no, Madog's the stable boy. But I don't mind. I'm often in and out of here, because—"

He hesitated, not sure whether to mention Elfgift.

"Because— ?" Halewyn prompted. Outlined in the stable doorway, he and his mule looked very alike – black silhouettes with long donkey-ears. Then Beelzebub shook his wet head till his ears and harness rattled.

"I look after – someone," said Wolf.

Halewyn touched a fingertip to his lips in a mimicry of thought. Then he pointed at Wolf. "The elf-girl!"

"How do you know about her?"

"How do I know? It's all around the countryside! Ooh, is she in here? Is this where you keep her? Let me see the elf-girl, do. Just a peek!"

He dropped Beelzebub's reins and advanced into the stable, craning his neck.

"No," said Wolf.

"Oh, why?"

Wolf didn't know why. "It's dark, and she's probably asleep." In fact, he could hear an abrupt crackling in the straw that suggested Elfgift was wide awake.

Halewyn was listening, head cocked. "That's her, isn't it? Show, show, show!" As if in agreement, Beelzebub stamped on the cobbled floor with his metal-shod hoof.

"Get out of the way then," said Wolf, flustered. "Let me go first!" He pushed in front of Halewyn and walked down the row to the last stall, calling quietly to Elfgift. It was so dark he could barely see his hand in front of his face, and he wished he'd brought a lantern. Halewyn was treading on his heels.

"She's here, but you won't be able to see much—"

Wolf almost jumped out of his skin. With a crack and a cascade of sparks, Halewyn struck a light. A sulphurous, yellow, smoky flame licked up. Elfgift's face gleamed half pale, half red, with huge startled eyes. She threw up a shielding arm and recoiled, screaming.

"*Put that out!*" Wolf yelled. He spat on his fingers, reached for Halewyn's taper and pinched it out. "You don't bring an unguarded flame into a stable, you fool!" He stamped out a glowing spark on the floor, shuddering as he thought of the heaps of dry straw surrounding them, the wooden stalls, the thatched roof. "Do you want the place to go up like a torch?"

"There's a thought." Halewyn sounded contrite but amused. "Truly I am a fool. I'm sorry."

"All right," Wolf growled. "There's an empty stall

here. Put the mule in it, and let's go." While Halewyn unharnessed the mule Wolf lingered, stretching out his hand. "Elfgift? It's all right." He'd been a fool to let Halewyn near her: the sudden appearance of his donkey-eared cap must have terrified her. "It's all right," he repeated soothingly. "Go to sleep again."

Small fingers crept out of the darkness and clung to his. "Go back to sleep," he whispered, and hummed the lullaby tune under his breath. "*Lullay, lullay little one. Sleep and do not fear…*"

And a moment later, out of the dark Elfgift hummed it back in a soft, hoarse voice that got inside his head and made his teeth buzz. And his skin popped up in goosebumps. And she didn't get the tune exactly right. But he clenched his teeth together and hung on to her hand. They were communicating. Elfgift and he were saying goodnight!

After a while she let go and he heard her curling up in the straw. He waited to be sure she was settled, then went out and rebolted the door. Halewyn stood in the glimmering drizzle, hanging his head so extravagantly that the donkey-ears on his cap drooped.

"I'm sorry," he said again. He pounded his thin chest. "*Mea culpa, mea culpa, mea maxima culpa*. Anything you'd like me to do in penance? Turn a somersault? Do three cartwheels across the yard, dodging the puddles? Sing a song standing on my head?"

Wolf couldn't help laughing. "No, it's all right. Just remember, flames are dangerous in stables and barns."

"Oh, I will. I'll be very, very careful." Halewyn perked up. "At least I saw her," he said buoyantly. "And now, take me to your leader."

Wolf shepherded him across the dark yard. Halewyn was fun.

The Hall was hot and bright and smoky, and full to bursting. It was clear that everyone had heard of Halewyn's arrival. Even the kitchen servants had squeezed in: Herbert and Bronwen and Gwenny. Argos came threading his way through the throng. He welcomed Wolf, but when he saw Halewyn he drew his lips back and growled, and his narrow hackles stood up like a scrubbing brush.

"Hush!" Wolf chided, pushing him aside.

Hugo was seated on the dais at the end of the Hall, magnificent in his chequered cloak. When he saw Halewyn he sat forward eagerly – and Wolf remembered what Rollo had said about the Crusades. How could Hugo look like that, when he had killed helpless prisoners? *The perfect knight,* he thought bitterly. *The crusader.*

Nest was seated beside her father. She had thrown on a clean white veil, and though her eyes sparkled more than usual, no one would guess she had just run up the lane hand in hand with a kitchen maid. Wolf was miserably thankful she hadn't overheard Rollo's bloodstained story.

Halewyn jogged Wolf's arm. "What are you glowering at? Watch me now, and learn how to make an entrance." He stepped forward with a flourish. "Greetings to you, noble lord, and to you, fair lady, and to everyone here, gentles and good folk all."

"God be good to you," Hugo said, smiling. "I well remember how you pleased us with your songs and tales, Halewyn, that time we were fellow travellers on the road through Anjou."

"My noble lord is gracious." Halewyn made another deep bow, adding softly as he straightened, "I promised you then I should see you again!"

And there were three batons in his right hand, like slender clubs. He tossed them up and began to juggle. He moved forwards, surrounded by a spinning halo. At the edge of the hearth he caught them and plunged them into the fire. They must have been dipped in pitch. He drew them out flaming, and danced across the floor, brandishing them at the crowd.

"*Real fire*, lords and masters. Mind your beards! Mind your long hair, maidens and wives!" With laughter and screams they scrambled away from him. Then Halewyn's hands flickered, and up went the firebrands, tumbling through the air in a brilliant fiery circle. He moved towards the dais, throwing them higher and higher. Wolf was breathless. How did he always manage to catch the handles and not the flaming ends? At last, in front of Lord Hugo and Nest, Halewyn caught the firebrands. He brought them to his lips and extinguished them – it almost looked as if he sucked the flames away. He knelt on one knee and bent his head till his ass's ears almost touched the ground.

Wolf clapped till his hands stung. Still kneeling, Halewyn put a hand to his heart. Next moment a flower was in his hand, a rose with delicate crimson petals. Humbly, timidly, as if he was afraid she would not take it, he held it out to Nest.

"For the beautiful lady."

Nest was taken by surprise. She coloured and glanced at her father. Angharad was tutting, but Hugo nodded. Nest took the flower. Then she flinched and dropped it into her lap. A moment later she was softly sucking her finger.

Wolf winced in sympathy. But Hugo was speaking. "Well done and welcome! I've sent for ale, bread and meat to refresh you after your journey. While we are waiting for it, talk to us of your travels. Where have you come from, and what brings you here tonight?"

"Thank you, lord." It went without saying that Halewyn would tell any scraps of news or gossip he had picked up. He perched himself on a stool near the edge of the dais. "I've lately come from Wenford…"

Wolf pricked up his ears.

"…where I stayed with the monks at St Ethelbert's." Halewyn was using a clear, formal style so that his words carried right across the Hall. "And there, to visit the abbot, came young Godfrey fitz Payne of La Blanche Land. I think his chaplain had died and he came to ask the abbot to appoint him a new one, which the abbot willingly did. There was talk of you, lord, since they said he is to marry with the lady your daughter –" here he bowed to Nest "– at Christmas. And hearing your name I remembered how I'd had the good fortune to meet with you on the road to Tours, and how you were pleased to laugh at my jests and listen to my poor songs, and I thought I would be glad to see you once again."

Wolf didn't attend to Hugo's reply. *Halewyn's seen Lord Godfrey!* He turned quickly to look at Nest, and she was already staring at him, her eyes huge. *We've got to get him alone and ask him questions!*

Food was brought, and Halewyn ate and drank. Then he opened his pack and brought out a small, box-shaped harp. He tested the strings. Everyone hushed, and Wolf sat up. He hoped, for Halewyn's sake, this wasn't going to be the tale of the dead woman that had upset Rollo.

It wasn't. First Halewyn sang part of the old story of Count Roland, who rode out to battle with the Saracens, laughing and tossing his lance into the air so that the white pennant whipped and curled against the blue sky. Wolf drank it up. This was the way a hero should behave!

Then Halewyn sang a drinking song that got everyone swaying and stamping their feet and trying to sing along. It got gradually faster and faster, till at the final chorus everyone tripped over their tongues and burst out laughing.

Wolf didn't quite forget his anger with Hugo, but he tucked it away for later. He had never had so much fun. Halewyn sang a few more songs and then rested. The household sat around the fire, telling ghost stories.

"…stand by the chapel door at midnight, and you'll see…"

"…a thing like a badger without a head…"

"…a wheel of fire, bowling down the hill…"

"Two hundred years ago," old Howell was saying placidly to anyone close enough to hear, "a pilgrim returning from the Holy Land discovered a mountain with a cleft in the rocks. Through the cleft he saw flickering flames, and heard the groans and cries of tormented souls. On hearing this story, the Abbot of Cluny appointed the feast of All Souls, so that prayers would be said for all the dead who have existed, or ever will exist, from the beginning of the world to the end of time…"

Wolf gazed into the miniature fairylands and hells of the fire. Heat chased across the embers, trembling from violet to scarlet, flowering into golden sparks when a log settled and fell. He picked up a stick and drew in the ashes.

Bronwen and Walter were talking about Halewyn.

"He must have ridden over Devil's Edge to get here," Walter marvelled. "Tonight, of all nights!"

"Did you hear or see anything strange, Master Halewyn?" called Bronwen, and everyone turned with a pleasurable shudder, thinking of the awful sights that might be met with on the mountain on All Hallows' Eve. "Walking fires?"

"The Wild Host," said Geraint, "the Devil with his hounds?"

"The Black Sow?"

But Halewyn shook his head. His smile was as wide as a friendly dog's. "I saw nothing stranger than myself."

Across the fire, Nest beckoned. Wolf got to his feet.

"Hush!" she whispered. "Look at this. Look!" She held out the rose Halewyn had given her, a ruff of crimson petals around a cluster of yellow stamens. He breathed a sweet, ecstatic scent.

"It's pretty."

"It's *real*!" Nest's whisper was intense. "A real rose! Where did he find it? We don't have any roses growing here."

"At the abbey they do," said Wolf. "He'll have brought it from there."

"In October?"

She was right. Even at the abbey, roses were rare, exotic flowers, carefully nurtured by Brother Osmund the herbalist. And they only grew in summer.

"I thought it would be silk or paper," Nest whispered. "But it's real. And when I took it from him, look what it did…"

"Pricked you," said Wolf, looking at the thorny stem.

"No, it *burned* me. I've got a blister, look! As if I'd picked up a spark!"

"That's impossible. Wait, I know." Wolf's face cleared. "He was juggling firebrands. A spark must have fallen on the rose as he passed it to you."

"Yes, but—" Nest stopped. "Maybe," she said, frowning. "But in any case, how could he carry a rose with him on a journey? It would never survive, Wolf."

As if to emphasise her point, one crumpled, silky petal suddenly shook to the floor. With a haphazard rush, the others followed. They lay on the rushes like splashes of blood. Nest was left holding the stalk. She looked almost ready to cry.

"Oh… but it was beautiful. Nobody ever gave me a rose before."

"May there be many roses in your life, my lady!" Halewyn appeared at her elbow. Nest darted him a suspicious look.

"How did you do it?" Wolf asked, pointing to the petals. "Where did you find a rose at this time of year?"

Halewyn looked at him. "Can you keep a secret?"

"Yes."

"So can I!" Halewyn's eyes were so mischievous, and his cap was so ridiculous, and he had such a funny way of putting his head on one side, that although Wolf felt foolish, he laughed too.

"All right. But – but Lady Agnes wants to ask you something."

Halewyn looked expectantly at Nest. Stiffly, reluctantly, she nodded. "Lord Godfrey of Blanchland." Her voice was nearly inaudible. "You saw him?"

"Certainly," said Halewyn promptly. "He stayed for nearly a week and went to Mass each day."

Nest's eyes could have burned holes in him. "What was he like?"

"He was very fine. He wore stockings striped in red and blue. He had a scarlet tunic and a mantle lined with spotted ermine."

"I don't want to know about his clothes! Is that all you can remember?"

Halewyn gave her a delicate glance. "Alas, I was

never close to the young lord. I never heard him speak. I could only admire him from a distance."

"But gossip about him must have been flying all over Wenford," Wolf burst out. "You must have heard something. Whether he's kind, or merry, or generous to the poor…" He stopped as Halewyn sent him a warning glance.

Nest whitened, and the hope died from her eyes. "I see." She snipped off the words like little pieces of unwanted thread. "Thank you."

Snip! Snip! Wolf eyed her anxiously.

Lord Hugo clapped his hands and called, "It's late! Master Halewyn shall give us one more song. And then we will bid one other good night."

Halewyn picked up his harp but held it loosely for a moment, as if thinking. Then he knelt on one knee and held out the harp to Hugo.

"Will *you* not sing, my lord?"

There was a sharp intake of breath all around the Hall. Hugo looked very startled. Then his mouth shut hard. He shook his head.

Halewyn seemed unperturbed. "Then you must make do with my poor voice once more. A love song!" he called out, glancing at Nest. "A love song for a fair lady!" He bowed to Hugo and sat down, bending his head over the harp, plucking a handful of notes like a shower of raindrops. He began to sing:

"*When all the spring is bursting and blossoming…*"

Nest's eyes flew wide open. "Wolf!" she whispered.

"What?"

"This is the first song my father made for my mother!"

Halewyn sang:

"*When all the spring is bursting and blossoming,*
And the hedge is white with blossom like a breaking wave,
That's when my heart is bursting with love-longing
For the girl who pierced it, for that sweet wound she gave."

Wolf stole a quick glance at his lord. Hugo's face was as hard and expressionless as it might look one day in the chapel, carved in stone on his own coffin. Halewyn had chosen this song as a compliment, of course – and yet, to sing it in Hugo's own Hall, in the place where it had been written, for the wife he had loved and who had died—

Halewyn's voice rose into the rafters, unbearably sad and clear:

"*And I hear the nightingale singing in the forest –*
Singing for love in the forest: 'Come to me, I am alone…'
Better to suffer love's pain for a single kiss

Than live for a hundred years with a heart of stone."

The song ended. Nobody breathed. Halewyn lifted his head. "And may each one of us dream tonight of his own beloved!"

Hugo's chair went back with a loud scrape. He stood, and the household rose with him, watching warily, not daring to clap or applaud till they saw how he reacted.

"That was well sung," he said thickly.

With a tingle of relief, Wolf joined in the clapping. But the evening was over. With hurry and bustle the servants set about preparing the Hall for bed. Candles were blown out; chairs and benches were cleared away; mattresses laid on the floor. In the middle of the turmoil Halewyn sat on his stool, stowing his harp away with a curious, half-hidden smile.

"Goodnight," Nest said to Wolf. Her eyes were on Halewyn, and she was frowning. Wolf watched her slowly climb the stairs to the solar, her long skirts drifting after her step by step. Halfway up she looked back, hesitating, but Angharad was close behind her and impatiently waved her on.

CHAPTER 12

Martinmas came, when the pigs and cattle were butchered to provide food for the winter, and the cookhouse steamed and smoked even more than usual as Herbert and his staff worked double time. Chains of sausages festooned the larders, and great hams hung browning in the smoke. Wolf was glad to see that in spite of the slaughter Morwenna was spared to root about the yard and lie basking in the pale sunshine beside Howell's door.

November slowly passed. The days drew in: the household rose at daybreak and went to bed an hour or two after sunset. Each night, Halewyn performed in the Hall, jesting or juggling or singing – and each night he ended his performance with some kind of love song. Not always one of Hugo's – there were many others – but always something intimate, something heart-sore and melancholy that spoke of pain and loss and longing.

Halewyn always addressed them to Nest, as if a love song could only be sung to a lady, but Wolf couldn't help feeling they had more effect on Hugo. At the beginning of each song, Nest would brace herself, enduring it with a pale, proud, expressionless face. But Hugo would listen, brooding, sinking further and further into himself. If the music hurt, it was clear that he welcomed the pain.

Everyone went to bed with these songs haunting their dreams and woke to another dark dawn. At morning Mass in the dark chapel, candles pricked the cold air and blazed at the head and feet of stone Eluned on her stone bed, and clouds of breath puffed from the mouths of the kneeling congregation as they said 'Amen'.

Then Wolf would cross the frosty yard to release Elfgift. She'd snatch the bread he brought, and skip outside to greet the world. She threw pebbles at the men-at-arms. She sneaked into the cookhouse to steal or beg scraps of food. La Motte Rouge was her playground. Wolf was equally entertained and exasperated by her, but no matter what he and Nest tried, they could not get her to repeat a single word –

or even to keep still long enough to listen. At night she would curl up in the straw while Wolf sang the lullaby, but that was a secret between the two of them. And meanwhile Hugo's impatience was growing, like a bowstring pulling tenser every day.

Once, going back into the chapel after Mass was over, Wolf found Hugo on his knees beside the stone effigy of Eluned. His forehead was pressed hard against the painted folds of its dress; his fingers were clasped over its unmoving stone hands, and he was muttering feverishly, like someone praying to a saint. Wolf stopped as if he had run into a wall. He backed quickly and quietly out, hoping Hugo had not seen him.

He couldn't stop thinking about it, with a cold twist of anxiety under his ribs. Christmas was approaching. There was no way Elfgift was going to talk by then. What would Hugo do? Wolf looked at happy, cheeky, confident Elfgift, and was afraid.

He didn't tell Nest. It would only upset her, and besides, she was spending more and more time with Mattie and Angharad, sewing clothes for her marriage. Wolf knew she was dreadfully nervous about Lord Godfrey's arrival, but she wouldn't admit it, or even talk about it any more. When Wolf tried to sympathise, she'd say coldly, "I'm not worrying, thank you. I'm perfectly all right." Snip! Snip! She was distant with Halewyn, too. Wolf guessed she was sorry she'd asked those questions about Lord Godfrey. She'd lowered her pride, and it hadn't done any good.

He said as much to Halewyn, trying to defend and excuse her. "Pride?" said Halewyn thoughtfully. "Yes. I suppose it's only to be expected. Pride is more important than anything else to a girl of her rank. You can't really be friends with her, not proper friends like you and me."

It warmed Wolf's heart to hear Halewyn claim him for a friend, but he couldn't let the comment about Nest pass. "She *is* my friend."

Halewyn gave him a pitying look. "If you say so!"

"What do you mean?"

Halewyn had shrugged. "Only that she's a rich lady, she'll be married soon – and then her husband will take her away and you won't have anything more to do with her. Still, good for you! You'll get a good present out of her before she leaves, I guess."

Wolf didn't reply.

Christmas drew closer. Huge piles of logs were stacked at the back of the Hall. Walter and Rollo went out into the woods and came back loaded with green branches of holly and ivy, which Bronwen and Gwenny wove into wreaths and long garlands to decorate the walls.

The Blanchland wedding party was expected daily. Every traveller riding along the road beyond the walls was eagerly scanned in case it should be Lord Godfrey arriving at last. But he was late, even though the weather was clear and the roads were in good condition. Two days before Christmas he had still not arrived, and the men began to grumble that this Lord Godfrey was hardly an eager suitor. Excitement mounted, tempers ran high, nerves frayed.

"Out! *Out*! GET OUT!"

It was the morning of Christmas Eve. Wolf and Elfgift had been watching a cart unloading exotic foodstuffs for Herbert – barrels of wine and sherry, a sack of fifty golden Spanish oranges, another of sticky brown Greek raisins. Wolf took his eyes off Elfgift for five minutes – and of course, she vanished into the kitchen.

Herbert appeared in the steaming doorway, brandishing an enormous chopper, and Elfgift rushed out shrieking, as if she and Herbert were playing a dangerous but thoroughly enjoyable game. She sprang into Wolf's arms, bright eyed and panting.

"Keep her out of here!" Herbert bellowed at Wolf. "Haven't I got enough to do? Don't you know that Lord Godfrey and his men ought to have been here *days ago*? Do you realise that *every day* we've been cooking enough food for *two households*, in case they turn up? Do you have the *faintest idea* how much *work* that is? And ALL you have to do is keep that – that *creature* – away from me!" He disappeared again before Wolf could answer.

"Hello!" Nest came out of the Hall, sounding amused. Wolf was glad of it: she'd been snappy and cross for the last week. She blinked in the bright, cold sunshine. "Fresh air! And we've finished the sewing at last. Angharad's gossiping with Mattie." She stretched. "I want to see *out*. I want to see something different from the walls. Let's take Elfgift up on the ramparts."

"Would you like that?" Wolf asked Elfgift. He set her down, and she scampered to the ladder at once. She loved to run all the way around on the boardwalk and come back to where she'd started. Wolf and Nest went once around the circuit with her. Then they let her run round alone, while they talked and looked out over the frozen fields.

Tall hemlock stalks in the ditch stood up like frosty starbursts; the earthern banks were blue-white wherever the sun had not touched. Beyond the ditch, the sloping ploughland was striped with frost down all the furrows. Wolf leaned on the stockade, looking over at the lane running between brown hedges to meet the old stone road, which bent away north and south, with ice flashing from the puddles. It was empty this morning. No sign of any riders.

"If only they would come!" Nest burst out with sudden vehemence. Her breath smoked and fled in the keen air. "It's so awful, waiting. I wake up every morning wondering if this is the day…"

Wolf grimaced. He thought it was dreadfully insulting that Lord Godfrey was so late. On the other hand, winter travel was always uncertain. "Maybe they'll come today."

"That's what I thought yesterday. And the day before that, and the day before that! Maybe something's happened. Maybe they won't come at all." She shook her head. "No, that's silly. I know they'll come. I just – hate – waiting!"

Elfgift came past, her arm up, trailing her fingers along the bumpy logs of the stockade. She now wore a woollen jerkin over her linen smock. Both were remarkably grubby, and so were her bare feet. The sunlight lit her stained cheek blood-red. She gave them one of her wild, weird smiles as she went by – her eyes wide and unfocused. It was as though she ran herself into a trance, going around and around the castle.

"Elfgift!" called Nest. "Say hello!" But Elfgift trotted on.

"She won't," Wolf said wearily. "You know she won't. She never says anything at all."

"Maybe that's not a bad thing," said Nest. Wolf looked at her, and she added in a sudden rush, "Well, is it? Think what she was like before. And look at her now! She's happy with us, isn't she? But if she starts talking, and my father takes her back under the hill..."

Wolf nodded. He thought of Elfgift the day he had first seen her, pallid and starving, with her puffball mop of hair. He remembered her strange, half-moon face peering out of the entrance to the old mines. *You keep clear of 'em, young master. They say the back door of Elfland leads down to Hell, and the rivers run with human blood.*

He said in a low voice, "Isn't it funny how things change? I was afraid of her when I first saw her. And now she's more like—"

"A little sister," said Nest.

"You're right," said Wolf, surprised. He lowered his voice even further. "And even though she can't talk, did you see how she ran to the ladder when we suggested coming up here? She understands a lot. She could probably understand if I asked her to lead Hugo into the mines. But I don't want to tell him."

Nest touched his hand. "Why not? He'd make you a squire; isn't that what you want?"

Wolf scowled. "Yes. But not like that." He shuddered. "You don't know what it's like down there. Wet and dark and cold. To make Elfgift go back – it's all wrong. I don't know what to do, Nest. New Year's so close. I don't know how much longer Hugo will wait."

Nest turned scarlet. "I was wondering if I could ask him to give her to me. As a sort of w-wedding gift. Then she could come away with me when I go. And maybe you could come too. If you w-want to, I mean. And we could both still look after her?" Her voice almost disappeared.

It sounded such an impossible dream, Wolf didn't know what to say. He cleared his throat. "Thanks. Maybe! But, Nest, your father isn't going to give you Elfgift. If our way of teaching her doesn't work, I'm afraid he's going to try –" he hesitated "– something else."

"He would never hurt her!" Nest cried.

Yes, he would! Wolf bit the words back. Let her go on thinking her father was the perfect knight… There was an awkward pause. In it, footsteps sounded on the nearest ladder, and Halewyn's donkey-eared hood rose over the edge of the boardwalk. He stepped on to the ramparts, carrying a short, painted stick with a bauble on the end shaped like a fool's head with a jesting, jeering mouth. He brandished it cheerfully, and it rattled. He bowed to Nest.

"Good day, madam! May I join you?"

Nest acknowledged him curtly. "If you wish."

Elfgift appeared around the curve of the ramparts, saw Halewyn, and turned back. After the fright of his first appearance in the stable, she had remained wary of him. "We were talking about Elfgift," said Wolf, missing Nest's shake of the head. "We were saying—"

The guard on the tower top moved with a winking flash as some part of his harness caught the sun. He was lifting his horn, and a moment later the note moaned out in warning. He stabbed an arm towards the north, and down the steep air Wolf heard him bawling faintly: "Horsemen!"

Wolf leaned out over the stockade, craning his neck so that he could see right down the road. Far off, half a mile away, a knot of jogging, jostling movement resolved into a band of horsemen carrying pennants.

"I can see them," he gasped, twisting round. "Nest, it's them, it must be! Lord Godfrey of Blanchland! He's here at last!"

Nest went perfectly white. "*Wolf!*"

"Look out!" Wolf dragged her roughly away from the unguarded edge of the boardwalk before she could step back over it and fall.

"He's here!" She clutched him. "What shall I do?"

"Don't worry," he gabbled idiotically. "It's all right…"

"It's *not* all right!" She covered her mouth with joined hands and stared at him with dilated eyes. "What shall I do? Oh, what shall I do?"

"I don't know," Wolf croaked.

"I never thought he would come," said Nest in a

high-pitched voice muffled behind her fingers. "I mean, I knew he had to, but I never really thought he would. Oh, sweet Saviour! What shall I do?"

Wolf looked down at the open gate. He repressed a mad urge to say, 'Let's run!'

Lord Hugo came striding out of the Hall, with Geraint at his heels and Bronwen scurrying after them both. He crossed to a point where he could look up at the tower and yelled to the guard, "Is it them?"

"Looks that way," the guard hailed back.

Hugo looked around. "Where's Agnes?"

Nest shrank against the stockade. Halewyn and Wolf exchanged glances. Then Halewyn swung up his arm in a wave. "Up here, lord."

Hugo tilted his face. "Agnes, come down; you'll need to change." She didn't reply and he said impatiently, "Bronwen, go and help Lady Agnes to descend." As Bronwen hitched up her skirt and began to scale the ladder, he called, "Take her inside to Angharad and then tell Herbert our guests are here. Geraint, fetch Rollo and the others as fast as you can. I want everyone turning out to greet them."

Nest was rigid as a stone saint, her hands still clasped over her mouth. Bronwen plucked her compassionately by the sleeve. "Lady? Lady, are you coming? Lady, you've got to get dressed."

Nest lowered her hands. "Get dressed?" she repeated stupidly.

"For Lord Godfrey, madam. Don't you want to look well for Lord Godfrey? And you can't meet him like this, out in the yard."

Nest sucked in a vast, sobbing breath, as if she'd been underwater. "I've got to get dressed. You're right. Inside, quick, before they see us!" She grabbed Bronwen's hand and they scrambled down the ladder and fled to the Hall like hunted deer.

"Wolf!" Hugo was still issuing orders. "Where's the elf-girl? Up there with you? Then keep her out of sight. The stables are going to be busy for a while. Take her—"

"I could take her to Hunith, lord," said Wolf. "She gets on well with Hunith."

"Good, and you can fetch Howell at the same time. Do that and come back. Ah, Rollo! I want you and Geraint to welcome Lord Godfrey. Make some kind of speech, and don't rush it; we need time to change. Then bring them all inside. Halewyn, you get out of the way, I'm not having my guests welcomed by a *jongleur.*"

He set off back to the Hall at a run.

Wolf looked around for Elfgift, and she was nowhere in sight: she might easily be the other side of the ramparts. The best thing would be to wait for her to come round again. And he wanted to see the horsemen arriving. He looked over the stockade again.

They were much closer already, swinging off the road to come up the lane. He could hear the horses snort as they stumbled over the hard, frozen ruts. There were ten or twelve riders wearing helmets and mailshirts. The horses, mostly bays and chestnuts, looked glossy and polished, and the bright harness gleamed against the leafless hedges. The foremost rider carried an upright lance with a blue and white swallowtail pennant fluttering from the shaft. Two more pennants brought up the rear.

Behind the first pennant rode Lord Godfrey, splendid in scarlet and gold. Wolf hoisted himself up, leaning eagerly over the stockade for a better look.

Lord Godfrey sat his proud, white horse with a careless slouch and glanced up at La Motte Rouge with an air of discontent. He called over his shoulder to the man riding just behind him. They were close enough now that the wind lifted the words clearly to Wolf's straining ears. "God's bonnet, Thomas! The lands are rich, but I hope the girl will please me better than her house. It must be at least a hundred years old. When it's mine I'll pull it down and build in stone."

A cold wind blew on Wolf's heart. How would Nest fare with someone so drawling and arrogant? He felt like rushing back to the Hall to warn her. But what was the point? She would find out soon enough for herself.

The cavalcade was very close, about to ride right underneath Wolf on their way through the gate. The pennant dipped. The man riding behind Lord Godfrey pulled off his broad-brimmed hat. Wolf looked down on a patch of shaven, ivory scalp ringed with iron-grey hair. The man passed his hand across his head, replaced his hat and looked up – directly at Wolf.

Cold, dark eyes opened wide in shock. With equal shock and in tingling horror Wolf saw and recognised the thin, straight nose with its flaring nostrils, the heavily marked black eyebrows, and the pale sarcastic lips – parting first with astonishment, then stretching over bared, brownish teeth in a smile of grim triumph.

Brother Thomas!

Wolf dropped to his knees on the boardwalk.

How did he know I was here?

He didn't. He's shocked, too.

Then why's he here?

With a great clatter of hooves the cavalcade crowded under the gateway and filled the courtyard. The pennant bearer stood up in his stirrups and bellowed, "Godfrey fitz Payne, lord of La Blanche Land, comes to do honour to Hugo fitz Warin, lord of La Motte Rouge!" At the noise all the hounds began baying and barking.

Rollo's voice lifted above the racket. "Welcome, my

lord," he bawled. "We've been eagerly expecting you. Did you break your journey at Wenford?"

Wolf buried his head in his hands. *Of course!*

Halewyn had seen Lord Godfrey at the abbey; he'd even said something about Lord Godfrey asking the abbot to find him a new chaplain. Wolf hadn't paid much attention at the time. *The abbot was glad to help,* Halewyn had said.

"I'll bet he was," Wolf groaned. "I'll just *bet* he was!" The abbot had clearly jumped at the chance to foist Brother Thomas off on someone else. He'd ordained him as a priest and got rid of him in one handy move.

So here was Brother Thomas, as large as life, sitting on his stout brown horse less than twenty feet away, pretending to pay polite attention to Rollo's speech. But Wolf could see him fidgeting and twisting about, trying to see if his runaway pupil was still on the stockade behind him.

He's not my master any more. Hugo is. Lord Hugo won't let him take me away. Not so long as I'm looking after…

Elfgift!

Where on earth was she? For a second his heart almost stopped. Then he saw her coming around the circle of the ramparts, her head turned to observe the shifting, stamping horses and the finely dressed riders. Wolf beckoned, but she was too interested in what was going on below to notice him.

"...AND AGAIN I SAY TO YOU, MY MOST NOBLE LORD – WELCOME!" Rollo had no idea how to project his words like a herald. He was using a sort of strained shout, like a sailor hailing an approaching ship. Lord Godfrey was tapping his saddle impatiently. Wolf realised he ought to get away before Rollo finished talking – before Brother Thomas could dismount. With a nervous glance at his old master's rigid back he ran to Elfgift, swept her up roughly and raced for the ladder. She seemed to realise that something serious was going on and clung to him. He half slid, half tumbled down the ladder, praying that Rollo would keep talking for just a few more minutes.

Rollo's voice cracked. "WELcome – to La MOTTE ROUGE!"

In the commotion of a general dismount, Wolf scuttled away towards Howell's house. A new voice struck across the hubbub like a whipcrack.

"That boy! Stop! Come here!"

It curled around Wolf's heart like a freezing lash, plucking him to a halt. He looked back, and Brother Thomas was thrusting his way between the milling horses, tall and terrible, one long arm outstretched.

"Hold that boy! He is a runaway!"

A gasp of fright escaped Wolf. It was a tiny noise:

nobody could have heard it but himself – and Elfgift, whose cheek was pressed to his. But he despised himself for it. All his old hatred for Brother Thomas came back with a rush. He hoisted Elfgift up and she gripped him, tense and quivering. He faced his enemy.

Rollo came striding over. "What's wrong?"

"This boy," said Brother Thomas thinly, "is a runaway from the abbey. He should be returned and disciplined, according to the Rule."

Wolf shuddered.

"Don't know anything about that," said Rollo, and to Wolf's astonishment he dropped one eyelid in the ghost of a wink. "You'd better speak to Lord Hugo about that. This is Wolf, this is. He looks after our elf-girl."

Something flashed in Brother Thomas's eyes. He looked curiously, even greedily, at Elfgift. "Aha," he breathed. "Lord Hugo's famous elf-child! I have heard of it. Let me look at it." He seized her chin in strong, bony fingers and twisted her face so that her stained cheek came into view.

Elfgift caught his wrist and bit sharply into the side of his hand. Then she once more wrapped her arms around Wolf's neck.

With a harsh scream, Brother Thomas shook his hand in the air. Bloody drops flew from it. "She bit me! The elf bit me!"

"You frightened her," Wolf cried. Brother Thomas

lashed out with his left hand, aiming a blow at Wolf's ear. Wolf swung away, still clasping Elfgift.

"Now, now, sir!" Rollo's face was stony. He caught Brother Thomas's arm. "You come with me and have that bathed. Don't you want to catch up with Lord Godfrey? He's already gone into the Hall."

Brother Thomas's mouth cramped into a straight line. "Not before I have seen this creature, this imp of Satan, safely locked up."

"It was your own fault!" Wolf snarled.

"Howell!" said Rollo in relief. Behind Wolf's shoulder, Howell pushed open the door of his house. The wind ruffled his fluffy white hair. When he saw Brother Thomas, his face brightened with surprise and pleasure. "Do I espy a brother of the church?"

"Lord Godfrey of Blanchland is here at last, Howell," said Rollo. "This is his chaplain, I'm guessing."

Howell beamed. "Howell Offeiriaid at your service, dear sir. Lord Hugo's chaplain and the priest of this castle. Unworthy as I am, I bid you heartily welcome."

Brother Thomas bared his teeth in a narrow smile. "I am Sir Thomas." Typical of him, Wolf thought, to assume the honorary 'Sir', which a priest could use. "I am chaplain to Lord Godfrey fitz Payne, and until lately I was master of the boys at the Abbey of Christ and Saint Ethelbert at Wenford."

Old Howell looked even more eager. "I very much hope you will honour me by staying in my house while you are here, sir. I am sure we have many things to talk about." He noticed Brother Thomas's hand. "But you have hurt yourself?"

"Bitten!" Brother Thomas snapped. "By *that*!" He pointed at Elfgift, clinging to Wolf like a knot on a rope.

"Little Elfgift? Dear me… she doesn't usually behave like that… mischievous, not spiteful… But step into my house, dear Sir Thomas, and my Hunith will find a healing salve for your hand." He bustled in, and Hunith rose from her stool by the fire, ducking her head in shy greeting.

Brother Thomas reared back like a horrified horse. "Who is this?"

"My Hunith," said Howell, startled.

"A *woman*?" Brother Thomas's voice trickled ice.

"My – my wife." Howell was beginning to sound upset. Hunith darted an anxious look at Brother Thomas. She might not understand the words, but Wolf could see she understood his tone and expression.

"You keep a *concubine* in your house?"

Howell's eyes were round with dismay in his apple-rosy face. His forehead wrinkled. "But no! – we are married – it is no sin…"

"Let's go and find Lord Godfrey," Rollo said doggedly to Brother Thomas.

"It is against church law!" Brother Thomas thundered. "A priest's woman is no wife but an abomination. The bishop shall hear of this. Put her aside – cast her out!"

Hunith fell to her knees, and broke into a flood of passionate Welsh, clutching a fold of Brother Thomas's robe pleadingly to her breast. He stepped back, tearing it out of her hands. "Touch me not, false temptress. Eve! Serpent! *Concubine*!"

Hunith's face crumpled. Wolf let Elfgift slide to the floor and aimed a kick at Brother Thomas. "Leave her alone!" he screamed. "Hunith's lovely! She and Howell are *married*! Leave her alone!"

"That's enough!" Rollo grabbed Wolf by the arm and shook him. "Wolf, shut your mouth. Don't let me hear you shouting at Lord Hugo's guests again. As for you, *sir* –" he bowed ironically to Brother Thomas "– anything you want to say about Howell or Hunith, you better say to Lord Hugo. *He's* the master here. And I reckon he'll tell you to mind your own business. Howell's been priest here for years, and so was his father before him." He held the door open. "Out!"

Brother Thomas's black eyebrows nearly disappeared into his hairline. He drew himself up, twitching like a furious cat, and stepped close to Rollo so that their chests almost touched. "I will indeed talk to your master about these *abuses*. And I will mention your insolence."

He held Rollo's eye, and Rollo stared back.

"You do that, sir."

Brother Thomas's lips turned down at the corners. He glanced at Wolf. "Also I will have this boy beaten and sent back to the abbey." He stalked out.

Rollo jerked his head at Wolf. "You too. Out." Wolf followed, breathing as if he'd been running a race. He looked back as Rollo shut the door and saw Hunith sobbing on the floor, and old Howell kneeling clumsily beside her, stroking her hair with shaking hands. They looked very old and frail. Elfgift crouched in the shadows, growling.

Halewyn pounced on them as they came outside. "Rollo, there you are! Lord Hugo wants you." Rollo strode past him without a word.

"That's right, hurry," Halewyn called after him, brandishing his rattle with a mocking clatter. "What a rough, rude fellow Rollo is… Is something wrong?"

"I hate him!" Wolf panted, pointing at Brother Thomas as he vanished into the Hall. "I hate him. I hate him!"

Halewyn's eyebrows rose. "You hate him. He certainly looks unpleasant. This sounds promising. Come on, tell me everything."

"If I told you everything I'd be here all day," Wolf said bitterly. "His name is Brother Thomas – oh no, sorry, *Sir* Thomas now – and he was my old master at the abbey.

He's the one the abbot picked to be Lord Godfrey's chaplain – remember? He's why I ran away. We all hated him; he was always beating us and shouting at us. And now –" he almost choked "– he's hurt Hunith."

"Hunith?" Halewyn sounded shocked. "That sweet old lady?"

"I don't mean he injured her. He shouted at her and told Howell to throw her out. He made her *cry*. And all she wanted to do was make him welcome!" Wolf was shivering with rage. "I'd like to kill him! I'd give anything to get my own back on him."

"Would you indeed?" Halewyn looked at Wolf. "Want me to help?"

"Do what?"

"Get back at him," said Halewyn. He shook the stick and the little fool on the end rattled as if in a fit of giggles. "I could make a fool of him. It's my job. I'd love to make his life very unpleasant. Shall I? Shall I?"

Wolf was taken aback by Halewyn's eagerness. He hesitated. Halewyn's eyes burned. The pupils glinted with inner light. Wolf turned suddenly dizzy.

The world fell away, like a trick box with collapsing sides. He felt himself dropping giddily over a huge, dark gulf, whirling through the air. His stomach lurched. He stumbled forward – and Halewyn caught him by the shoulders. He looked up groggily.

Halewyn grinned down at him. For a moment Wolf saw him as a predator in his eared hood, like some strange, thin animal on its hind legs, sharp-toothed, panting with anticipation. He recoiled. His heart started knocking a warning.

"Wolf, are you ill? For a moment there I thought you were going to faint."

Wolf's lips parted stickily. He didn't speak.

Halewyn gave him a mocking glance. "You're not going to turn all monkish on me, are you? What are you worrying about? I'm not suggesting doing anything very bad – and even if I were," he added sarcastically, "you'd have plenty of time to repent of it afterwards. We'll play a few tricks on Brother Thomas, that's all. Take him down a peg or two. He deserves it, and it'll be funny. Come on, let's teach him a lesson."

Teach Brother Thomas a lesson!

It was a tempting thought. Wolf took a deep, steadying breath. He didn't know what had come over him. Halewyn was the same as he'd always been, thin and freckled and ridiculous in his donkey-eared cap. And he was offering Wolf the chance of a lifetime.

"Could we?" he asked. "You're serious?"

Halewyn rolled his eyes. "Of course we could. Think of all the things he's done. Beaten you. Made Hunith cry, and humiliated good old Howell. Are you going to let him get away with it? Don't you want *revenge*?" Halewyn paused. "Or are you too much of a monk after all?"

"We'll do it," said Wolf with savage eagerness. "I'll do whatever you say!"

CHAPTER 13

"Your servant, sweet lady." Lord Godfrey placed a slow, emphatic kiss on Nest's cold hand, leaving a moist print. He looked at her, raising his eyebrows. "Or should I say – your prisoner?"

"P-prisoner?" Nest attempted to smile, and surreptitiously rubbed the wet mark against her skirt. Beside her Angharad beamed sentimental delight, for Godfrey was very handsome. He was tall, dark-haired, with blue eyes, a fresh, rosy colour, and full red lips. He made Nest feel plain and small and insignificant, even though she was wearing her new gooseberry-green gown, and her best necklace of crystal and coral beads.

"Of course – for have you not captured my heart? But

I am happy to be the prisoner of so fair a jailor." Godfrey fanned away a yawn with long, white fingers, and a blush burned up into Nest's face. *Prisoners? Jailors?* He didn't mean a word of it. This was fashionable nonsense, the way they talked at court. Nest had never flirted, she couldn't chatter, she didn't know how to make the proper witty response. She felt miserably inadequate.

"But since I am at your mercy," Godfrey elaborated, "I hope you will not be cruel?" He arched an eyebrow, adding an exasperated glance that seemed to say, *Oh come on – play the game!*

Nest twisted her fingers in desperation. What could she say? *Have you ridden far today?* It was dull, but possible. She rehearsed it: *Have you ridden far?* It wasn't very interesting, and she already knew the answer. All the same...

"H-have you ridden far today?" she quavered.

He replied promptly, "I never noticed. I whiled away the miles in a delightful dream – thinking of you!"

"Oh," said Nest faintly.

Another dreadful silence fell between them. Nest hunted for something – anything – to say. Her mind presented her with a clean white blank, like unwritten paper. Why couldn't someone help? Why didn't Angharad say something, when for once Nest would have been glad to have her launch into one of her long speeches?

Have you ridden far?

"Have — have you ridden far today?" she asked hopelessly — and knew from his incredulous face that she'd already said it. He would think she was an idiot! She wanted to die. Time had stopped. She would be frozen in this moment forever...

The Hall door opened with a gust that fluttered the tablecloths. In marched a tall, stern-looking priest with a ring of steel-grey hair and fierce black eyebrows. Rollo followed him, and the door clapped shut with a bang that delivered Nest from her agony.

"Who is that priest?" she was able to ask.

"My new chaplain. I'll bring him to meet you." Godfrey strode away in obvious relief.

As if a spell had ended, everything began to move and change and happen. Angharad clasped ecstatic hands. "Oh, my lucky little lamb, *what* a lovely man your father has chosen for you!"

"Well, Nest?" Her father appeared by her side. "Now that he's here at last, do you like him?"

"Ah, my lord," Angharad cried before Nest could get a word in, "I'm sure she's tumbling into love with him already, although she's far too shy to say so. So tall, so handsome, so attentive! *The journey seemed short,* he said to her, *for I was dreaming of you.* Oh!"

"Is it so?" Hugo smiled at Nest.

"He said something like that," she muttered, hot-cheeked. "But he didn't—"

"Hush! He's coming back!" Angharad clutched Nest's arm.

Godfrey reappeared with the priest, a tall man in his fifties with an ascetic, bad-tempered face. Before anyone could greet him he broke out in a harsh, complaining voice, "My lord, your elf-child has bitten me!"

They stared at him, astonished. He thrust out his hand for Hugo to see. "Blood, look! And this man of yours –" he gestured to Rollo, who stood back with arms folded "– has spoken to me with insolence. I demand that you punish them both!" He spoke with the confidence of a man accustomed to inspiring fear in everyone he meets. Hugo's face went cold.

"Who are you to make demands of me, *fellow*?"

The priest seemed shaken. He took a step back and looked sulkily at Lord Godfrey.

"This is Sir Thomas, my chaplain," Godfrey explained.

"Is it?" Hugo said with indifference. "Well, Thomas, the elf-girl shouldn't have been anywhere near you. I thought I told Wolf to put her away."

"*That* boy?" The priest turned, pointing dramatically: and there was Wolf, standing near the door with Halewyn. His colour was high and his eyes were angry: he lifted his chin with a hard defiance that Nest had never seen in him before.

"That boy is a liar and a runaway, and not to be relied upon. Did you know that he had escaped from Wenford Abbey, where he used to be under *my* charge? He should be whipped and sent back."

So this arrogant, intense, thin-lipped man was Wolf's old master! No wonder Wolf had run away. Nest tried to catch his eye, to signal shock and sympathy, but he wasn't looking. He was staring at Thomas with something close to hatred.

Hugo shrugged. "You should bathe that hand. Angharad, send for a basin of hot water. And let us sit down to our meal." He looked around, frowning. "Where is Howell? Not here? Then, Sir Thomas, perhaps you will be good enough to say grace?"

Nest was longing to exchange a word with Wolf, but he kept his distance and avoided meeting her eye. Soon she was sitting stiffly between her father and Lord Godfrey, and Wolf was yards away on one of the lower tables. The first course was served: a white soup of minced chicken and almonds. Whenever Nest looked at Wolf, he was talking rapidly to Halewyn, his elbows on the table, his head low. She could guess what it was about. Every so often, one of them would fling a quick glance at Brother Thomas on the High Table.

Nest felt forlorn. She shrank into herself, trying not to let her elbow touch Lord Godfrey's, and pushed her spoon drearily through the creamy soup. Lord Godfrey drank a lot of wine and talked across her to her father, in a louder and much more natural voice than he had used before. "The elf-girl, Hugo – I should like to see her. Why don't you have her brought in to amuse us?"

"She is not very amusing," said Hugo briefly.

Godfrey bit into a sweet pastry. "How did you find her? What's the story?"

"I came across her while I was out hunting wolves."

"It is all very marvellous," Godfrey said, spraying crumbs, "but what makes you keep the creature, if not for entertainment? Especially if she bites?"

"Because—" Hugo fell silent, and Nest saw his fingers whiten around his cup. She looked up, startled – surely he wasn't going to tell the real reason? – and caught him staring into space with a tormented frown. Lord Godfrey and Brother Thomas exchanged glances. Then Hugo blinked and said quietly, "To see if she can be taught to speak."

Godfrey laughed – too loudly. "What, is she dumb? I'll lend you Sir Thomas. He must have beaten Latin into dozens of youngsters at the abbey. He'll have her singing psalms in a week or two." He folded his hands together in mock prayer. "*Oh Lord, open my lips*! Eh, Thomas?"

Brother Thomas leaned from the end of the table. "I scarcely think that the words of the psalms are fit for the mouth of an elf-child. Still, it's possible I could make her talk."

Hugo looked at him. "How?" He sounded sceptical, but Brother Thomas was not to be deterred. He fitted his fingertips precisely together. "As you would expect of a man in my position, I have read many books. Although everyone agrees that elves are stubborn and deceitful, I know of ways in which they can be tricked or shocked into speech."

As Brother Thomas's loud arrogant voice carried across the Hall, Nest saw Wolf raise his head. Their eyes met, their lips twitched in shared anticipation. Here it came again – the porridge and the eggshell!

"Red-hot iron should do it," went on Brother Thomas. "Heat a poker or a horse-shoe, and brand the elf-child with it."

Nest clutched the edge of the table. "How can you *say* such a cruel thing?"

"Cruel?" Brother Thomas drew his dark eyebrows into a frown. "Madam, you are a very young lady." *And therefore ignorant*, his tone seemed to say. "Perhaps you do not understand the nature of elves. They deserve no mercy. They are the accursed remnant of the angels who fell with Lucifer, for whom God Himself has decreed punishment. To deal with such spirits, one must be as harsh and merciless as they are. In any case, they do not have real bodies. The shapes they take are mere illusions."

"Now *that* must be true!" Halewyn called out from the lower table. "The elf-girl gave you an illusionary bite, with illusionary teeth, didn't she?"

A titter of laughter followed this remark. Brother Thomas went pale with anger. "The elf-child is corporeal, that is to say she has a physical body, not a spiritual one. Probably she is not entirely a demon, but the offspring of a demon and a mortal."

Godfrey's munching jaws slowed. "Is that possible?"

"Certainly, my lord. God allows demons to put on mortal shapes, though there is always some flaw, some mark by which they can be recognised – hooves, or horns – that red stain on your elf-child's face. Between the moon and the Earth live false spirits called *incubus* and *succubus*, which roam about tempting women and men into sin. The sorcerer Merlin was the child of a woman and an incubus. Saints without number have been tempted by succubi, in the form of seductive women."

"Have they really?" Godfrey drawled. "I didn't know saints had so much fun."

Nest glanced at her father. His expression was grim. She was suddenly sorry for him, having to listen to all this about elves and devils, when he thought her mother was in such danger... She plucked his sleeve. "Father, let's not talk of devils on Christmas Eve!"

He turned to her in surprised relief. "You're right, Agnes!" He clapped his hands. "This is sad stuff. Halewyn – entertain us. Sing something, or tell us a tale."

Halewyn eeled his way backwards off the bench, tall and thin and extravagant in his bright red and blue clothing. He picked up his harp, but instead of striking the strings he wandered towards the High Table holding it loosely in one hand, his pale face alert. Everyone watched, expecting some foolery. He leaned his head close to Brother Thomas. "Have *you* ever been tempted by a succubus?"

Nest was furious. She wanted Halewyn to distract attention from the priest, not concentrate on him. Brother Thomas stared rigidly ahead, obviously hoping Halewyn would move on. But Halewyn hadn't finished.

"But of course not, Sir Thomas. The Devil isn't stupid. Do you think he would tempt you with beautiful women, or gold and jewels – things you can easily refuse, because you don't want them? No. Temptation should be… tempting. That's the whole point, really." He added lightly, "And you know, sir, I'm so ignorant, I've always thought that men ought to have a little fellow feeling for devils. They're not so different from us. Out of all Creation, only men and devils know how to be *truly wicked*. Isn't that so?"

Two bright spots glowed on Brother Thomas's

cheekbones. He stretched sarcastic lips in a mirthless smile. "The fool thinks he is a philosopher!"

"I'm a *fool-osopher*!" cried Halewyn, with a caper. "But I think my *fool-osophy* is worth more than your wisdom!"

As a scatter of applause greeted the pun, he spun away and bowed to Lord Hugo.

"Now my lord," he said gaily, "At this time of the year it's customary to have a night of foolery, when 'the mighty are put down from their seat and the humble are exalted'. And as the best fool among you, I hereby appoint myself your Lord of Misrule! Here is my crown!" He whipped a paper crown out of his pocket and set it crookedly over one donkey ear. To shouts of encouragement, he drew himself up on tiptoe like a crowing cockerel. "Will you take me for your Pharoah of Folly and Master of Mischief?"

"Very well," said Hugo, laughing. "Give us your first command!"

Halewyn's smile was wicked. "Out of your seat, then, Hugo – it's mine now!"

Nest's hand flew to her mouth. Rollo, who had been serving Hugo's wine, leaned from behind with a mutter of warning. But Hugo seemed bent on entering into the spirit of the thing. He stood up easily, and Halewyn flung himself down in Hugo's great chair.

Hugo made an elaborate bow. "And now, King of Comedy? What is your will? How shall we proceed?"

Halewyn cocked an eyebrow. "Hugo, you have written a song or two in your time —" Nest gasped at this effrontery "— but since All Hallows' Eve until now, I have not once heard you sing. And they say you are worth hearing!" He watched Hugo's face change. "Since our positions are now reversed, *you* shall entertain *us*." He held out the harp.

The talk in the Hall faded and hushed. For an unbreathing moment, Hugo stared at the harp. Nest sat up, every nerve-ending prickling. *He won't! He can't!* Surely he wouldn't let Halewyn get away with this? After all, the reversal of roles was only a joke. Her father was still lord: he could do what he liked! She waited for him angrily to order Halewyn out of his sight.

"*You know you want to*," added Halewyn softly.

Hugo slowly stretched out a hand and took the harp. He sat on the edge of the dais and set it against his shoulder. Tentatively he plucked one string, and the note struck the silence like a drop of silver water.

Halewyn leaned forward, resting his chin on his fist. "I have sung plenty of your songs, Hugo. Let me see if you can remember one of mine. It's maybe a year or two since you heard it, but a good tale lives in the memory. A tale of love —" he looked from Hugo to

Godfrey and Nest, and dark laughter flashed in his eyes "– a tale of woe. The story of good King Orfeo!"

Rollo sucked in a hissing breath. Hugo bowed his golden head. Like a man in a dream he sat plucking idle notes, and the hush stretched until Nest's nerves were as tight as the harp strings, and she could hear Argos' teeth rattle and knock on the bone he was chewing beneath the table.

"There was a king and there was his queen," Hugo began at last, half singing, half chanting in a quiet, clear voice, "and their names were King Orfeo and…"

"Queen Herodys," said Halewyn softly.

Hugo nodded to him over the top of the harp. "Now King Orfeo was the best harper of his day. Whenever he played, the birds would cease to sing, the waters cease to run, the very clouds wandering over the blue sky would pause to listen to him. And King Orfeo loved Queen Herodys and she loved him, and so they were happy, happy, happy." The harp strings sobbed.

"But as nothing mortal lasts forever, so one day King Orfeo went out hunting. And Queen Herodys went with her ladies into an orchard. And in the hottest part of the day when the sun stood at noon and the shadows under the apple trees were very deep, and the grasshoppers ticked away the moments, the lord of Elfland came riding by with all his company. And saw

Queen Herodys half-asleep in the shade, and struck her to the heart with his cruel dart, so that she vanished away. And nothing was left to show where she had been but a great grey stone."

A great, grey stone.

Sorrow took Nest by surprise, splashing right over her. It was true. This was what death did. Took away the person you loved and left you with a stone. Her nose prickled, her eyes filled. *Oh, Mam! You died so long ago, and still I miss you!*

Hugo plucked a handful of soft, lamenting notes. "When King Orfeo came home and found everyone in his house weeping and crying, he swore he would never rest until he found his lady. And they begged him not to try, 'for the lord of the underworld has your lady now, and no man can go there.'

"And King Orfeo said, 'Yet I will go.'

"And they told him, 'Each step you take into the underworld will be a year from your life.'"

Nest shivered. This was true too: you could lose years of your life in grief. Did her father understand what he was singing? Didn't he see that the tale was telling him *what would happen* if you tried to follow someone who'd died?

"But King Orfeo said, 'What do I care for the years of my life if I live them without my love?' And he went into the orchard where the elf-lord had struck his lady, and he played his harp until the grey stone itself cracked in two for pure grief. And the way opened into the underworld."

Hugo's fingers flickered in a series of notes that sounded like hasty footsteps descending in a spiral, going down and down. "And King Orfeo went into the underworld to look for his Queen. And each step he took was a year from his life, but on he went."

The music went slow and quiet.

"Now deep under the hill he found a green meadow, lit by a light as though the sun had not quite risen, or had just set. And through the meadow a river flowed, and the colour of that river was dark red." Hugo's voice was suddenly harsh. "For all the blood that's shed on Earth runs through the rivers of Elfland!"

Was that in the story? Or was it something her father had just added? Nest remembered Wolf's vision of a slow rust-red river, looping through a green country in the deep mines under Devil's Edge.

"And King Orfeo found a castle on the river bank, as fine as the walls of Paradise. And in the castle was a splendid hall, and in that hall the lord of the underworld sat on a high seat. And beside him sat Queen Herodys, pale and still. And all through that hall ran a whispering and a groaning and a weeping.

"Then the lord of the underworld said to King Orfeo, 'Who are you?'

"And King Orfeo said, 'I am nothing but a poor minstrel, who must make my living by playing in many a lord's hall.' And he began to play such blissful music that everyone in the hall thought they were in Paradise."

Now Hugo bent low over the harp and began singing to himself as if no one was there: so quietly that Nest could hardly hear. She strained her ears. It was a song about a lady riding through a meadow. "*Her petticoat was of linen, of silk was her dress. Her slippers were made of mayflowers, her feet to caress.*" He sang in a low, crooning voice that raised the hairs on the nape of her neck. And when he had finished...

"When he had finished, the lord of Elfland said, 'By my head, your payment shall be whatever you ask, for we have never heard such music before.'

"Then King Orfeo said, 'King of Shadows, give me the lady who sits beside you.'"

Nest leaned forward, as tense as if it was all really happening, so intent on her father that she was only dimly annoyed by Lord Godfrey fidgeting, tapping his foot, twiddling a spoon and catching it.

What would happen? How would it end?

"'By my head,' said the lord of Elfland, 'I wish you had asked for anything else. But the lady is yours, for it would be a black shame on me to break my promise.'

"So, joyfully, King Orfeo took his Queen by her

hand and led her away out of the hall and the castle and across the green meadow and up the path that led to the light. And they returned to their own castle and their own lands, and lived long and happy.

"And if they have not died… they are living there still."

Hugo swept his hand over the strings in a sudden discord and bent his head. Lord Godfrey dropped the spoon with a muffled clatter. With a shifting, stirring, cautious murmur, everyone in the Hall wiped tears from their faces. The murmur swelled into muted applause.

Nest's head throbbed. She pressed her fingers to her temples.

Is that how it ends?

Halewyn turned his head as if he had heard her thoughts. His eyes were narrow and bright as a sleepy cat's. Nest shook her head in distress.

That can't be how it ends!

She'd never heard the story before, but she knew in her bones that something was wrong. It so, so obviously should have ended sadly.

CHAPTER 14

Godfrey caught Nest at the foot of the stairs and squeezed another kiss on her reluctant hand. "Goodnight, fair one. I shall dream of you!"

"Sh-shall you?" And she fled, tripping on her gown.

In bed she lay open-eyed and miserable, pressed back to back with Angharad, who had shared the big four poster with her ever since her mother had died.

Once upon a time the simple fact of Angharad's warm, ample presence had been enough to scare away all Nest's night terrors and calm her fears. But she wasn't seven years old any more, and it was a long time since she had told Angharad her troubles.

Godfrey.

She didn't like him. With a shrinking of every fibre in her body, she knew she never would. His kiss lingered on her hand like the touch of a snail.

And he thought she was dull. Somehow she hadn't expected that. Tears of humiliation prickled in Nest's eyes. The last glimmer of a hope she had barely admitted even to herself – a hope that some miracle would happen, that she and Godfrey would fall headlong in love as her parents had done – vanished like a twist of candle smoke. *Have you ridden far today*? She buried her face in the pillow, muffling a gasp of agony. How stupid she had been! But he made her stupid. When he looked at her he didn't see Nest. He saw Lady Agnes: plain, tongue-tied and boring.

She tossed and turned. *Something else, think of something else…*

Halewyn.

That was no better. What was he up to? And why? He was funny, he was clever, he was popular – at least, Nest acknowledged bitterly, *Wolf* seemed to like him – but what sort of a person turned up on All Hallows' Eve to conjure burning roses out of nowhere, and to sing love songs he had no right to sing – songs that disturbed everyone so? As for that tale tonight, the tale of *the dead woman who came back* – it was as though he had made her father look deep into a dark mirror. Had he cast a spell over Hugo? Was he really a wandering *jongleur* – or some sort of magician? Why had he come?

Think of something else.

Godfrey…

Maybe he won't marry me.

But of course he would: it had been arranged for too long. Neither of them could break it off now without causing terrible offence to the other's family. Besides, love and liking had nothing to do with it. She was her father's heir, and the wide lands of La Motte Rouge would pass with her to Godfrey, after her father's death. That was why he was courting her; that was why he was saying all those slimy things…

The thought made her shudder. She turned over, drew her knees up to her chin and wrapped tense arms around them. *Sweet blessed Saviour, help me to want to marry Godfrey.*

But it was no good: she didn't *want* to want to marry him.

What do *I want?*

She rolled over again. Beyond the bed curtains, her mother's map of the world was no more than a dark blotch on the wall. She couldn't make out any details. But it glowed in her mind's eye like a landscape seen from a high window – patched with seas and islands, ringed with ocean, guarded by angels. Braided with rivers running out of Paradise – Nilus and Ganges, Tigris and Euphrates. Sprinkled with cities: Rome, Jerusalem and Babylon. Inhabited by marvellous peoples – by Jews and Christians and Saracens, by giants and pygmies. Bursting with wonderful creatures – giraffes and camels and dragons, lions and unicorns and talking trees.

Oh, I want the world! And I want to go on learning new things as long as I live!

A floorboard creaked.

Nest's heart jerked. She prised herself up on her elbow and peered over the edge of the mattress, hooking back the curtain. A black shape moved away from her across the dark space of the room. Her father had come out of his room, wrapped in his mantle. With a squeak and a thump he pushed open the shutters of the north window and knelt there, elbows on the sill, gazing out and upwards. She heard him groan.

He's looking at the hill, Nest thought. *Looking at Devil's Edge and thinking Mam's hidden away there, somewhere underneath it.*

And I'm still not supposed to know.

She was suddenly furious. *Wolf knows, Rollo knows. I'm his daughter – and Mam's too. Why hasn't he told me? He ought to have told me!*

Now was the chance. No one else awake, no one to overhear. A chance to talk to him properly. She swung out of bed and her bare feet landed silently on the floor. She was wearing her nightgown, and her unbraided hair tumbled over her shoulders. She tiptoed over the boards. *Mustn't wake Angharad.* As Hugo knelt with his back to her he almost blocked the small window, but rivulets of icy air flowed past her ankles and she heard a wolf howling somewhere on Devil's Edge.

"Sir," said Nest in a whisper. She laid a hand lightly on his shoulder.

He twisted around so suddenly she jumped. Still on his knees, he stared up at her, mouth and eyes dark and startled.

"*Eluned*?" It was a harsh, unbelieving whisper.

Nest turned to ice. "No!" And she felt for the first time, dimly, that something in Hugo was broken, past mending. "It's not her. It's me. Agnes. I wanted to talk to you."

"Agnes?" said Hugo as if awakening from a dream. He added, "Nest – don't cry."

He'd not used her Welsh name in years. "Dada," Nest whispered.

They sat on Hugo's bed. He pulled the curtains closed, and it was like being in a dark and private tent. Nest curled up her feet, and her father tucked the fur cover around her shoulders. "Or you'll freeze. Now, what's the matter?"

She said in a quick, breathless voice, "Dada. Is it true you think Mam was taken by the elves?"

"Who told you that?"

"I overheard someone talking." *You.*

He didn't answer for a moment. "Do you never dream of her, Nest?"

Her heart thumped. "Not often. Or if I do, I don't remember." She hesitated, knowing the answer, asking anyway. "And you?"

"Constantly. She comes to me constantly." His voice was quiet. "Just now, before I woke, I dreamed I was underneath Devil's Edge, in a great hall crowded with people. They were all richly dressed, but not one of them would speak to me. Each one moved aside as I approached, or turned his face away." He gripped her hand. "Then I saw that many of them were men I used to know, men who died of disease in the siege. Some were maimed, horribly injured. Their faces were all mottled with blood. In the middle of them, I caught sight of your mother. She was very pale, and gazed at me reproachfully. I tried to reach her, but she disappeared into the crowd and I couldn't find her. Do what I could, I woke. I left her there!"

"Oh, father—" Nest longed to comfort him. "It was a dream. Only a dream! She's not really under Devil's Edge…"

"What else can the dreams mean?" Hugo paused. "Elves!" he said with hatred. "Thieving, hungry elves, stealing away what we love! Especially at the in-between times, the hours between life and death, between night and day – like that New Year's Eve seven years ago when your mother lay sick. Seven years! Seven wasted, stolen years!" He struck the bed with his fist. "I'll do anything – anything at all, to bring her home!"

Nest felt a shudder of awe. Almost she believed him. Between Heaven and Hell, Earth and Elfland, where was her mother now? In the double darkness of the curtained bed she gasped, "But it's dangerous!"

He put his arm around her, and she leaned against him. "Yes, it will be dangerous." He hesitated. Was he wondering whether to tell her the rest of his fears? She felt him decide against it. "But if I went all the way to the Holy Land to fight for Christendom, I can venture into Elfland and come back again." He paused. "And if I never come back, at least you won't be alone. You'll be safe, Nest. Married, with Godfrey to look after you."

Nest sat up with a jerk.

I don't want Godfrey to look after me!

She couldn't say it straight out. Maybe there was a way of leading up to it.

"How did you meet my mother?"

He said vaguely, "Oh, there was a council at Gloucester to make peace with the Welsh princes. A number of marriages were arranged. My father and hers made the agreement between them. It was a way of building alliances."

"I see," said Nest bleakly. "And hadn't you ever seen her before?"

"Never." A smile came into his voice. "But when I did – beautiful? She took my breath away. As beautiful as Helen or Blanchefleur out of the old tales. From that day on," he added formally, "my heart was in her keeping."

It sounded like something Godfrey would say. But Hugo meant it.

"What if you hadn't liked her?"

"How could I not have liked her? Agnes –" he spoke gently but firmly "– everything will be all right for you, just as it was for us. You know this has been arranged for years. Your mother wanted you to marry Godfrey; that's why she had the boy come to visit us. You've met him before, remember?"

"But it was ages ago," Nest said in a small, incredulous voice. "I was five."

And she suddenly understood.

Mam never intended this to happen. She meant there to be lots of visits, I'm sure of it. She wanted me and Godfrey to get to know each other slowly, and if I didn't like him, she would have arranged something else. But then she died, and Father went on the Crusade, and there were no more chances.

He's making me marry Godfrey because he thinks she

wanted it. And because he wants me safely out of the way.

Anger rose in her like thin smoke.

He may have loved her, but did he really know her? Any more than he knows me? She wasn't Helen of Troy, and she wasn't Blanchefleur. She was my Mam.

Eight years ago she was in this room painting the map of the world, humming cheerfully, and pretending to dab gold paint on Nest's nose.

It's all about him, isn't it? His songs, his love, his grief. Mam was clever and funny and real. She painted pictures and read and wrote. She taught me about the stars and the planets. But nobody thinks of that now. Nobody sees her except through his eyes. He's made her into a dream, a shadow, a sad storybook lady. He hopes he can bring her back from the underworld, but the more he talks about her, the less real she gets. A shadow, that's what he's chasing. That's what he's looking for, and that's what he'll never find.

She opened her mouth to say so.

And from outside in the dark yard there came a succession of agonising, blood-curdling shrieks, and a man's voice shouting in angry terror.

Hugo was out of the room and down the stairs before Nest could even blink. She grabbed her cloak and ran out after him, just as Angharad sat up in the big bed, crying, "Nest, Nest?"

"I'm with Father!" Nest called over her shoulder. She paused on the landing, looking down on a Doomsday scene as waking rows of sleepers sat up, shaking off their blankets, scrambling to their feet. Outside, the screaming and shouting continued. Some of it sounded very piggy to Nest; but now there were other noises too: dogs barking, and the horns of the guards blowing, and even a disturbed cockerel crowing its head off in the dark.

She dashed downstairs and threaded her way across the floor. Hugo had left the Hall door open in his haste. A cold draught rushed in, brightening the embers. She hurried after him.

And it was snowing. For a second she stopped, caught up in childish excitement. Flakes spun into the light from the doorway and blew away in flurries over the hard-packed mud. Nest ran along the side of the Hall towards the chapel, where all the noise was coming from. As she reached the corner something caught her cloak. A voice near her knees said in gruff alarm, "Oy, missis – watch out!"

Morwenna the pig bolted past with an ear-splitting squeal and a drumming of hooves. Nest reeled, fended herself off against the house wall and looked down. The hearth-hob peered up out of a patch of dead weeds. Its eyes glowed like eerie wandering sparks. "What you doin' out here, missis?" it muttered hoarsely. "This an't no place for you."

"Don't *you* start telling me what to do," Nest hissed. "I want to see what's happening!" She tugged her cloak out of its fingers and stole silently into the black shadows under the eaves of the granary. The hob melted after her, grumbling.

The chapel yard was alive with shadows and silhouettes and flaring torches. Lord Godfrey was there – Nest pulled her hood further over her head – and Hugo and Rollo and Geraint, and even old Howell, all shouting at once in an indecipherable tangle of Welsh and French. A shriek rose above it all.

"The Devil! The Devil in the shape of a pig!"

Nest stood on tiptoe to see Brother Thomas backed up in the chapel porch, waving his arms wildly. "Devils! Devils and pigs!" he screeched. The torchlight gleamed on the whites of his eyes.

The cry was taken up at once. "The *Hwch ddu gwta*! He's seen the Black Sow!"

No, he hasn't! It was Morwenna, Nest thought.

Hugo grabbed Brother Thomas by the shoulders. "Splendour of God! Calm down, man. That was no devil!"

"It was Morwenna," shouted Rollo roughly. And Howell nodded his frail white head.

"Morwenna – t'was only Morwenna, my good pig…"

"Good pig?" screamed Brother Thomas. "I was surrounded! A ring of little black piglets with fiery eyes, dancing on their hind legs! Imps of the pit, mocking me…"

Fiery eyes? Nest turned suspiciously. The hob was crouching just behind her. Sure enough, its eyes cast a faint glow on the ground, for the snow was beginning to stick, whitening the frozen mud. She could just see its scrawny limbs, clad in some tattered garment of balding rabbit fur.

"Did *you* do this?"

"Go on, blame me," muttered the hob sourly. "No I never! And missis, I'm telling you, you want to watch out—"

Then Nest saw Halewyn and Wolf. They were on the far side of the crowd, and even from here, even in the dim light and the dizzying flakes of snow, she could see that they were laughing, clutching each other's arms, almost falling against each other.

So they had done it. Nest didn't know how, but they were obviously enjoying some trick they'd played. Why hadn't Wolf told her? Did he think she wouldn't approve?

"Oy!" The hob was plucking at her cloak with urgent, twiggy fingers, but she ignored it. She felt cold and defeated. Perhaps Wolf was right to think so. Perhaps all of them were right, him and Lord Godfrey and her father and everyone. Perhaps she was just stupid and stiff and proper, and only fit to be married off.

Brother Thomas yelled something more about devils over the buzz of arguing voices, and she saw Wolf hide his laughing face against Halewyn's shoulder. He wasn't looking for her; hadn't missed her. She didn't want to be here any more. She stepped back.

"Oy!" yelped the hob. "Mind your great feet, missis; I an't got toes to spare."

Nest turned on it with tears in her eyes. "Stop saying *Oy*! Stop calling me *missis*! Stop tugging at my cloak! And if I stepped on you, it's your own fault for creeping about under my feet. I'm going in."

The hob grabbed a double handful of her cloak and hung on, growling like a dog. The growling frightened her a little. She realised at last that the hob was both scared and angry. It hauled on her cloak, fist over hairy fist, till she had to bend down.

"You an't going to leave your friend Wolf alone with that jester feller?" it whispered.

"Why not?" said Nest, bitterly.

"Use yer head, gal! You only got to look at them two to see who's behind all this, plain as all that writing you likes to bury yourself in. Din't you see Morwenna? Tarrified out of her skin, she was. I reckon that lad's in trouble. *Piglets with fiery eyes*? How d'you suppose they done it?"

"Well, but—" Nest remembered the burning rose that Halewyn had given her, and hesitated.

The hob was nodding: its hair stood on end like a small haystack. "Ar! Think about it – ask yourself!"

That rose. Not a shrivelled little bud, but a full-blown rose breathing an air of confident summer. And it had burned her fingers…

"He'm a wrong un, I reckon," the hob whispered. It tugged her cloak to make her bend down even further. "Why do he wear that comic cap with the ears, eh? He even sleeps in it, and it an't that cold by the fire at night. What d'you reckon he's hiding?"

Nest shivered. "What do you mean?"

The hob prodded two fingers up past its own sloping forehead and waggled them. "Pokey, pokey!"

"*What – do – you – mean?*" Nest said between her teeth.

"You ask young Wolf if he's ever seen what's under it, that's all," the hob said wildly. "I an't accusin' anyone, mind! I an't saying nothin' more!"

It was snowing harder. Though Brother Thomas was still ranting about devils in the chapel porch, a stream of less interested spectators had begun hurrying back to the warm Hall. As the yard emptied, the wind came moaning through, brushing the dry snow up into everyone's eyes in a tingling scatter of cold, white flakes.

Crouching at Nest's feet, the hob clawed its hair and groaned. "*Ach*! *Now* we're for it, an' no mistake. Pore foolish creature, an't she got *no* sense at all?"

For as the spray of snow cleared, there was something in the yard that hadn't been there before. Glowing faintly, wrapped in a mist of twinkling icy dust, the White Lady stepped silently towards the chapel, with that unsettling air of not quite touching the ground.

Brother Thomas saw her. He made a strangled noise. As she drew nearer and nearer he pressed himself back against the door of the chapel, groping for the door handle. Not fast enough. The White Lady reached him, paused, leaned forward, and murmured something in a voice like the barely audible tinkle of a brook at midnight.

Brother Thomas found the handle. "*Succubus*! Begone, foul spirit!" he howled; and as the door swung open he fell backwards through it. As he vanished into the candlelit interior, the White Lady peered bemusedly after him. The light from the doorway shone through her and lit her whiteness to a moony glow.

"*How-ell-ll*!" yelled Geraint urgently, and Nest saw her father look around and beckon. "Howell, where are you? Howell, you deal with this..."

Old Howell hobbled forwards. "Come along now, my dear," he began. "You come your ways. There's nothing in there for you."

The White Lady turned her head right round on her shoulders, like an owl. Some of the Blanchland men backed hurriedly with hisses of fright. "I can't get in…" she moaned, and now her voice was like the wind whining under the door on the darkest night of winter. "I can't remember. I can't get in… I can't remember."

"Never you worry," Howell soothed her. "You come with me. I know where you belong. You'll feel fine after a little splash in the cistern. You come with me." He set off across the yard, still talking comfortingly, and she drifted slowly after.

The hob relaxed. "*There* you go. Get along with you, go with Howell," it muttered. "There an't much left of her nowadays, but she's bin here longest of us all. Longest of us all!"

Brother Thomas leaped through the chapel door, clutching a candle in one hand, a cup in the other. "The place is accursed – plagued with devils!" he shouted. "First the piglets – then the succubus! But I shall banish her, as I banished them!"

Shouts broke out. "Leave her alone!"

"Go for it, Thomas – get her!"

"That's no succubus! That's our *ladi wen*!"

"It is a succubus!" shouted Brother Thomas. "But fear not. See?" He waved the cup. "Holy water!"

And he threw the entire cupful over the White Lady.

"*Oooooh!*" The hob cringed.

A terrible scream streaked through the night. For a moment after it stopped everyone stood with hands clapped to their ears, as if their heads might suddenly split in two.

And something fled across the yard, sobbing heartbrokenly and dwindling as it went. As it passed her, Nest was sure it was a woman, the White Lady with her face hidden in her hands. But then it was no bigger than a thin child, or perhaps a very old, bent little woman, hobbling away. Before it reached the corner of the Hall it was more the size of a bounding white hare, which changed in mid-leap to a little scuff of snow, which fell away into powder. And there was nothing left.

CHAPTER 15

Brother Thomas stood as if shocked at his own success, his hand still half raised. Then he fell to his knees. "Praise be!" He bowed his head.

The snow came on thicker.

At Nest's feet, the hob stirred. "Gone!" it said in a stunned voice. "After all this time. Gone forever. Gone!"

"Gone!" voices echoed. Men were joining Brother Thomas, kneeling beside him in the snow.

"Praise be!" Brother Thomas cried loudly. "Praise for this miracle! Men of La Motte Rouge, it is no wonder that you have been troubled by such creatures. See the wickedness of your priest, Howell? See how the succubus, the evil spirit, followed him like a lamb following a shepherd? Oh deliver us from evil shepherds who live with concubines against the law of the church!"

"That's a lie," Geraint shouted. "Howell and Hunith have been married this forty years!"

"Forty years of sin!" Brother Thomas rolled his eyes to Heaven.

Roger Bach dropped clumsily to his knees and held up his clasped hands. Stephen le Beau copied him. Some of the Frenchmen from Blanchland also knelt, but the Welsh were drawing aside, with dark looks and upset voices. Across the windswept space of the yard, Nest saw Wolf standing slack-jawed beside Halewyn. He wasn't laughing now.

"The poor creature!" mourned Howell, standing shakily by the corner of the Hall, his knuckles to his mouth. "The poor, poor creature. She never did any harm. And now she's gone!" Geraint put a sheltering arm around him.

"You know what else has gone?" said the hob bleakly to Nest. "The luck of this place. The luck of the lord."

"Join me in prayer!" cried Brother Thomas. "Pray that I shall be your shepherd, until the bishop appoints you a new one. Pray that I shall unlock the elf-girl's stubborn tongue, so that your lord may bring his wife home out of the vile durance of the elf-kingdom. Pray…"

"How do you know that?" Hugo demanded.

You told him! Nest thought fiercely. *After that song tonight do you think there's anyone who hasn't worked it out?* She waited for Brother Thomas to explain. Instead, kneeling in the snow, he flung his arms wide. "God told me!" he exclaimed. "God has sent me here to help you!"

"*How?*"

Brother Thomas rose to his feet. He was as tall as Hugo, and just as impressive in his long black robe. Surrounded by the upturned faces of the kneeling men, he looked like a stern saint sent to chastise sinners. It was probably how he saw himself.

"Give me the elf-girl," he said with harsh confidence. "I will make her talk."

Wolf stood shocked in the cold wind at the other side of the yard.

It had been great, at first. Sneaking out with Halewyn, crouching in the darkness, gleefully watching Brother Thomas stride towards the chapel for the night prayers – as Wolf had known he would. "It's easy to frighten people in the dark," Halewyn had said with a glinting eye. Close by in a corner of the yard, Morwenna lay on her side in the mud, lapped in black shadows, snoring gently. Halewyn undid a brooch from his tunic – a brooch with a long, sharp pin. He passed it to Wolf. "Stick her with this."

"But—"

"Quick!" Halewyn hissed, and Wolf jabbed with the pin. Poor Morwenna had leaped up and careered across the yard, squealing with pain and shock. And Brother Thomas had screamed – and jumped the wrong way. Morwenna knocked him down. And then Brother Thomas began yelling about pigs and devils, and Halewyn had whispered, laughing, "If that's what he wants, let's *give* him pigs and devils!" And with a snap of his fingers, a whole farrow of little black shadows scattered out across the yard...

And Wolf had been filled with furious delight. It had been so funny to see Brother Thomas cowering in the chapel doorway with an arm over his face. Wolf had a sore crease across his stomach from trying to hold in the laughter. And then the White Lady had come walking across the yard – and it had all gone wrong.

"Give me the elf-girl!" Brother Thomas drew himself up like a tall, black pillar. "I will make her talk!"

"No!" Wolf ran into the torchlight, snatched Hugo's hand, and dropped to his knees on the frozen ground. "No, lord, don't! He'll burn her! Don't let him hurt her!"

"*Insolent* boy!" Brother Thomas fixed a blistering glare on Wolf. Spit glistened on his pale lips. "Worthless, quarrelsome, lazy little troublemaker!"

Hugo tore his hand free from Wolf's and laughed –

a fierce, mad laugh. He looked dangerous in the torchlight – a sort of monster. One side of his body was black, the other half splashed with colour. His breath curled out into the freezing air and the flames lit it to gilded clouds. "Wolf? Wolf isn't insolent. He just hasn't learned the meaning of fear – have you, Wolf?"

"Don't let him touch Elfgift!" Wolf shouted.

"Splendour of God!" Hugo roared at him. "If he thinks he can make the elf-girl speak, why shouldn't he try? *You* haven't been doing so well!"

"I've been doing better than you think! She can't talk, but she understands what we say—"

"*Does* she?" Hugo's eyes were narrow slits. "Why haven't you told me that before?"

Wolf lost his head. "Because she's only little. And she can't talk, so she can't tell you anything. And she'd think you were taking her back forever." A terrible illumination came to him. "It's true, isn't it? You don't just want her for a guide. You think you can exchange her for Eluned." He choked. "You're a—"

Rollo grabbed Wolf by the ear and hauled him yelping to his feet. "You insolent young jackanapes, don't you speak to Lord Hugo like that!" He turned to Hugo. "I'll sort him out, sir." And he dragged Wolf away. With that pinching, agonising grip on his ear, Wolf had no choice but to go with him, bent almost double.

"Let go! Let me go! I'm not afraid of Hugo!"

Rollo let go Wolf's ear, grabbed his shoulders and slammed him against the Hall door. Wolf's head hit it with a crack. He bit his tongue. Salty blood filled his mouth. Rollo's face swam close to his.

"Then it's time you were," Rollo breathed. "What did he say to you? '*Wolf doesn't know the meaning of fear?*' Are you proud of that? You young fool!" He held Wolf for a moment longer then released him. Wolf stared at him, panting.

"I saved your skin back there," said Rollo, "and you're not a bit grateful, are you? Get it through your thick head: here on his own land Hugo can do anything he wants. Mostly, he doesn't. Mostly, he's a reasonable man. But about Lady Eluned he isn't reasonable at all. And you want to get in his way? Fear is useful, Wolf. *It tells you when to run.*"

Wolf wiped his mouth. His tongue was immensely sore. But he saw, with great surprise, that Rollo liked him. How had that happened?

He said in a muffled voice, "He'll let that beast burn Elfgift. And he'll give her to the elves."

"That's what you think," Rollo grunted. "Hugo's never used torture yet."

Wolf couldn't help himself. "No? But he's killed innocent people. You told me so yourself."

Rollo's gaze was level and hard. "I've killed them too, Wolf, but you're not upset with *me*. You think about that. Now, I've wasted enough time on you. I'm going in."

He shoved the Hall door open and vanished into the warmth. Wolf loitered on the doorstep, shocked and miserable. The snow pattered on his face and shoulders. A hand tapped his arm.

"Wolf, it's me!"

He whirled. Nest appeared out of the darkness like a ghost. "What have you and Halewyn been doing?" she demanded. It sounded like an accusation. Wolf pulled away.

"Getting back at Brother Thomas. I knew you wouldn't understand."

Lights were bobbing towards them. Everyone was coming in.

"The hob says you shouldn't trust Halewyn. The hob says—"

He hunched his shoulders. "Well, too late. I have! Goodnight, Nest."

"Wolf, what's wrong?"

"What's *wrong*?" he said in a raw, breathless voice. "What's *right*? Didn't you hear your father? He's going to let that – that brute – hurt Elfgift. He's—"

"No he isn't! Of course he won't, not when he's had time to think. He'd never hurt Elfgift! He won't!"

The snow swirled between them like pale curtains. "Yes he will. He's a soldier; he's killed plenty of people in his time. Why should he care about hurting one more?"

"How *dare* you!" Nest's voice rose and cracked. She swept past Wolf into the Hall and turned. Trickles of melting snow slid out of her hair and dripped to the floor. "I've got no time for you when you're being so *stupid*!" Her dark eyes flashed. "You'd better listen. There's something *wrong* about Halewyn. Don't trust him. He's not safe! And I'm trying to tell you: the hob says to ask—"

The door pushed open behind Wolf. Nest had only time to hiss, "*Have you ever seen Halewyn without his cap?*" Without waiting for a reply she whirled away.

In came the rest of the men: Hugo and Lord Godfrey and Brother Thomas, Geraint and Roger and Halewyn, all powdered with snow and stamping their feet. Argos came snaking in past their legs. Wolf flung himself down on his mattress and pulled the blanket over his head to escape notice. Hugo went off upstairs. Lord Godfrey settled into a rather grand four-poster bed that had been set up on the other side of the room. The others made themselves comfortable, and Halewyn lay down on a mattress beside Wolf's. Wolf turned on his side to look at him. Through the dim rosy gloom of the firelit Hall, Halewyn winked.

Anger shot through Wolf. After everything that had

happened, Halewyn could treat it as a joke?

"I thought you said you could help!" he whispered bitterly. "But you've made everything worse!"

"Have I?" Halewyn's voice was cold as a draught across the floor. "Before you go blaming me, think. Who destroyed the White Lady? Brother Thomas. Who said Elfgift ought to be burned? Brother Thomas. If I bring out the worst in people, is it my fault? I gave you what you wanted. I give everyone what they want."

"But I didn't want any of *those* things to happen." He saw Halewyn was laughing silently. "It's all gone wrong!"

"What did you expect from the Lord of Misrule?" said Halewyn. "You wanted revenge, and I gave it to you. You had it, and you enjoyed it. Was it my fault, what happened next?" He rolled on to his back and folded his arms behind his head.

Wolf clenched his fist and thumped his own forehead in desperation.

Somehow it steadied him. For the first time since Lord Godfrey rode in under the gateway – had it really only been hours ago? – he stopped obsessing about Brother Thomas. He began to worry about Halewyn, instead.

Halewyn had arrived on All Hallows' Eve, riding a bad-tempered mule called Beelzebub. He had met Hugo before and told him the tale of *the dead woman who came back*. He had handed Nest a flower that burned her fingers. He had sung songs that kept Hugo's mind fixed on love and death. And tonight he had terrified Brother Thomas with an illusion of little black dancing piglets, hellfire squirting from their triangular eyes and laughing jaws.

He peered through half-closed eyes at Halewyn, who appeared to have dropped off to sleep.

Wolf found he was thinking very clearly indeed. He saw that he had liked Halewyn too easily. For a pleasant smile and a joke, he'd managed to ignore all these strange things. As for Elfgift, Wolf remembered how reluctant he'd been to let Halewyn see her, the night he arrived. Elfgift had screamed. And she'd been wary of Halewyn ever since.

Wolf began to feel like a frightened swimmer being swept along in a strong current. He had an awful feeling about where it was taking him.

What had Nest been saying? *Don't trust Halewyn,* she'd said, *there's something wrong with him.* And a message from the hob: *Have you ever seen Halewyn without his cap?*

What was that supposed to mean? Wolf lay thinking. Halewyn's cap. A close-fitting hood, really, with cloth donkey-ears sewn on. Had he ever seen Halewyn without it? No, he didn't think so. Not from the very first time Halewyn appeared at the All Hallows' fire, and everyone mistook him for a horned—

A horned—

Very cautiously, Wolf sat up.

The fire was burning low. Great shadows reared up the walls. Hardly breathing, he leaned over towards Halewyn, praying that the straw wouldn't crackle.

Halewyn lay with his face half turned away. And yes, he was wearing his hood. Wolf had never noticed before that Halewyn slept with his hood on. Why would he do that?

Something Brother Thomas had said about demons came unbidden to his mind. *God allows them to put on mortal shape, but always with some flaw, some mark by which they can be recognised. Like hooves, or—*

Or something you could hide underneath a fool's cap with ass's ears?

The Lord of Misrule.

Wolf hugged himself and shuddered. He rocked to and fro, sucking air though his teeth as though he'd tasted something bitter, because Halewyn must be – he was – well, Wolf was almost sure he was...

He had to be sure.

He threw a scared glance around the vast room. No one was awake. He was on his own, for none of the snoring sleepers could help him. He crossed himself, muttered a prayer, and stretched stealthy fingers towards the nearest, upwards-pointing donkey ear.

He wanted to feel if there was anything – *hard* –

inside, and he was picturing goats: goats had the sort of small, knobbly, curved-back horns which would fit nicely into the lower part of those long, floppy ears. His fingers floated out as light as smoke—

Wolf stopped breathing. Halewyn was not asleep. There was something altogether false about the way he lay, too motionless, eyes shut – or were they ever so slightly open? It was a trap. Touch him, and—

Those eyes would fly open and spill an awful yellow light. Halewyn would seize him, and then—

Wolf remembered his sins. He had run away from the abbey, he had been disobedient; the saints were angry with him; he had not repented.

He drew his hand away. He pushed the blanket down and climbed to his feet, fearfully aware of every sound: the quiet rustle of the straw, the brushing of cloth against cloth. The crickets were singing their shrill wincing songs across the hearth; a fire-eroded log slipped and settled; Argos whimpered and twitched in his sleep. Wolf's shadow brushed across Halewyn's face, and the eyelids flickered, with a glitter under the lashes. Wolf froze. Looking down now at Halewyn, he wondered what he had ever thought was friendly about that face. The wide mouth held a secret smile, but not a pleasant one. The corner of a tooth showed, caught over the lower lip.

Carefully, silently, one step after another, he tiptoed towards the door. He lifted the latch as quietly as he could and slipped out into the night.

It was still snowing. The cold closed around him like a fist. Wolf fled soft-foot through ankle-deep snow, skidded across the yard, and thudded against the chapel door. Panting and shivering he wrenched it open, squirmed in as soon as the gap was wide enough, and banged it shut.

Safe! The candle-flames bent, streamed, and stood up straight again as the gust from the door died. The calm, stern saints regarded him from the walls.

He flung himself down on the smooth flagstones in front of the altar. With one cheek pressed to the cold stone, the dazzle of the candles filling one eye, he lay and let the silence wash over him. The chill penetrated to his bones. He shivered in spasms. Shivering, relaxing, shivering again, he thought about his sins.

You couldn't make yourself repent. That was the trap he was in. If it was truly a sin to run away from the abbey, he wasn't sorry for it. He was glad. And shouldn't it cut both ways? Brother Thomas certainly wasn't sorry for the things *he'd* done.

Wolf decided to be completely honest. He raised his head and said in a loud, firm voice, "*Miserere mei, dominus.* Lord, have mercy. I'm sorry I stuck a pin in poor Morwenna. I'm sorry I was mean to Nest. But I can't be sorry for running away from the abbey. It wasn't my choice to be a monk, Lord. Is that all right?"

He listened. In the spinning, singing silence of the empty chapel, he felt Christ and His angels gravely assenting.

He sat up, filled with relief. Perhaps, after all, he hadn't done anything terribly bad.

But what about Elfgift?

The answer did not come at once. He waited, his breath coming in small puffs, his fingers freezing, thinking of Hugo's terrible and desperate quest to bring a dead woman back; and how all his hopes hung on Elfgift. And then he thought of Elfgift —scrambling up and down the ladders, playing hide and seek around the buildings, stalking chickens, teasing cats. He thought of this morning, when Herbert chased her out of the kitchens, and she'd jumped into Wolf's arms, panting and laughing. She wasn't really frightened, just pretending – and Herbert was pretending too: he had a soft spot for Elfgift, Wolf was sure.

She trusts us. Not just me and Nest; we've taught her to trust people. I wouldn't hand a dog over to Brother Thomas, let alone Elfgift.

How could he save her? *Even if we ran away, there's nowhere to go…*

But there was. The answer slid into his mind like a dagger. *I could go back to the abbey.*

Wolf scrambled to his feet. He stood still, while the candle flames shimmied, and the saints on the walls peered from the swaying shadows.

Take Elfgift to the abbey? Bury himself in that life of rules and silence?

"I can't!"

Stay here, then, and see what Brother Thomas does to Elfgift. Your choice.

A sort of fiery calm descended on Wolf. He lifted his head. His shoulders straightened. It had to be done, and he would do it. So be it.

Amen, he said silently. And with a loud squeak and a rattle, the chapel door pushed open, letting in a rush of cold air and a glimpse of bluish, pre-dawn dusk. A stooped old figure hobbled slowly through. The candlelight shone warm gold on a ring of wispy white hair.

"Howell! What are you doing here so early?"

"It is Christmas Day," said Howell simply.

Christmas Day! Wolf had actually forgotten. Christmas Day! He began to smile back, and the smile twisted, and he found himself almost in tears. Howell patted his shoulder.

"You've been keeping vigil, I see?" His old face crinkled in benign approval. "Good boy, good boy."

Wolf rubbed his eyes. "How's Hunith? Is she all right?"

Howell was pottering about, snuffing candles and lighting new ones. He looked at Wolf over his shoulder. "There's kind of you to ask. Yes indeed, she is much better."

How could Howell look so ordinary, so *happy,* after everything that had happened? "But Howell, the White Lady!"

Howell's face clouded. "Poor creature; that was a bad business. But all things are in the hands of the Eternal Creator." He bowed to the altar. "And after all that fuss, Hunith and I came in here and knelt down quietly together, and we soon saw that poor Sir Thomas was sadly deluded." He shook his head with a troubled frown. "I am very much afraid he has allowed pride, yes, and even cruelty, to blind the eyes of his soul. We must pray for him, Wolf," he added earnestly, "indeed we must."

Poor Sir Thomas? Wolf gazed at Howell in awe.

And suddenly he laughed. He stretched his arms wide, till his muscles cracked. "Merry Christmas, Howell. I'd better go; there's something I have to do." He didn't say what; it wouldn't be fair.

Old Howell raised his hand. "God bless you, boy, and a merry Christmas!"

CHAPTER 16

Out in the chapel yard, Wolf's feet crunched in frozen snow, and the whole world was blue and dim and trembling on the edge of dawn.

He'd been going to run straight to the stables. Now he glanced at the Hall, where Halewyn was presumably still sleeping, and shivered. He didn't dare go back inside.

But if he just disappeared, what would Nest think? They'd almost quarrelled last night. He had to see her, warn her about Halewyn, tell her what he planned to do, and say goodbye. Then he remembered their pact, made weeks ago – to meet on the tower on Christmas morning, to see the angels dancing in the sun.

He'd completely forgotten about it: maybe she had

too. But it wouldn't take long to find out. He turned and ran around the back of the Hall. The bridge over the ditch was a white arch of snow. A single set of footprints had been trodden into it, a little bit smaller than his, and went on up the steep steps of the mound.

Wolf's heart leaped. He ran up the steps till he had to stop, puffing. He was higher than the Hall roof, higher than the chapel. Far across the snow-filled valley the sky was changing from blue to the palest apricot. He hurried on, slipping and stumbling. When he reached the door at the bottom of the tower, it was ajar, and clods of snow had been stamped off on the dark floor just inside. The ladder ran up into the gloom. He climbed steadily, rung after rung, till his head and shoulders emerged into the chilly little room at the top of the tower. Snow had gusted through the open windows and doorway and coated the boards with white powder.

"Look out!" said Nest quietly. "It's slippery."

"You remembered!"

"So did you!"

They beamed at each other.

"I wasn't sure you would," said Nest, "but I came in case. Angharad's fast asleep, and everyone's still snoring after last night. Where have you been? You weren't in the Hall."

"No," said Wolf grimly. "I went to the chapel. The hob was right about Halewyn!"

Her eyes opened wide. "Did you look? Does he – does he really have horns?"

Wolf remembered that awful moment last night in the firelit Hall. "I don't know. I was going to find out; I thought he was asleep. And then I knew he was only pretending." He shuddered. "I liked him. I thought he liked me. And all the time he was just worming his way into my confidence. Trying to steal my immortal soul!"

"*Your* soul," said Nest hotly. "My father's more like! Rollo was right about that tale he told. It's been like a curse. He wants to tempt my father under the hill. He preys on people's weaknesses."

"Not any more!" said Wolf.

"No! When my father hears this, he'll fling Halewyn out! We've got to tell him. We've got to warn him."

Wolf said in a low voice, "Yes. But you know, Halewyn didn't have to do so very much. We did most of it ourselves. Guess what I feel worst about?" He choked between a laugh and a sob. "I stuck a pin into poor Morwenna!"

"But you're sorry for it," Nest sighed. She picked up a cloth bundle tied with string, and thrust it at him. "Here – this is for you. Take it!"

Mystified, Wolf undid the knots. Out fell a long-sleeved tunic. A linen shirt. Warm, tight-fitting hose for his legs. And a fine woollen cloak lined with rabbit fur. By now there was enough light in the sky to see that the tunic was blue and the hose were green. They were new. Nest must have been making them secretly for weeks. He looked up at her, speechless.

"Merry Christmas," she said gruffly.

"I can't believe you did this," he said in a hoarse voice. "Thank you." He looked at the clothes again, fingering the good cloth. "Nest – I came to tell you—"

A gleam of pink light touched her face. "No!" she pleaded. "Don't tell me yet. Remember why we came? Look, the sun's nearly up!"

Wolf swept snow from the rail. They leaned on it, looking east. Every moment, the colour in the sky grew stronger. A vast cloud stood high over Crow Moor. It flushed rose and peach and gold and began to brighten beyond colour, into pure light. Out of nowhere a small wind ruffled their faces.

Christus natus est! Christ is born! Far below their feet a cock crowed, wild and shrill. A goblet of fire too bright to look at rose over the rim of the world. Fields and woods leaped to life. Rays of light struck across the valley, and the snow-crusted edge of the rail where they leaned turned all to diamonds.

A lump came into Wolf's throat. Poised here on the

tower, high above the world, his hard decisions and troubles seemed tiny and unimportant.

Nest grabbed his hand. "Oh, Wolf," she breathed. "Look."

Above the joyful, blazing disc of the sun, the sky was like hammered silver. White sparks appeared in it, like morning stars. Wolf squinted between the bars of his fingers. Far, far away, leaving streaks and curls of fire, the angels danced like a flock of birds before the sun, their immeasurably distant wings flashing.

Nest and Wolf gazed from their snowy eyrie, dazzled and silent. They went on watching, until between one eye-blink and the next the angels melted away into the brilliance of the sky.

A rook flapped overhead, cawing.

With a deep sigh, Wolf shook his head. Somewhere out of sight below, a door scraped open. Someone coughed. People were waking, and there was no time to lose. "Nest…"

"I know." She turned, her eyes bright and unfocused, her cheeks flushed. "We can't stay up here. We've got to go down."

"But I've got to go even further. I'm going back to the abbey. I came up here to say goodbye. I can't let Brother Thomas get his hands on Elfgift. I must take her away."

"I see." She spoke quietly, but she turned pale.

"I mean, I'm responsible for her. Who saw Elfgift in the first place? Who told Hugo about her? Who fetched her out of the mines?" He thumped his chest. "Me!"

"Yes, I see. I do see, Wolf. She needs you." She added tightly, "It will be all right. In the end, everything will be all right."

Wolf looked at her. "Nest, I hope—" He wanted to say something like, *I hope you'll be happy,* but he couldn't go on. "Don't get married to that stupid lord! Surely, if you begged your father—"

"I tried. He didn't listen."

"Do you mean you *told* him you don't want to marry Lord Godfrey? Hugo never minds if you talk to him straight. Try again. Tell him you can't stand Godfrey. Tell him—"

"Can't you see none of that matters?" Nest burst out. "Whether I like Godfrey or not, I have to marry someone. I'm my father's heir. If it wasn't Godfrey it might be someone worse. I'd never get to choose."

"Oh Nest…"

"Don't worry about me. I can do my duty."

When Nest started talking about duty in that clipped, brittle voice, Wolf knew not to argue. It wouldn't do any good, and he didn't want to end their friendship on another quarrel.

"Goodbye, then." Awkwardly he added, "I'll never forget you," and turned away.

Below, hooves clopped a quickening pace across the yard. They glanced down. Two riders came into sight, heading at a hasty, slithering trot for the open gate. In the lead was Halewyn on his mule. After him came Hugo on his black horse. White Argos ran beside him, a ghost-dog against the snow. With one arm Hugo held a jouncing, child-like figure in front of him on the saddle.

"Halewyn!"

"*Elfgift!*"

"*Father!*" Nest shrieked.

Halewyn's mule was already through the gate. Hugo spurred his horse. It sprang forward under the gateway.

Nest grabbed Wolf by the arm. "Oh, we're too late. He's gone with Halewyn! They're taking Elfgift away!"

"Not if I can help it." Wolf flung himself at the ladder.

"You'll never catch them on foot," Nest wailed. "Wait! Take my pony!"

"But—" Halfway through the trapdoor, Wolf shut his mouth with a snap. How hard could riding be? Everyone did it. "Right!"

He hurtled down the ladder, waiting at the bottom in jiggling impatience as Nest came more carefully down. Together they jumped and slid down the steps, raced across the bridge and around the back of the Hall. How quickly the world came to life after daybreak! The Hall steamed and smoked. Sparrows hopped around the cookhouse. From inside came a noise of clattering dishes. Herbert was already busy. *Christmas Day*, Wolf thought. *Oh, what a Christmas!*

They dodged into the stables. Madog was there, sweeping. He jumped round when he saw Nest. She snapped something in Welsh, and then, as he didn't immediately move, stamped her foot and repeated it. Madog nodded hurriedly. He dropped the broom and vanished into the harness room.

Wolf looked at the bundle of new clothes Nest had brought down from the tower. Much better for riding than his long, monkish robe. He ducked behind the partition, tore off the robe, pulled the blue tunic over the shirt he was already wearing, and stuffed his legs into the green hose. He threw the cloak over it all and tossed the robe into the straw just as Madog reappeared. Goggling at Wolf's finery, he clapped the saddle and bridle on to Nest's pony, and within a few minutes was leading it out.

Wolf stared at its swaying, hairy sides and gulped. He poked a toe into the stirrup. The pony sidled away and he followed, helplessly hopping.

"Grab the saddle, Wolf! Grab it and pull yourself up!"

With a clumsy scramble he managed to obey. And there he was on the pony's back, feeling higher than he had on the tower. The pony kicked, and he clung to the saddle. Nest's anxious face floated below.

"How do I make it go?" he demanded.

"Oh, Wolf!" She wrung her hands. "Can't you ride at all?"

Wolf was about to admit that perhaps he had better get down and run after Hugo on foot. But just then the Hall door opened. Brother Thomas came out. Seeing a boy on a pony he strode towards the stable, dark robes swishing. "You, young sir – where is Lord Hugo?" He stopped. "*Wolfstan!*" he exclaimed, not seeing Nest. "What are you doing on that horse? *Thief!*" He rushed forward, long sleeves flapping. And the pony, which had been cooped up in its stall for days, shied and bolted.

Wolf flung himself forwards and hugged its neck. The yard whizzed past in a white blur. He heard shouts, felt rather than saw the gate looming, and shut his eyes. The sound of the hooves drummed hollow on the bridge and then muffled again as they hit the lane. Here the pony stumbled, and he nearly flew over its head. But it was a sure-footed little beast. It recovered, pitching Wolf back into the saddle. He had lost the reins. The pony went down the lane in a series of plunging salmon leaps. He wound his fingers into its coarse mane and hung on for grim death.

Where the lane reached the road, the pony slipped on icy stones under the snow, and its haunches went down. It picked itself up with a heave and a twist, and luckily turned the right way, hurtling after Hugo and Halewyn. At last its wild pace slowed to a bone-rattling trot, and finally to a brisk, bouncing walk.

Wolf hauled himself straight and fished for the reins with trembling fingers. When he had them in his hands he felt better. They were something to hang on to, and he knew in theory that if you pulled on them, the pony should stop. He looked behind, and La Motte Rouge was already half a mile away. He was astounded at the distance the pony had covered. He looked ahead down the white road. Far off, two black horsemen moved like scuttling spiders.

He screwed up his eyes. It was hard to tell from here, but he thought they were strung out, one behind the other, not riding side by side. Hugo on his black horse seemed to be nearest. The more distant figure was Halewyn: Wolf could see two twists of ears suggesting a fool's cap. Or curving horns.

"*Is* it Halewyn?" Wolf was struck with doubt. "It looks like him, but he seems bigger. Even the mule looks bigger. Oh! He's gone!" The rider had turned his mount and leaped off the road into the shadows of the snow-pocked woods. And, a short time later, Hugo followed. They were going up Devil's Edge.

Well, at least they wouldn't see him following; and he couldn't lose them. All he had to do was follow Hugo's tracks. Riding wasn't so hard after all. The air was sharp on his cheeks, but he was warm from the gallop. He looked down at his colourful clothes. Brother Thomas had called him *young sir*! Whatever lay ahead, he was well-dressed and on horseback. For the first time ever, he knew how it felt to be a squire riding after his knight!

They passed a fold of the hill where a stream ran down through a culvert under the road. Here the pony stopped and flung up its shaggy head, staring into the woods. Wolf shook the reins, and flapped his legs against its sides. "Gee up! Gee!" The pony swelled as it took an enormous breath. Its nostrils cracked. Suddenly it let rip with a deafening shrieking neigh, a sound like a brass trumpet. Wolf was so shocked he almost fell off. Like an echo, an answering neigh rang faintly from the woods.

The pony quivered. And Wolf just had time to notice the tracks turning off the road, and a kicked-up trail leading steeply into the woods. He'd nearly missed the place where Hugo had left the road and ridden up through the trees! How had the pony known? But of course, it was following its stable-mate. And first there was a four-foot ditch to cross, edged with dead hemlock and teazles. Ice glimmered at the bottom.

The pony flung itself at the ditch. Wolf grabbed its mane with both fists, dropping the reins again. The world turned topsy-turvy. Then the pony was hurtling uphill in a series of floundering jumps, tossing its head and heaving with its haunches. "You mad animal," Wolf muttered, clinging fiercely. "Mad!" And he thought of Nest. He'd seen her riding it; it had always looked quiet. But perhaps that was just because she was a wonderful rider! His respect for her soared.

The slope eased. The pony trotted, its shaggy legs pumping through the snow. Wolf sat up, bouncing. Ahead, the dark ridge of Devil's Edge glanced at him between bare branches. The trees stood back. In the centre of a glade, he saw a tangle of charred branches – the mark of an old bonfire. On the uphill side of the glade Hugo's black horse was waiting, untethered, reins trailing. It looked at them with pricked ears. The pony squealed and tore across to greet it. While the two animals nuzzled, Wolf swung a stiff leg over the back of his saddle and dropped shakily into the snow.

He knew this place. That old bonfire was the one that Hugo and his men had lit after the wolf hunt. For a cold moment, it was as if everything that had happened between now and then had been a dream.

But Hugo's horse was here, and a line of crisp footprints led away under the thorn trees. A man's straight stride and a wavering patter of paw-prints. No marks of a child. Hugo must be carrying Elfgift in his arms…

Wolf faltered. Where was Halewyn?

The snow was trampled by more than one set of hoof prints, but none of them led away. In fact, they might all belong to Hugo's horse and his own pony. There was no sign of the mule anywhere. And now he came to think of it, had there been more than one set of hoof prints along the road? He hadn't noticed. He wasn't sure.

With growing unease, Wolf set off after Hugo through the scratching hawthorns. The wood didn't look much as he remembered it. It was so bright, filled with snow-light. After a while he saw fresh prints. Something with cloven hooves had come out of the woods on the left, followed Hugo's trail for a while as if curious, and then – apparently satisfied – split off to the right. It wasn't a deer. It had been walking on two legs.

Deeply thankful he hadn't come in time to see it pass, Wolf hurried on uphill, his boots filling with snow. And there in front was a mound of snow-covered rocks, and the cliff rising out of tangled brambles like a stern, grey forehead. He wiped sweat out of his eyes. Not far ahead stones tumbled. Somebody was moving about at the foot of the cliff. And then Argos came weaving down over the rocks, his coat only slightly creamier than the snow, his golden eyes ablaze with welcome.

"Hugo!" Wolf shouted the name like a challenge, and the echo bounced back off the rock face, flat and menacing. "*Hugo!*"

CHAPTER 17

"Wolf!"

Hugo spun around, swinging Elfgift down. He stood balanced on rocks not far from the mine entrance, gripping her by one thin arm. She didn't stand. She fell into a sort of crouching huddle at his feet.

Using hands as well as feet Wolf scrambled over the snowy rocks. He had no plan, except to do exactly what Rollo had told him not to do. Get in Hugo's way.

"I've come to get Elfgift."

Hugo said quietly, "You can't have her."

Wolf shook his head; he was still getting back his breath. "Where's Halewyn?" he demanded.

"How should I know?"

"You followed him. He led you here. I *saw* him!" Wolf insisted as Hugo frowned. "He rode ahead of you all the way."

"Are you mad? I came alone."

Wolf's heart turned to ice. "No you didn't. Whether you saw him or not, he brought you here. Sir, you can't take Elfgift into the mines."

"*Can't*?"

"Because you won't. Any more than you'd let Brother Thomas hurt her. Rollo says you're better than that, and so does Nest." He added passionately, "You are, aren't you?"

"Ah, God." Hugo's eyes were hard and bright. With a shock Wolf saw that the brightness was unshed tears. "The things we must do, to be men! What a place the world is, Wolf! Ringed with angels, and as rotten as an old tooth. Don't mistake me for a hero. In the Holy Land I raised my sword for Christendom – where Peter was forbidden to raise his sword to defend Christ – and if all the blood I helped to spill has soaked down through the earth, the rivers of Elfland must be foaming full.

"And Heaven's a bright, cruel place, where God and his saints sit in stainless bliss. They turn grief and doubt away from the gates, like shabby, bandaged beggars. They'll never let me in.

"But Elfland – I wander through Elfland every night.

It's full of outcast angels and men I saw die in the wars, and unbaptised babes, and travelling companions left behind on the road. I've seen the twisting path that leads there. I've been lost on it ever since Eluned died. I've followed it in dreams: a maze of false turnings.

"Now I have to go down that road in very truth. It starts *here.*" He nodded at the gaping black slot in the cliff at his back. "I need your elf-girl. As a hostage – as a guide—"

"How do you even know Lady Eluned's there?" Wolf cried. "Nest thinks she's not. And Howell, Howell says she's in Paradise."

"And if she's in Paradise," Hugo sounded deadly tired, "I've lost her forever."

He took a fresh grip of Elfgift's arm and tried pulling her to her feet, but she hung limp and set up a pitiful, high screaming like an animal in a snare. Hugo set his teeth and dragged her towards the black mouth of the mine, still screaming.

"Stop it! Oh, stop it!" Wolf rushed at Hugo, seizing his elbow. Icicles dropped from the cliff, shattering on the rocks. Argos sprang around, barking.

Hugo let go of Elfgift's arm, looking sick. "You're right. I can't do it."

Elfgift took off like a rabbit. She tore past Wolf almost on all fours, using her hands for balance over the rock spill. He glimpsed her eyes, wide with terror in her blotched face – then she vanished into the trees. Argos flew after her.

"Elfgift! Come back!" Wolf leaped after them. His foot went into a hole under the snow and he fell on the rocks. Picking himself up painfully, he saw Hugo turning towards the mine.

"No! Hugo, don't!"

Hugo looked back. His face lit to a teasing, surprisingly gentle smile. "Fine feathers, Wolf. Did Nest give you those clothes? You were never cut out for a monk, were you? Tell her to give you two silver marks from me, in payment for your services."

"You can't go in there alone!" Wolf was torn with grief and panic. He wanted to rush after Elfgift, yet he couldn't leave Hugo.

"Why not? You did! Am I less of a man than you?"

"But you waited outside for me – I knew you were there."

Hugo paused. "Watch for me, then, if you will. Wait by the entrance."

"But I've got to find Elfgift!" Wolf cried.

"Wolf!" Hugo took him by the shoulders and shook him. "*Do what you must.*" And with that, he ducked in under the low overhang of the cave mouth.

Wolf knelt, shivering, watching Hugo vanish. It was

as though the cave ate him. One moment he was there: the next, gone. Wolf was alone. The cliff dripped silently on to the back of his neck.

He got to his feet. This was a bad place: he'd always thought so. Even through the snow he could smell the odd, sour smell that he'd noticed before.

He jumped over the rocks and ran down the slope. Elfgift's trail, overlaid with Argos's, went looping away into the woods.

"Elfgift!" Nothing stirred. Fog was gathering under the trees. "Elfgift!" He whistled for Argos, long and shrill. The dog did not come back.

Wolf shoved his hands through his hair in agonised uncertainty. What to do? He could follow the tracks, but who knew if he could ever catch them? Perhaps he should stay here. If he waited patiently they might return. Argos might, anyway: and then he and Argos together would be able to find Elfgift.

But waiting patiently wasn't in Wolf's nature. He clambered back over the stones. He jiggled from foot to foot. He bit his nails. He glanced at the wood. He glanced at the mine. Horrible to think of Hugo, buried in there! Perhaps he hadn't got far. Perhaps he was already coming back. Wolf threw himself down and stuck head and shoulders into the opening. The cold stone was forbidding, pressing close on every side.

"Hugo?" he called. "Hugo?" No answer.

He listened, remembering the last time he had been here. He thought of Hugo leaning into the darkness, calling for Eluned. He thought how he'd hoped to be Hugo's squire. He thought of Hugo's tired, teasing smile.

If I were really his squire, I would have gone with him.

So the decision made itself. Light with relief, he dropped his fine new cloak on the rocks. If Elfgift came back she would see it, and know where he had gone. She could use it to keep herself warm until he came out again. He threw a last look at the snowy wood, filling his eyes. Then he bent under the stone lintel and crawled into the mine.

Almost immediately the outside world became difficult to believe in, like a fantastic story. Only the stone was real, and the dark; his body blocked the daylight like a stopper in a bottle. He scuffled and slid down the first slant of gritty mud. He knocked his head on the roof and hastily bent double, then dropped to hands and knees.

How far had Hugo got? He called, and his voice sounded flat, trapped. "Hugo!"

Somewhere ahead, miraculously, a gleam of yellow light appeared, curling around the edges of the tunnel. Wolf saw where he was going: a short, downhill crawl under a drooping bulge of rock. He crabbed his way painfully along over glistening, pointed stones, and emerged in a wide chamber with a low, uneven roof, no more than three feet high. The floor was an undulating expanse of mud, stones and shallow puddles. Hugo was sitting in the middle of it with a fat, stumpy candle. The flame winked like a star.

He nodded at Wolf, as casually as if they were passing each other in the yard. "So you came." The nonchalant welcome made Wolf glow more than speeches of gratitude. "Is this the place where you found Elfgift?"

"Yes. But I never saw it before." Wolf looked around in wonder. His breath floated out in damp clouds. The ceiling was ribbed and arched like the roof of a mouth, and lots of little white drops clung to it like pimples. He looked down. Near his left hand was a broken, brownish curve. He picked it up. "This bit of broken pot – I remember putting my hand on it."

"That's not a bit of pot," said Hugo. "It's a piece of someone's skull."

Wolf flung it from him with a start of horror. He scrubbed his hand against his sleeve. "Whose?"

"Who knows?" Hugo's voice was quiet and grim. "And there's a jawbone here. You can tell it's old. Maybe someone crawled in here to die. Maybe someone the elves lured in and enchanted."

Wolf threw a nervous glance around. The edges of the cave disappeared into darkness.

"But this isn't the place where I saw the wall open up," he whispered. "That was further on. I was following Argos, and Argos was following Elfgift."

"Which way?" Hugo asked.

"I don't know." Being able to see was confusing him. He closed his eyes and pointed. "That way, I think."

"Let's go and look." Hugo lifted the candle. Awkwardly, one hand raised, he began crawling across the stones, and the chamber seemed to tilt and tip as the shadows lurched after him. Wolf followed in his dark wake. The roof descended towards them and Hugo knocked his head. "There – is penance in this," he said with a gasp of pained laughter. "To crawl on the naked knees over sharp stones – it is good for us, Wolf. It teaches humility." He began to murmur the *Paternoster*.

Wolf joined in. They crawled on. Presently, Hugo checked. "Dead end."

Wolf peered past Hugo's arm. The candlelight flickered on a hollowed-out rock wall, pocked with dimples and scarrings that looked like old tool marks.

"This is it! This is where I caught her. She was trapped against the wall. What do we do now?"

Hugo blew out the candle and the darkness was absolute.

"We will wait."

Hot, sooty smoke wreathed past Wolf, filling his nostrils. He gasped like a fish. The shape of the candle flame reappeared, repeating itself on the darkness, greenish and unreal, sliding up and down wherever he turned his straining eyes. *Corpse candles!*

He'd forgotten how terrible this place was. Why had he returned? Why had he been so mad? He touched Hugo's sleeve. "Light the candle!"

Hugo laid an arm lightly across Wolf's shoulders. "Keep up your courage, young Wolf. Suffer a little darkness for me and my lady." After a while he added, "If I'd had a son like you, I wouldn't have put him in a monastery."

It was the ultimate accolade. Pride could go no further. But Wolf thought loyally of Nest. "Your daughter's just as—" he began.

"Hush. Listen!"

To what? Tense and quivering, Wolf obeyed, his eyes uselessly wide, his mouth open, his ears straining. What could he hear? Nothing. And then a steady drip of falling water. And then a far-off murmur, like voices speaking many rooms away. Or even low laughter. Prickles raced over Wolf's skin.

"You hear it?" Hugo breathed. "Rumours from another level. Deeper down." And suddenly he shouted: "Open up!" In the confined space the noise was terrific.

Wolf cringed, clapping his hands over his ears.

"Open up! Open up!"

Breathless, Wolf waited for the walls to split open. For the enchanted green fields of Elfland to float glowing into view.

Nothing happened. With a sharp chipping sound, sparks fell like seeds and grew into a pale, tender flame. Hugo had relit the candle. He moved it around sharply.

"Look!"

Wolf looked. There was a little tuck of darkness at the side of the floor.

"Down there?" he gasped. "But it looks tiny!"

Hugo swam the candle closer. The shadows moved back, and Wolf saw that the side of the passage they were in dropped sharply towards the mouth of this new tunnel, in a steep downward step.

Hugo lay down and stretched his arm under the edge. The candle flame shivered. "See?" said Hugo softly. "There's a current of air. It goes somewhere. Here. Take the candle, and then pass it to me when I ask you. I'm going to look."

He tipped himself head-first into the dip and wriggled forward. Wolf held the candle, watching Hugo squirm his shoulders under the rock shelf, then half his back. At last he heard a muffled grunt – Hugo was asking for the candle! He held it as low as he could, trying to pass it under the edge of the rock close to Hugo's side. Somehow Lord Hugo managed to grasp it. He moved it ahead of him, and darkness swallowed Wolf.

He crouched, trying not to panic. Listening to Hugo gasping and struggling was worse than doing it himself. At last – it seemed an age – the sound of boots grinding on stones and trickling gravel ceased. Hugo's voice, less muffled now that his own body wasn't blocking the hole, called quietly, "I'm through. It'll be easier for you. You're smaller."

Wolf took a shaking breath of the damp, sour air. He groped towards the edge of the slope and tipped himself down it as he'd seen Hugo do. At once he felt committed. His heels were higher than his head, and his body bent in a bow-shape. He kicked violently, slithering forwards and down over cold, wet mud. Protruding stones grazed his knees and hips. The layer of rock above pressed his shoulders like a hand forcing him down. But once his head and shoulders were well into the tunnel, he could see the faint glow of candlelight on the other side, fifteen or twenty feet away. With renewed vigour, he began kicking himself on.

"What's it like?" he panted.

"Bigger," Hugo's voice floated. "You can stand up."

Wolf was glad to hear it. He wriggled on like a

worm, making so much noise that he only dimly heard Hugo swearing. "Wolf – hurry! The light!" His voice faded to a mumble.

"What?" Wolf felt a cold splash of terror. Was the candle going out? Then a strange greenish light washed into the crack he was lying in, and faded.

Hugo spoke again, "*Oh!*" His voice vibrated with wonder and alarm. What had he seen? Icy with fear, Wolf dug elbows and toes into the gritty ground and squirmed on.

Then he heard Hugo say quite clearly, "Wolf, be quick! I have to go."

"Wait!" Wolf scrabbled and strained towards the light. There was that smell, the acid smell of the elves: sharp on his tongue. "Wait for me. Hugo, wait!" Gasping, sweating, streaked with mud, he dragged himself out of the constricting tunnel and collapsed on his stomach on a smooth rock floor. Hugo's candle burned on the ground in front of him, shooting rays into his eyes.

Hugo was not there.

Wolf scooped up the candle and scrambled to his feet. He turned around, sure Hugo must be standing close, hidden in the shadows. His own enormous shadow revolved behind him. Panting like a dog, Wolf raised the candle high so that his shadow shrank and cowered underfoot. No Hugo. He was in a narrow gallery, about five feet high, part natural rock, part squared by tools. He could only see a few yards each way.

"Hugo!" he screamed. "*Hugo!*"

He ran – not knowing which way to go, he just ran – and the candle fluttered wildly and almost went out. He dropped to a fearful, pacing stride, shielding it with his hand. He had no flint, nothing to strike a light. If the candle went out, he was lost – unless Hugo came back.

"*Hugo!*"

The passage ended suddenly in a small, blunt chamber like a fist at the end of an arm. No way out. He passed the candle along the roughly marked walls to be sure. Just a concave surface of rock glistening with seepage of slow, brown water, and a wet, gritty floor. Hugo must have gone the other way: *must* have. Wolf turned, leaving the blind space to its eternal darkness and went swiftly back.

"Hugo?"

His voice frightened him. It was lonely, lost. It was the voice of someone who no longer expects an answer. The passage was longer this way. His hopes rose. Then an end loomed dimly into the candlelight.

Unbelieving, Wolf carried the candle right up to it. It was not curved this time, not a chamber: simply a wall where the tunnel stopped. He thumped it, and his fist didn't even make a noise. Solid rock.

Terror overtook him. He had just enough sense to put the candle down before flinging himself against the rock, pounding and kicking it, and screaming, "Hugo! HUGO!" At last, bruised and dizzy, he slid to the floor.

He was in a place where people got lost – lost—
a maze of false turnings…
they'll draw you down deeper than you want to go…
draw you down deeper…
lost – lost—
nobody knows you're here…
nobody cares—

It seemed that a thousand dry voices were whispering in his head. The sound prickled on his skin in pins and needles. Clutching the candle, he stared down the passage into shadows as black as the centre of an eye. Where was Hugo?

Lost, lost, said the muttering, shifting voices of the elves.

The flame dwindled to a blue bead, and at once the darkness was all around him, a fingertip away. In a fright, Wolf tilted the candle. Hot tallow fat ran over his hand and the flame recovered, struggling up in a smoky spire.

Wolf coughed, and his heart pounded. If the candle could not live here, neither could he. The acidic, elvish smell caught in his throat. If he lingered, he would never get out. He would die right here at the end of the tunnel – unless the elves opened the walls and drew him in as they must have done for Hugo. He had to find the crack he and Hugo had crawled through.

"Quick," he mumbled.

Wolf, be quick. Hugo's parting words. *Be quick, be quick! I have to go.*

(*Before the candle dies, before the shadows catch me...*)

As he stumbled along, shielding the unsteady flame, the shadows harried him. They crawled past him along the floor, ducked down in front of him, shrank around corners, leaped up behind him. It was like blundering through crowds of faceless, angry ghosts. He nearly missed the way out altogether. But there it was, an unappealing slit at floor level, brimful of darkness like black ink.

Wolf, be quick!

Wolf flung himself down, panting uncontrollably. He gripped the candle in one fist and thrust it into the opening. He squirmed after, dragging himself along by his elbows, wrenching his way through the tunnel. His lungs were raw from breathing the rancid, cellar-cold air; his fingers were numb and bleeding. *Be quick! Be quick!* He got to the halfway point and began to kick and struggle upwards. The worst part was not being able to see the end. Everything ahead was dark.

Wolf, be quick! The candle flame was shrinking again. Sobbing, grunting, swearing, Wolf hauled himself on. For the last time the flame trembled like a blue water drop. Then, as if invisible fingers had reached over his shoulder and pinched it, it went out. For a second a tiny red-hot spark remained glowing, the only visible thing in this world of night. It faded.

Wolf shut his eyes. It was better than trying to see. He scrabbled and clawed his way on. He began to be giddy. The passage held him in its fist. Which was the right way? Was he still heading out? He could never turn around. At last his groping hands knocked on stone ahead. In despair he reached left and right, patting and fumbling. More stone.

Wolf laid his aching head down, exhausted. This was the end. The long struggle was over. He'd lost Hugo; he'd lost everything.

Lost… agreed the whispering voices. *Lost…*

Beyond fear, Wolf lay stretched in the tunnel. Weariness soaked through him, and he welcomed it, sinking into cold sleep.

CHAPTER 18

Ignoring Brother Thomas's furious cries, Nest ran to the gateway to watch her grey pony bolting down the hill with Wolf clinging to its back. At the road it nearly fell. She clapped her hands over her face and watched through her fingers as it recovered and went tearing off along the snowy road with Wolf miraculously still in the saddle.

The men from the gatehouse behind her crowded out to see.

"He'll break his neck!"

"Where's he off to in such a hurry?"

A hand tapped Nest on the shoulder. "Don't cry for him, my lovely – there's other lads in the world!"

Nest stiffened. She spun around. "Were you speaking to me?"

One of Godfrey's men stood there, wiping a smirk from his face. "Your pardon, lady." He winked. "I only meant to say, our Lord Godfrey'll soon cheer you up!"

Nest realised she was surrounded by men. More than half of them were strangers. They stared at her, nudging each other. And Brother Thomas came striding up like a tall, black scarecrow. "After that boy, some of you!" he shouted. "He stole a horse!"

"No he didn't," Nest contradicted. "I told him to take it!"

"You?" Brother Thomas demanded. "And why, may I ask?"

Her chin came up. "Lord Hugo went out – on his own business, and I sent Wolf after him."

Brother Thomas's black eyebrows met. He bent over her.

"That was *most* unwise," he said softly. "The boy is quite untrustworthy. I say he *has* stolen the horse. He will not come back. As I said before, madam – you are very young. After you are married tomorrow, I trust you will leave such – impetuous decisions – to the better wisdom of your lord and master."

Nest was stung. "Perhaps I will not be married tomorrow," she said in a hasty, breathless voice. "My father has ridden away on business. I cannot be married until he returns."

Brother Thomas lifted an eyebrow. "Do you not expect him to return by tomorrow?"

"Of – of course I do!" Nest stammered.

"Then *of course* the marriage will take place. And since, I am sure, nothing short of death would prevent Lord Hugo from returning in time for your wedding –" Brother Thomas raised the other eyebrow "– if he does *not*, naturally Lord Godfrey will honour his promise to make you his wife, and take you under his protection."

Is he threatening me? Nest braced herself to meet Brother Thomas's steel-cold gaze, and it was like meeting the eyes of some merciless bird of prey. Once she was married, Brother Thomas would be her own priest and confessor. He would exercise religious authority over her. And he knew it.

She looked down, intimidated and appalled. Brother Thomas smiled. Without taking his eyes off her he snapped his fingers at Madog. "Boy! Fetch me the elf-girl."

As Madog, who spoke only Welsh, gaped nervously at Brother Thomas, Rollo came pushing brusquely through the crowd. He bowed to Nest with grim formality. "Allow me to escort you back to the Hall, my lady."

Nest caught a breath of relief. She stepped gratefully

ahead of him, and he muttered, "The elf-girl's not there, is she? Has Hugo gone off with her?"

"Yes," she murmured.

"*Hell*!" Rollo controlled his voice. "And Wolf's gone chasing after? Mind you, Hugo likes him. If anyone can fetch him back..." He opened the door for her and bowed her through. "It's all that *jongleur's* fault. I swear this time I'll tear his head off."

"He's gone too."

"Has he? *Has* he?" Rollo drummed his fingers against his thigh. "All right, madam, without your father here I'd rather you didn't wander about. There's as many of Godfrey's men here as there are of us – and no one in charge. I'd go after Hugo myself, but I couldn't leave you and feel easy..." He whistled through his teeth. "It might be better if you kept out of sight. It's nearly time for Mass. Afterwards, though, if you don't feel like sitting through the feast, why don't you go to your room with a headache? With any luck, your father will be home by dark." He didn't sound as if he believed it. "If you need me, send for me."

Nest nodded, unable to trust her voice. She swept across the Hall and ran upstairs. Angharad was there. Nest hurled herself across the room and buried herself in her old nurse's comfortable bosom.

"Dearie, whatever's the matter? There now! There

now! My pet, my *cariad*! What's wrong?" Between hiccups and sobs, Nest poured it all out. Angharad listened in growing concern. "Your noble father gone off with the elf-girl? And all because he thinks your good mother, God rest her, was stolen away by the elves? Bless me, the man's a fool after all. I never knew a man who wasn't. It's true that the night she died, poor soul, I heard the wild hounds passing overhead baying and belling, a noise to make you shiver; but fenced around by holy candles as she was, and the holy name on her lips, how could anything evil touch her?

"And whatever shall we do if he's not back by tomorrow? How can you get married, if your father's not there?"

Nest sat up, wiping her eyes. She was ashamed of herself, but there was comfort in telling Angharad everything. It felt like being small again – though she knew Angharad was powerless to help. "They'll make me marry Godfrey whatever happens. If Father doesn't come back they'll say he's dead and Godfrey needs to p-protect me. And if he does come back, Father expects me to marry. That's why he left. He thinks I'll be h-happy…" Tears welled up again.

Angharad shook her head. "Well, maybe he's right! Lord Godfrey's a handsome, courtly young man, and if it's what your father wants…"

"I hate Godfrey!"

Angharad clucked. "He's been paying you a lot of attention. You might be a little shy at first, but you'll get used to him, my dearie, never you fret. Come along, now. It's Christmas Day. Put on your fine new mantle. We'll go to Mass and we'll pray for your father to come safely home. I'm sure it will all come right. You'll see!"

She gave Nest a smacking kiss, opened the door to the top of the stairs and pushed her gently out. Voices floated up from below. Angharad and Nest stopped, transfixed. Brother Thomas was talking to Lord Godfrey.

"…taken the elf-girl already," he was saying in his harsh, penetrating voice. "Rode off this morning, before anyone was up."

"Hugo's mad," Godfrey grumbled. "To make such a fuss over a wife! After all, there are other women in the world."

"Indeed," Brother Thomas agreed with distaste.

Nest peered over the rail. The pair were standing directly beneath her, but the canopy that hung over the dais hid them from sight. Every word, however, was clearly audible.

Brother Thomas continued meaningfully, "But why need you care? You'll marry the daughter tomorrow, and if Hugo never returns…"

"I'll be the lord of La Motte Rouge. True!" Godfrey sounded more cheerful. "Pity the girl's almost an idiot – and plain, too – but she'll do. I don't want a wife with opinions, and if I wish to be entertained I know plenty of other ladies who will be glad to do it. Yes. If Hugo's set off on some crazy quest into Elfland, let him stay there."

"God has brought us here," said Brother Thomas piously. "There is work to be done."

"Quite," Godfrey coughed. They moved away.

Angharad and Nest looked at each other. "*Well!*" Angharad breathed. Her eyes flashed with indignation. "Well, *really!*"

Nest took Rollo's advice. She and Angharad retreated to the solar after Mass, and bolted the door. A tear-stained Bronwen brought food upstairs to them, which Nest refused to eat. Tense and sick, she knelt by the window in the whistling draught, staring out at the white yard and darkening sky, hoping against hope to see her father and Wolf come riding in.

From below came laughter and sounds of merrymaking as Lord Godfrey and his men feasted. It was cold in the solar – but she'd rather freeze up here than be warm down there. The afternoon wore on. Once she heard Godfrey shouting drunkenly, "Where's my bride?" and one of his men yelled, "I'll get her!" There were cheers. Heavy feet stampeded up the stairs. Angharad rushed to make sure the door was properly bolted. Nest stood rigid. Then they heard Rollo roaring: "Off those stairs or I'll drag you down!"

It sounded as though he really did, for there was a crash, and a series of bumps and curses. A voice wailed, "– it was only a joke!"

"Disgraceful!" Angharad panted.

Nest said nothing. She was ice-cold with fright and disgust.

"Disgraceful behaviour! When Lord Hugo hears about this—"

"If he ever does," interrupted Nest, "it will be too late. This time tomorrow, I'll be married."

Angharad was silenced. Nest went to the reading stand, lit the candle, turned a page of the book. Her eyes slid over the words without taking them in. Her fingers shook with grief and fear and futile rage. How dared her father go off like this? How dare he leave her with no choice, except to marry a man she'd only just met, a drunken, avaricious fool who thought she was an idiot?

Oh, where are they? Wolf, and Father, and Elfgift? What's happening to them now?

It grew dark outside. The turmoil below gradually sank away. Christmas day was ending. Angharad climbed into bed to keep warm, and fell asleep, but Nest paced up and down like a prisoner. Was it only this morning that she and Wolf had stood on the tower and seen the angels? It seemed a lifetime ago.

There was a scratching in a corner of the room. The hob came creeping out of the shadows, weird eyes glowing. "I reckoned you'd be hungry," it said hoarsely. "I've brung a pie." It stretched out a sinewy, hairy arm and offered her one of Herbert's neat little glazed meat pastries.

Nest realised that she was starving. She bit into it and the hob watched with slightly envious approval. It cleared its throat. "That was a dinner, that was. Herbert did us proud. In a rare old temper he was, mind – your father not being here. Still, Lord Godfrey insisted. *I'll be the lord here tomorrow*, he says, *an' if you want to keep your place, you'll cook for me.* So Herbert had to. Roast boar. Venison. A boned goose stuffed with apples and figs… You missed a treat, stuck up here."

"It was too noisy," said Nest. Her voice was loud in her ears. She hadn't spoken for hours.

"It *was* noisy," admitted the hob. It eyed her. "Looking forward to tomorrow? Getting wed?"

Nest wrapped her arms across her chest. "Of course I'm not."

Wild-haired and tufty, the hob sat hugging its knees on the boarded floor. It smelled of smoke, and storerooms where cheeses are kept and sausages hang. It smelled of her childhood.

"What about all that stuff you said you wanted to do?"

"What stuff?" Nest said sharply.

The hob made a vague gesture. "*Great things*, you said. Stuff about stars. You know. Planets. Rats."

"*Rats?*"

"There's always rats," the hob mumbled. "Wasn't it rats? So why marry this Lord Godfrey, if you don't want to?"

"It's not as easy as that."

"Easy? Who said easy? I thought you wanted to do something hard."

It waited. After a while, as Nest did not answer, it slipped away. She sat on the floor, her chin in her hands, thinking. At last she got up and went over to the reading stand. *Lives of the Saints.* Tracing the lines with a finger she read to the bottom of the page, turned it, turned another. The candlelight shone on her dark hair and frowning, intent face. Long after midnight, rigid with cold, she blew out the candle and climbed into bed, pressing her freezing feet against Angharad's warm bulk.

She fell asleep and dreamed of her mother. Eluned was standing by the north wall holding a broad paintbrush. She looked at Nest sadly, and slowly began painting out the map of the world with sweeping white strokes.

With Angharad behind her, Nest walked to her

wedding down a narrow path someone had shovelled through the snow and scattered with ashes. By the time she reached the porch where Godfrey was waiting, the bottom of her dress was dirty and her thin shoes were soaked. She didn't care. Her father had not come back. Wolf and Elfgift had not come back. It was beginning to snow again as they entered the chapel. Brother Thomas lurked just inside the door.

"The first sin of Eve," he announced without preamble, "was disobedience."

He shook his finger at Nest. "Never disobey your husband in any way. For if our first mother Eve had not committed the sin of disobedience, neither sickness nor death would have entered the world."

The altar twinkled with candles, but the flames did nothing to heat the air. The cold silence was broken by coughs and sniffs, and suppressed sobs from some of the women. Behind Nest, Hugo's household crowded in. Lord Godfrey's men lined the walls. Above their heads the painted saints looked down with calm, stern eyes. Nest stood stiffly in her warmest cloak, staring straight ahead. Angharad held her left arm. Godfrey stood to her right, looking smug.

"The second sin of Eve was that of idle speech." Brother Thomas glared around, looking especially at Angharad. "Chattering with the serpent Lucifer, who was too cunning for her weak and foolish brain! She should have kept silence."

Angharad dabbed red-rimmed eyes and snorted indignantly, but she held her tongue.

"The third sin of Eve" – Nest closed her eyes and wished she could close her ears too. Her stomach fluttered with nerves. She wished it was over – "was of plucking and eating the forbidden fruit. For by that deed we were all delivered into the perils of death and Hell!" Brother Thomas rolled the words on his tongue and fixed Nest with a shrivelling stare as though she and she alone was responsible for every one of Eve's dreadful faults. "Avoid the sins of Eve. Be modest, silent, virtuous, prudent. Acknowledge your husband's authority, for he is wiser than you." Godfrey smirked. "Obey him in all things." Nest stared back.

"And now," said Brother Thomas. The shuffling and coughing quietened. He turned to Godfrey. "Godfrey, do you take this woman, Agnes, for your wife?"

"Yes," said Godfrey promptly.

"Agnes, do you take this man, Godfrey, for your husband?"

Nest's heart banged so hard, she thought everyone must be able to hear it. Her hands shook. She looked Brother Thomas straight in the eye. She opened her mouth.

"Marry Godfrey? I'd sooner die!"

For a split second, his astonished, scandalised face was the sweetest thing she had ever seen. She shot out an arm, pointing to the saints on the wall, and instinctively everyone wheeled to look. "Saint Agnes was beheaded," she said loudly and rapidly, "for refusing to marry a pagan. And Saint Winifred was decapitated for refusing to marry a man called Caradog. Her head rolled downhill and where it stopped, a spring of holy water gushed out of the earth. Saint Margaret wouldn't get married either. She was swallowed by a dragon which got indigestion when she prodded it with a crucifix, and hiccupped her out. And Saint Catherine…" She was shouting now, shouting to be heard over the hubbub. "Do you think a single one of those saints would have taken your advice? *Do what you're told, don't talk, don't use your brain*? Sir Thomas, is there anything a woman *may* do?"

The anger in his eyes was frightening. He raised his hand as if to strike her.

"She said YES!" Godfrey bawled. He seized her arm and pulled her towards him. "The girl agreed to marry me!"

"I said NO!" Nest tore free from Godfrey and dodged behind Angharad. Godfrey grabbed for her again, but Angharad was as solid and wide as a bolster. "You leave her alone!" she screamed. "You just leave my lady alone!"

A knot of her own men surrounded Nest. Tough old Rollo and dark-haired Geraint, stout Roger Bach and skinny Stephen shouldered in to protect her, to get her out of the chapel. They swept her towards the door. Some of Lord Godfrey's men were there, barring it. Rollo flung himself on the nearest. Roger Bach dragged the door open. Daylight streamed in.

They burst out into the yard where snow was falling as steadily as white flour shaken through a sieve. Rollo slammed the chapel door behind him and hauled on the iron ring. Blood trickled from a cut eyebrow. "Help me!" he yelled. Stephen snatched up a shovel propped against the chapel wall. He thrust the wooden handle through the iron ring and braced it, levering the door shut.

"Nice work!" gasped Rollo. "Keep it shut as long as you can. No bloodshed though." He grabbed Nest's hand, yanking her towards the stables. "You might have warned me you were going to do that," he panted. "What now? Where do you want to go?"

Nest hadn't thought. Now she knew. "The convent! I want to go back to Our Lady's In-the-Wood."

"Sanctuary," said Rollo. "All right. *Madog!*" he bellowed. "*Horses!*"

"Be quick," begged Nest. "They'll break out of the chapel any minute!" A crash and an outburst of yells confirmed her words.

Madog hurried out with two horses. Rollo threw Nest up on to the nearest, and sprang up himself. By the time Nest had arranged her skirt and gathered up the reins, Madog reappeared with two more horses. Geraint and Roger mounted. The animals tugged and pranced.

"Ride!" shrieked Nest.

As the horses surged out of the gate, Lord Godfrey's men poured across the yard from the chapel. They didn't shout; they ran for the stables. Looking over her shoulder, Nest saw Madog sent flying by a back-handed blow from Lord Godfrey. Then she had to concentrate on her riding.

The four big horses hurtled down the lane, excited to be out, plunging and jostling, kicking up a freezing spray of snow. They reached the road and began to gallop. Cakes of snow flew past Nest's ears like white birds. She felt alive for the first time in weeks. Her veil blew across her face and with an excited laugh she pulled it away and flung it to the winds. Her hair streamed loose. She leaned forwards, urging the horse along.

Rollo drew alongside. "They're after us!"

Nest glanced back. At least half a dozen riders were coming down the lane. Not so fast, though. Not at such a break-neck speed. The falling snow made everything dim and soft, but she saw Lord Godfrey out in front.

Behind him rode the hooded shape of Brother Thomas in sweeping dark robes.

"If we stay on the road they'll catch us. Follow me!" Rollo spurred towards the woods. The four horses bounded up the slanting hillside into the woods. Branches raked past. White-gloved twigs threw handfuls of snow down their necks.

The ground dropped away behind. Dark-stemmed pines rose from the slope like ship masts. The horses struggled, snorting, kicking their way up. The gradient changed. They burst out of the trees. Ahead of them stretched blank, featureless moorland, rising and vanishing. The snow fell all around them, dusting the horses' dark manes.

"How can we ride over Devil's Edge in this?" shouted Roger Bach. "And it'll be dark before long."

"Go back if you don't like it," Rollo bellowed. He slapped his steaming horse's neck and began to ride up the hill, winding between gorse bushes and snow-capped rocks.

There were shouts in the wood behind them. Nest clapped her heels into her horse's sides. They galloped over a rise and into the wind, which swept down from the ridge. The horses plunged into a dingle deep with snow-covered heather. Nest nearly fell. They heard mocking shouts from behind.

Rollo looked back. "They've seen us. If we can beat them to the top, we've still got a chance. Aim for the ridge, as straight as you can!"

Nest murmured encouragement to her horse, patting his neck. "Come on, boy. Come on!" The horses floundered valiantly uphill, struggling through the snow-filled hollows.

"We've gained a bit!" Geraint shouted. Lord Godfrey and his men had fallen behind.

The wind grew keener: the snowflakes swarmed like white bees. In this failing light it was easy to imagine things moving, like white hares with white hounds behind them, racing silently across the slopes.

And there! Flickering in and out of sight over the dips and hollows, something like a white, dancing child. It spun over a ridge and vanished, reappeared over the next, drawing nearer, ever nearer. Beside it leaped another of those ghostly snow-dogs – but this one looked more solid than most. Nest could see its lean body arching and stretching as it galloped across the slope. It was running against the wind!

The snow-dog barked.

"Argos!" shrieked Nest. "Rollo, it's Argos – and Elfgift!"

The dog reached her, shivering and leaping with joy. "Oh, Argos," cried Nest, bending down to him. He jumped and kissed her hand. "Where's Father? Where's Wolf?" She looked up. "Elfgift!"

Bare-foot, bare-legged, the childish figure stood warily poised on top of a drift. She looked so weird and wild, with her smock fluttering, and the wind-driven snow snaking past her, that Nest felt a shiver of awe.

"We're wasting time," yelled Geraint. Lord Godfrey's half-dozen riders were strung out through the deep heather only a few hundred yards below.

"We can't leave her!"

"We can't take her," Roger Bach howled. "She's bad luck. Where's Hugo? What's she done to Hugo?"

"Stop!" Lord Godfrey bawled, spurring up the slope. "Bring back my *wife,* Rollo! Or I'll hang you from the tower!"

"God's *bones!*" Rollo kicked his horse forwards. Elfgift whirled as if to flee, but he reached down, caught the back of her smock and swung her up in front of him. "Now – ride!" he roared.

The horses bounded on. Argos sprang wearily beside them. Nest twisted in the saddle to look back down the bitter hillside. Wild emotions stirred in her. Rage at having to run like this. Desperation about Wolf and her father. If only Elfgift could talk! If only she could explain what had happened! She longed to turn back, to gallop madly down the hill to search for them.

"My lady! Keep up!" shouted Rollo over his shoulder.

The tangled heather gave way to barren grassy uplands where the wind-scoured snow was only a few inches deep. With renewed vigour the tiring horses cantered towards the skyline, where cruel rocks showed their black teeth along the crest of Devil's Edge.

CHAPTER 19

I have to go, Wolf thought drowsily. *I have to go...* He heard music, quiet harp music, and the music drew him away from this place where his body lay cramped in the stone. What had happened to the walls of rock? They were smokily transparent, like horn or glass. He stretched out a hand and they dissolved into greenish light. He floated through...

...and it seemed to him that he was following a little river *like one of the wild streams that flow off the moor.* The chattering of the dark water as it swirled over its stony bed blended with the harp music. All the stones in the stream were round, smooth pebbles like the tops of skulls. Wolf followed the stream over a slow curve of moorland. It was dark above him and to the sides: he couldn't see any horizon or edges or sky. He wasn't afraid, but the place gave him a ghastly, sick, dream-like feeling that was worse than fear. Someone was walking beside him, but for a long time he didn't look to see who it was. But at last he did, and it was Hugo, and he was playing a harp, and that was where the music came from.

"So you came," said Hugo.

"Of course I came," said Wolf. "I'm your squire." And his voice sent ripples up and down the moorland so that it tore apart and rippled away like candle smoke, and the sick, ghastly feeling got worse, and he and Hugo passed through into a doorway so huge and dark, Wolf felt like a gnat or a fly floating into a cathedral.

Inside was very quiet, but it was a restless quiet. In the dimness he felt things brushing against him, and heard the rattle of wings overhead, and saw the glint of eyes – and faces he half recognised peering out of the gloom. A boy ran silently across the shadowy floor, and Wolf was almost sure it was a boy he'd known at the abbey, who'd fallen sick and died...

This was a dream, right? On impulse he bent to touch the floor. It was cold and hard: smooth stone with a layer of fine gritty dust. It was real.

Hugo had not waited. With a shiver Wolf brushed

the grit from his fingertips and hurried after, afraid of losing him. His feet tapped on the flagstones, setting off a landslide of pattering echoes, and he slowed and tried to walk quietly, quietly. At the end of the hall was a stepped dais, and on it a throne, hung about with long black banners. Somebody was sitting on it. It was Halewyn.

He sat in a huddle, his feet drawn up, his chin in his hands, and stared at them with dark eyes. "Welcome, Hugo." His glance trailed on to Wolf, with a glint of laughter. "And your faithful squire."

"You, here?" Hugo breathed.

Wolf pushed up close to Hugo. "Don't trust him. He's a—"

Halewyn's eyes sparked. "What? Dare you say? Dare you name me? Where were you when I was made? When Lucifer, that shining angel, fell from Heaven, I fell with him. I saw him plunge like a meteor, burning – before the winds caught me and tossed me away. And I found this place of shadows to be my kingdom. How do you know what I am? Be careful, Wolf. I will be whatever you choose to call me."

He turned to Hugo. "Play for me, harper!"

Hugo's fingers jarred on the harp strings.

"Play," Wolf whispered urgently. "Hugo, play – for Eluned's sake!" And Hugo sat on the steps of the dais and bent over his harp. He began to play. As the music rippled from his fingers, a cold, greenish light flowed into the hall. Gold gleamed from the throne and green gems glinted on the black banners. Green streaks and veins ran over the black marble floor. Fans of branching tracery swept into the roof like green frost. There was dancing in the hall behind them, Wolf could sense it, though not for his life dared he turn around to see who or what was dancing.

"*Though I died and went to Paradise, I would come back To be your lover,*" Hugo sang, and bent his head. The moment the music ceased, the green light faded. The hall was dark again, restless, shuffling, whispering. *Lost, lost…* Up in the roof something shook gigantic wings. Halewyn lifted his hands and clapped slowly and deliberately, wakening flat echoes.

"Well played, Hugo. What do you desire?"

"Release my lady." Hugo's voice shook. "Every seven years you send a living soul to Hell. Let it not be her. Give me my Eluned. Give me my love."

"Your love," Halewyn repeated softly.

Wolf stared about. His heart beat hard and his mouth was dry. He had seen no lady here. He looked at the dais and the throne, and there was no lady anywhere: nothing but the stirring shadows of the banners as they moved gently in the fanning draughts. Chills ran down his spine. Hugo's eyes were fixed on the dais, as though by sheer force of longing he could conjure the person he loved out of the dark.

"She's not here," said Halewyn.

Hugo stood like a stone.

Halewyn leaned forward from the throne. Horns curled back from his brow: not goat's horns, but the budding branching horns of a young stag.

"Eluned's not here," he said softly, and echoes swept around the hall: *Not here. Not. Not here. Not here.* "She never was." *Was. Was she? Never was, was.*

"You were a fool to think so. The old, mad beggars on the roads, they're my people. The cast-off children nobody wants. The babies abandoned in ditches. The guilty, the lost, the wanderers, the refuse of Heaven – they all come down to me, to crawl into this crack in God's creation where they can wrap a few rags of make-believe around them to keep warm." His voice sank to a whisper. "Heaven has forgotten us, and, for one little payment every seven years, Hell turns a blind eye. You belong here, Hugo, lost with your dreams in the dark. Welcome. Abandon hope. Play for us again."

With a terrible, snorting grunt, Hugo fell to his knees. He doubled over and slapped the dusty floor, touching his forehead to the ground. Wolf ran to him. Hugo uncurled. He flung his arms wide and threw back his head.

"Eluned!" he howled. "*ELUNED*!"

The vast space of the hall exploded with the shocking clatter of wings. Hooves scraped and boomed on stone. Sparks glittered and spat in the shadows. Halewyn rose to his feet. He grew as he rose: he was taller than Hugo, taller than any man; on his head the horns spread and branched into spikes and prongs.

"Run!" Wolf shrieked.

"Run!" cried Halewyn, laughing. "Run, Hugo. See how far you can get! For I am Lord of Lies and Master of Shadows and Hunter of Souls!"

Wolf seized Hugo's arm and tugged it. Hugo stumbled up. Wolf dragged him across the hall: but now there was no hall, only a jostling darkness without up or down. They blundered through, and were on the moor, where the bloody stream ran. Behind them horns wailed, harsh and shrill and deadly: they heard the yammer of hounds. "The hunt is up!" cried Hugo. All the skull-stones in the stream rolled around to look at them, dark and empty eyed, chattering with loose jaws.

"Run!" And they ran – into night, into black stony passages, into smaller and smaller spaces, scrambling through closing chinks of rock with the hunt snarling at their heels – ducking, bending, crawling on hands and knees through room after contracting room, squeezing into earthworm tunnels beyond hope of light…

Wolf reared out of the dirt like a caterpillar. He grovelled forward, met solid rock and reached upwards, straining. His hand went into space overhead. So it wasn't a dead end after all, but the bottom of the steep step he had wriggled over on the way in. He had been lying stretched at its base. For how long? He didn't know. He dragged himself up between the rock edges and knelt on all fours, shivering. "Hugo," he called. He forced himself to remain calm. "Hugo, are you there?"

A gasping groan answered him, and sounds of scrabbling and wrenching. " Hugo!" Wolf cried. "Be quick!" He didn't bother to ask how much of this had been real. In the darkness he had found Hugo: that was all that mattered. He was filled with sharp urgency. The air of the mine pulsed. "They're coming!"

Hugo felt it too. He tore himself out of the squeeze. "Don't wait for me. Go!"

There was a noise under the ground, like stone jaws grinding. Tremors ran through the darkness. They crawled blind and desperate over the stone-strewn floor. At last the weave of the darkness wore thin. Wolf took the lead. He burrowed upwards like a mole under the slanting rocks. Then he saw the irregular shape of the entrance. A glitter of light on stones and the flash of water dropping. A breath of snow blew down to him, a living draught of air. And he was out.

Hugo crawled out behind him. They staggered to their feet. From the mouth of the mine came a muttering rattle, like fingers tapping on the hollow skin of a drum.

"Run!"

The cliff trembled. Snow cascaded from the ledges. They stumbled downhill over the loose rocks. It was still snowing. Wolf shuddered with joy at the white, fresh world.

They burst into the clearing. The horses had strayed. Hugo whistled. He whistled again, and a shrill whinny came from the woods. In a moment, his black horse came cantering up the dingle, its ears pricked. The grey pony bustled along behind it.

"Ride!"

"I c-can't get up," said Wolf through chattering teeth. Hugo grabbed him and flung him up. He mounted himself, and wheeled to face the hill. "Goodbye, Wolf. Go home. Back to the castle…"

"Not without you!"

"There is no more shelter in this world for me. The Wild Host will drive me like a leaf before a tempest until they hunt me down. I won't lead them to my daughter, or let you share my doom. They'll follow me, not you. Live to serve some other knight, a better man than I." His voice broke. "My wife is dead. I will never go home again. Go back, Wolf. Pray for me."

Unseen behind the trees, the face of the cliff collapsed with a rush and a roar. Rocks bounded into the dingle, crashing into the stream. Snow burst into the air like spray. Hugo gave a shout. His black horse bounded up the hill. The pony tossed its head and leaped after. Wolf grabbed steadying handfuls of mane.

Hugo shouted over his shoulder, "I said, go back!"

"No!" Wolf shouted. "Anyway, I can't!" There was no time to say more. The black horse clattered across the stream and leaped up the bank on to the moor. The pony hurtled after. Wolf's teeth rattled in his head. Icy water splashed his legs. Then with a jerk and a lurch he too was on the snowy uplands.

Hugo was already many yards away, galloping up the moor. The pony put its head down and tore after him. Wolf clung on for dear life. Snow flew in his face. He lost his breath. He bounced up and down, landing back in the saddle each time with a grinding jolt. Rocks, gorse bushes, heather-filled hollows – the pony jumped, twisted and scrambled over them or past them. Suddenly the wild pace slowed. Hugo had drawn rein. The pony rammed its nose into the coarse hairs of the black horse's tail.

"Riders!" said Hugo in a strange voice, staring at the skyline. "There are riders up on Devil's Edge!"

Nest and Rollo, Roger and Geraint cantered north along the Edge. The steep ridge was like a knife dividing day from night. To the west, the plunging sun struggled for life through a turbulent fog of yellow snow clouds. To the east, darkness climbed the sky on gigantic wings. The wind cut to the bone. Nest glanced into the western valley. The convent was down there somewhere, but it was invisible: the woods were buried under a brownish haze. The eastern valley lit to a vast blink of light. Nest flinched. A growl of thunder rolled across the moor.

From behind came breathless shouts. "Rollo, you bastard. Come back!" "Come back or else!" And Brother Thomas yelled something about the wrath of God.

The eastern valley dimmed and vanished behind a sweeping curtain of hail. Then with a hissing rattle, hailstones hurtled out of the sky. The horses shied. A bright flash lit the hail: for a moment the world was a brilliant multi-dimensional white. Nest was dizzy. Which way was which? Thunder tore the sky apart.

On its crashing rumbling heels, two riders galloped out of the blizzard. First was a man on a big black horse, which reared up, neighing. After him came a careering grey pony with a boy clasping its neck as he rode. It slid to a halt, nearly throwing the boy off. Nest screamed.

"Father! *Wolf*!"

"*Hugo*!" Rollo bellowed.

"Nest!" Hugo's voice split with horror. "What are you doing here?"

More horsemen came blundering out of the storm. The hail redoubled its fury. Pursuers and pursued could only bend gasping under the onslaught, while the horses milled, trampling the white, slippery ground.

The shower went hissing away over the ridge. They could raise their heads again. Nest found herself next to Brother Thomas. Every crease of his black robes was filled with white hailstones. Lord Godfrey kicked his horse forward and seized Nest's reins. His dark hair was plastered to his head and he bared his teeth with fury. "You come with me, you little vixen—"

Nest cried out, jerking at the reins. "Father, help me!"

"Leave her alone!" Wolf yelled. And Hugo pushed his horse menacingly close.

"*Take your hand off that rein, Godfrey*!"

Godfrey's face went smooth with shock. "*Hugo*?"

He recovered. "Hugo! Thank God you're safe! I'm rescuing your daughter. These men of yours snatched her from the very steps of the altar and went riding off with her…"

"It's a lie!" Nest shrieked.

"*Oh, my God,*" Roger Bach interrupted in a wailing cry. He lifted a quivering finger and pointed. "*Look!*"

Carried by the bitter east wind, a mass of cloud the colour of charcoal was blowing across the valley. Its ragged fringe reached out high overhead, forming and reforming like the smoke from a bonfire. It took the form of a band of dark horsemen, trampling the air. When the lightning flashed behind them, the shapes lit up in glowing strands and veins. They formed and reformed, lifting ghostly horns, which shredded away into streamers. Black hounds with gaping jaws raced ahead of them, the front runners failing and fading like breakers on the shore: forever renewed by the piled ranks behind. From somewhere beyond the world a yelping gabble carried on the wind. Horns sang out in a searing music. Thunder rolled.

"Riders in the sky!" cried Geraint.

"Devils!" exclaimed Brother Thomas in horror.

Lord Godfrey let go of Nest's reins.

"Ride for your lives," he screamed. "For your very souls!"

He clapped his heels into his horse's sides and galloped away along the ridge. With a thudding scramble of hooves, everyone followed, friends and enemies together, galloping over the rising and dipping spine of Devil's Edge.

"Slow down!" Rollo bellowed, riding neck and neck with Nest. Elfgift clung to the saddle in front of him. "Slow down!" Ahead, Lord Godfrey's white horse stumbled, almost throwing him. Stones poked through the snow.

"We're on the Devil's Road!" Rollo yelled. "If you gallop over this you'll lame your horses – or break your necks. Slow down!"

Roger Bach turned on him. "This is your fault, Rollo! You've still got the elf-girl. Throw her down! I *told* you she'd bring bad luck!"

"The elf-girl?" Brother Thomas rode his horse jostling alongside and gazed at Elfgift in incredulous horror. "*Fools*! No wonder the Devil is hunting us. Cast her off! Throw her down!"

He drove his horse into Rollo's, and dragged Elfgift sideways from Rollo's saddle. Rollo struggled to hold her. For a moment she dangled between the two horses, kicking. As their paths diverged, Rollo had to let go.

"I will save us!" yelled Brother Thomas, and flung

Elfgift to the ground. As she tried to get up, he spurred his horse at her. "I will smite her down," he shouted. "I will trample her under my feet as Michael trampled Satan!" The horse reared to avoid Elfgift, but its foreleg caught her a glancing blow and knocked her down again.

"Leave her!" Brother Thomas yelled, wrenching his horse's head around. "Let the Devil take his own!" Flapping his arms and legs, he urged his mount into a gallop. It hit the rocks and went down, throwing Brother Thomas over its head.

Wolf saw Elfgift fall. In horror he tugged the reins. The grey pony was tired, but it was frightened and had no intention of stopping. It tore on. Wolf kicked his feet free from the stirrups and fell off. He hit the snow, bashing his knee on a stone. For a moment he nearly blacked out with the pain. He got up, and with one hand clapped to his gashed and bleeding knee, started back at a hobbling run to the place where Elfgift lay limp as a rag doll. The sky behind her was as dark as night.

The Wild Host broke against the hill and rushed up over the snow. Their shapes flickered and flowed into one another, continuously changing, opening and closing slow wings, showing dreadful faces which twisted and melted. Wolf saw bounding black goats with uncoiling, drifting horns: horses with hissing, wind-combed manes. Still they came on, huge as a tidal wave, rolling on the wind, straining forwards. Whips of lightning crackled across the valley, and the music of the horns and the hounds together was like sobbing souls in agony.

Wolf reached Elfgift and tried to pick her up. His knee gave way and he fell. He dragged her into his arms, looking up. The stormy riders were almost on top of them. Overhead a vast, cloudy projection poked forwards a ragged, grinning mouth; crazily, it reminded Wolf of something. Of Halewyn's mule. He looked up further, with the same feeling of dizzy, ghastly sickness that he'd had before, as though the mask of reality had been ripped off. He saw the rider.

"You can't have her," he screamed into the wind. "Elfgift's mine!"

"And mine!" Hooves came stamping into the snow beside him. Nest jumped from her snorting, terrified horse. As soon as she let go of the reins it bolted. She flung herself down next to Wolf. They clung together, looking up.

"Oh, my goodness!" Nest wailed.

Halewyn towered halfway up the sky. His horns were branches of flickering lightning. His eyes were like the night behind the stars. The wind sighed through him and gave him a voice – a voice that raised goosebumps all over their skin.

"She was *mine*, until you stole her away. If you want her, you must pay me, soul for soul. And who cares enough for that? Who gives himself for her?"

A man's voice yelled, "I will!"

Hugo dismounted beside them. He slapped his horse to send it away, and planted his feet firmly in the snow, gazing upwards.

"Father, no!" screamed Nest.

Hugo turned to her with a brief caress. "Let me do this, Nest. I gave life to you but I have taken many more. More than you know." He looked up. "I will run no further, Lord of Shadows. I have spilled enough blood – taken enough lives. Time to atone. Let the elf-child go."

"You – Lord Hugo of La Motte Rouge?" said Halewyn. His voice seemed to tremble with laughter, and the seething mass of dark riders shook their spears. "Lord Hugo's soul for a little elf-girl's, the least of my cold children? There's a fine bargain. *Let it be so.*"

The dark wave toppled forwards. Wolf hugged Elfgift tight. She tried to burrow into him. He hugged Nest. They cowered into the snow, hiding their eyes as the Wild Host crashed over them. Freezing winds tugged and plucked at their clothes. Wolf heard distorted voices, echoing and dim; shouts and clashes like the sound of a far off battle. Heavy footfalls padded around them. Something panted hot and close in his ear.

"Don't look!" Wolf muffled his face in Nest's shoulder. "Don't look!" And he and Nest and Elfgift clutched one another tighter and tighter. He could feel Nest shaking, Elfgift pressing close. A knot of warmth grew between them. And, at the heart of the warmth, a buzzing, wordless hum. A tune. A lullaby.

> *"Lullay, my little young child,*
> *Sleep and do not cry:*
> *Your mother and your father*
> *Watch at your cradle side…"*

Goosebumps pattered over Wolf's skin. "*And there they will abide*," he sang softly.

He sucked in a huge breath and opened his eyes. The others were opening their eyes too. They looked at each other speechlessly, close, close in the darkness. A wreck of clouds blew overhead.

With a cry, Nest flung herself aside. Hugo lay limp in the snow beside them. She knelt over him, feeling for his breath, clasping his hand. "Father, don't die!

Oh, God," she cried passionately, "where are your angels? Send us your angels, quickly!"

Wolf stood up. He gripped Elfgift by the hand. Horses and riders lay scattered over the Devil's Road. He thought they were all dead. But one by one they were rising, picking themselves up. A scarecrow of a man tottered upright in the snow, shaking his fist, screaming: "The wrath of God...! Sinners, repent! Let the Devil take his own...!" His torn black robes streamed in the wind.

Someone tapped Wolf on the shoulder. He turned with a start, and then backed with a shaken gasp, gripping Elfgift. It was Halewyn, riding his black mule, no different from the first time they'd met. He cocked an eyebrow at Wolf. "It's just too tempting," he said thoughtfully. "Hugo? Or Brother Thomas? What did he say? *Let the Devil take his own*? And the fee to Hell is due on Saturday. I really can't resist..."

He rode forward. Over his shoulder he added, "Goodbye, Wolf. Until we meet again!" The mule twisted its head and gave Wolf a sneering, open-mouthed grin. It was all on fire inside. He could see right down its throat.

Halewyn spurred over the snow. He reached Brother Thomas and snatched him up with the deadly grace of a cat pouncing on a mouse. He swung him over the mule. Brother Thomas's heels kicked. His head and feet hung down. Black mule and black rider sprang away. They rode down over the snowy rocks, galloping over the Devil's Road as if they were not touching it. A thin, trailing scream hung in the air. And they were gone.

Light burst over the ridge. On the very edge of the western hills, the dying sun struggled through two layers of cloud and shot level rays across the valley. The snow turned silver and gold.

With Elfgift clinging to him, Wolf limped to where Nest knelt. She had somehow dragged Hugo's head and shoulders into her lap, and looked up with a tear-streaked face as they approached.

"Is he…?"

Hugo's eyes were open. There was a great black bruise on his forehead. The sunlight touched his face, as if with a brush dipped in gold.

"Eluned," he whispered, smiling. He reached out his hand to someone standing just above him.

And closed his eyes.

Wolf stood, swallowing tears, squeezing Elfgift's hand. Nest bowed her head, hiding Hugo's face in her long, black hair. "He's dead. He's dead! Oh, where are God's angels?"

The sun was almost below the hills. The valley was a

solid mass of clouds, lit by the last of the sunset to a fiery floor. The falling snow flashed like crystals. Pushing through the frail curtains of falling flakes, enormous shining shapes came stepping across the valley.

"Nest." Wolf cleared his throat. "I think— " He stopped, shuddering with awe. "I think they're coming now."

CHAPTER 20

The convent of Our Lady's In-the-Woods turned out to be much as Wolf had imagined it: a small, stone building with a slate roof, a few outhouses, and a walled garden currently buried under a foot of snow.

Mother Aethelflaed, however, did not much resemble the bewhiskered crone he had vaguely pictured whenever Nest had mentioned her. She was a tall, smooth-faced, stately woman with keen grey eyes, who wore her black habit and white wimple with an air of efficient authority, and who could not be more than thirty.

Her household was so well run, in fact, that not even the late-night arrival of Lady Agnes of La Motte Rouge, along with eight exhausted men, a boy, a strange-looking dumb child, and a quivering, miserable white dog, could disturb her calm control. Not even when Agnes seized her hand and dragged her outside into the snow, babbling about angels.

"They went before us the whole way – like huge, pale pillars, lighting up the snow! We'd never have got here without them. The wood is all drifted through with snow: you can't see any of the paths. They led us all the way. Godfrey couldn't see them. He never stopped complaining. But we could see them! Me and Wolf, and Elfgift! Look, look. Look where they're going away!"

Mother Aethelflaed looked. And certainly there were some odd milky shafts of light over the wood – like sunbeams striking through dusty air – only it was midnight – and the dust was snow – and the shafts of light were moving. She didn't have time to wonder about it.

"Father's dead," said Nest, and burst into tears.

Mother Aethelflaed gripped the girl by the shoulders and pushed her gently into the house. The nuns were already gathering, flinging on their mantles. Some were building up the fire. Others headed out purposefully to take care of the horses.

"Hot drinks," said Mother Aethelflaed. "And then all you men must sleep in the stable–"

"I say!" Lord Godfrey was looking ghastly, but he stirred in protest. "I'm Lord Godfrey fitz Payne of Blanchland, you know! I'm betrothed to Lady Agnes. In fact, we're nearly married!"

Mother Aethelflaed lifted an eyebrow. "Betrothed is *not* married. And if Lord Hugo is dead, it's not very likely that you'll be married any time soon. In any case, I shall have to know a great deal more about all of this before I give my consent."

"*Your* consent? On whose authority?"

Mother Aethelflaed looked him up and down till he squirmed. "Agnes has been delivered to this house by angels, Lord Godfrey. I think that is sufficient authority. Meanwhile *all* you men will sleep in the stables."

"Except Wolf," Nest hiccupped. "I want Wolf."

Mother Aelthelflaed's eyebrows rose a fraction higher. "And Wolf is…?"

"Me," said Wolf hoarsely, huddled by the fire with Elfgift on his knee. Mother Aethelflaed relaxed. "Certainly, Wolf may stay." Her eyes travelled to Argos, pressed against Wolf's legs, his wet, curly coat steaming. A faint smile touched her lips. "And Wolf's dog, too." Her fingers brushed Elfgift's flaming cheek. "And this…" She paused. "Who is this little girl, Agnes?"

"Elfgift!" said Wolf and Nest together.

Later, much later, after the weary men had been despatched to the stables, and Mother Aethelflaed and the nuns had gone to their beds, Wolf and Nest and Elfgift sat by the fire.

Nest's eyelashes were still wet. With her arms around her knees, she stared into the golden embers.

"Father's gone to Paradise," she said, as though trying the statement out. "He has – hasn't he?"

"Of course he has," said Wolf.

Nest turned her cheek sideways and looked at him. "You're not sure."

Wolf was too tired to lie. "How can anyone be sure? But I think he'll be all right. Because – well – because we loved him. And he saved Elfgift. And he was brave, and he was sorry for what he'd done..." There was a painful lump in his throat. He could feel Hugo's arm around his shoulders, could hear his voice saying, *If I'd had a son like you, I wouldn't have put him in a monastery...*

Neither of them spoke for a while. At last Wolf asked, "What will you do, now that you don't have to marry Lord Godfrey?"

Nest turned back to gaze once again into the fire. A very small, dreamy smile appeared on her lips. "I'm going to ask Mother Aethelflaed to send me on a pilgrimage," she said. "To some distant shrine, to pray for my father's soul."

Wolf stared at her. "Where?"

"Maybe Rome. Santiago de Compostela. All the places on my mother's map. Jerusalem…" She stretched her arms, and tipped back a shining face. "Just think! We could go anywhere. Even the Earthly Paradise. It's here on this world, if only we could travel far enough to find it!"

"We?" asked Wolf. His heart beat fast.

"And we can take Elfgift," Nest went on. "Maybe at some shrine or other, there'll be another miracle. Maybe she'll learn to speak!"

"We?" said Wolf again.

Nest looked at him, her skin ivory and gilt in the firelight. "If you'd like to come," she said with diffidence. "I mean – couldn't you be *my* squire? If that's not too silly?"

Wolf caught an uneven breath. He started to laugh, though there were tears hiding in the laughter. He put out a hand, and Nest gripped it hard.

"What do you think, Elfgift?" he asked. "Would you like to come with us?"

Elfgift looked up, her eyes sleepy slits against the bright fire.

She nodded.

TROLL fell

KATHERINE LANGRISH

"The Gaffer," Uncle Baldur whispered, *"is the King of Troll Fell, see? And he lives up there under the crags, not far away. And naughty little boys, why, he likes to tear them in pieces! So watch your step, laddie."*

Peer's life has changed for ever. Left an orphan, Peer is dragged off by his gruesome uncles, Baldur and Grim, to their dilapidated mill near the dark and mysterious Troll Fell. Peer soon makes friends with a house spirit, the Nis, and Hilde, a lively girl from the neighbouring farm. When he discovers his greedy uncles are plotting with the ruthless trolls, he and Hilde are plunged into a terrifying adventure. The Grimssons will do anything for gold, but they haven't counted on Peer and Hilde's determination, or the cunning nature of the trolls...

HarperCollins Children's Books

www.trollfell.com